Mistress, Inc.

Also by Niobia Bryant

Mistress No More
Message from a Mistress
Show and Tell
Live and Learn
The Hot Spot
Give Me Fever
Make You Mine
Hot Like Fire
Heated

Heat Wave (with Donna Hill and Zuri Day)
Reckless (with Cydney Rax and Grace Octavia)

Mistress, Inc.

NIOBIA
BRYANT

KENSINGTON PUBLISHING CORP.
www.kensingtonbooks.com

DAFINA BOOKS are published by

Kensington Publishing Corp.
119 West 40th Street
New York, NY 10018

All Kensington Titles, Imprints, and Distributed Lines are available at special quantity discounts for bulk purchases for sales promotions, premiums, fund-raising, and educational or institutional use. Special book excerpts or customized printings can also be created to fit specific needs. For details, write or phone the office of the Kensington special sales manager: Kensington Publishing Corp., 119 West 40th Street, New York, NY 10018, attn: Special Sales Department, Phone: 1-800-221-2647.

Dafina and the Dafina logo Reg. U.S. Pat. & TM Off.

First trade paperback printing: June 2012

ISBN-13: 978-0-7582-6529-6
ISBN-10: 0-7582-6529-8

10 9 8 7 6 5 4 3 2 1

Printed in the United States of America

For those who love the power of books to
entertain and enlighten

Mistress, Inc.

Prologue

"I am standing outside the gated community of Richmond Hills, which has been shocked by tonight's fatal shooting inside one of the community's affluent homes. The police and the medical coroner are on the scene investigating the apparent self-inflicted shooting. The name of the deceased is being withheld at this time, but it's being reported that the shooting occurred in the home of his alleged mistress—just a block down from the home he once shared with his estranged wife. It seems the violence tonight was the culmination of the deceased stalking his mistress after she tried to end the affair. After being distraught by strangling her, the victim delivered one fatal shot to his head by a 9mm gun registered in his name. A next-door neighbor happened to be walking by when the gun was shot and rushed inside to discover the bodies. And that was an act of sheer luck for Jessa Bell, as her neighbor, who is definitely a hero, was able to perform CPR and revive her until the paramedics arrived on the scene. She is now in stable condition at Fairmount Hospital. I will continue to report on this scandalous crime as details continue to unfold. This is Maria Vargas reporting for WCBL. Now back to you—"

Click.

The television set quickly faded to black. I didn't really need to watch the news report to know what happened. It was my life—or nearly the end of my life—that they speculated upon and spread like the clap in a whorehouse. As if almost dying wasn't enough, now my reputation would get skewered as my sins were put on Front Street. They might as well slap the scarlet letter on my chest and push me back into the mid-1600s.

Sighing, I turned my head on the lifeless pillow to look out through the slats of the blinds of the hospital room's window. Nothing but the moon or some light reflecting on a huge silver mechanical device on the rooftop of the shorter building next door filled my vision. Not a blessed thing to distract me from my thoughts, my reflections. My sins. My death.

I shivered and pressed my fingertips to the bruises on my throat as a vision of Eric's face filled with anger and murder flashed before me. I shook my head a bit trying to free myself of the vision, only to have it replaced by the brief memory of Eric's blood and brains seeping from his head as they rolled my weak body past him on the stretcher.

Tilting my head up on the pillow, I bit my bottom lip as tears filled my eyes. I closed my lids, but the tears still raced down my cheeks.

I almost died tonight.

That was a chilling fact . . . and I felt it to my bones.

Karma is and always will be a bitch.

I betrayed a friend to have Eric—*her husband*—in my life.

And I learned the hard way you have to be careful what you ask for. The man I fought to win at any cost became my enemy instead of the love of my life. He tried to kill me because I turned my back on *his* half-lies and part-time love.

Again, I see his face above mine as he tried his hardest to kill me.

I knew that the three friends I turned into enemies would probably gloat or toast with cocktails how the tables had turned on me. How being the mistress of someone's husband had almost killed me. Tonight I was just a few seconds short of being able to spill all my sins directly to God—or the devil—and that scared the shit out of me.

You have to change, Jessa Bell, I told myself, forcing my hand away from the bruises on my neck and ignoring the tenderness of my throat as I swallowed.

Releasing a heavy breath, I reached out to the side rail and pressed the button to call for the nurse.

"*Yes?*" someone said over the intercom after a few moments.

"Is there a chaplain on duty?" I asked, my voice slightly hoarse.

"*Yes. Would you like for me to call him for you?*"

I paused. The end of your life was all about heaven or hell.

"Yes," I whispered, trying to ease the use of my tender vocal cords. "Tell him there is a sinner who needs his help getting saved."

Chapter 1

Funerals were all about saying good-bye.

Most times it was a necessary part of seeking and receiving closure. Of course, the ending of a life for the deceased, but also the closing of a chapter—or, in some cases, a book—for those grieving. Closure.

And although she knew that it was quite scandalous and bold for her to be there, Jessa Bell felt like she needed to see Eric's body in that casket. Because of him, that day could have also been the day people came to either wish her well into heaven or curse her straight to hell. She needed the closure.

And no one was going to stop her from getting it. No one.

Eric was dead.

No one but God or Satan could have him now. Not her and not Jaime.

Jessa released a shaky breath. When she thought about their friendship, she missed him. When she thought about their lovemaking, she could almost forgive him. When she thought about him choking the life from her body with his eyes filled with rage, she wanted to see him slam-dunked straight into hell.

She still couldn't believe she never saw the craziness inside of him. He had always been the steady one. The reliable one. Even when she couldn't depend on her husband, Marc, because he traveled frequently for business, she knew she could call on Eric.

And after Marc's sudden death from a motorcycle accident, her friend had been her rock. And that had nothing to do with sex and love. All of that came later—unexpectedly, but satisfyingly. As if it was meant to be from the very beginning and they just didn't know it.

If I knew it all would end like this, I never would have crossed that line. Jessa squinted her eyes as she looked at the crowded parking lot of the church and then turned her head to take in the small group of news reporters standing outside the fence with cameras rolling.

The murder-suicide attempt had rocked the small affluent town and dominated the news for the last week. Every detail. Every flawed facet. All of it. Even down to the message she sent to her three friends taunting them all about running away with one of their husbands.

There was nothing the news media hadn't dug up from her Richmond Hills neighbors—and her ex-friends—and then spread like manure. Her name and image had been splattered all over the newspapers, Internet, and television.

Thank God they have a good picture of me.

With one last breath, Jessa slid on her oversized designer shades before opening the door to her cherry red Jaguar to climb out, smoothing the severe cut of the pencil skirt she wore with a sheer black blouse with long balloon sleeves and a mandarin collar. It was the end of summer, but the temperature was still in the mid-eighties. She suffered the heat with the collar of her blouse to cover the bruises that had darkened to an ugly purplish color.

Pushing her jet-black hair behind her ear, Jessa made her way toward the church on her five-inch heels, tucking her clutch under her arm. She felt some fear and anxiety as she neared the small crowd of people slowly entering the church.

This was a bold and brazen move. She knew that. But there was no turning back. There was no need for shame. Everyone knew. Everyone judged. But still she had to live. There was no need to hide.

I am a victim in all this.

Still, she was thankful that everyone was focused forward and didn't even notice her coming up on them.

"Excuse me, Ms. Bell. Ms. Bell!"

Jessa stiffened as the news reporter began calling out her name.

"That's her. I know it's her," another reporter said.

A few of the churchgoers turned and spotted her coming up the steps of the church. She notched her chin higher as their faces filled with disgust, confusion, anger, or pure curiosity.

As she neared them standing in the open double doors of the church, the men and women moved back from her, opening a gap between them as if she were Moses and they made up the Red Sea. There wasn't an available seat in the entire church, just standing room only. A murmur rose through the church that was distinguishable even above the solemn organ music playing.

Jessa's steps faltered a bit as every head in the church turned to eye her. She was glad for the dark shades she still wore as her eyes shifted about the church until they landed on the sight of Jaime jumping up from her seat on the front pew.

Here we go, Jessa sighed inwardly as Jaime made a step but was stopped by her father reaching up to grab her arm and then whispering something to her.

Jaime waved him off, pointing her finger at Jessa like it was a gun. "Are you kidding me, Jessa? Are you really this stupid or uncaring or unaware that you would show your face?"

A collective gasp went through the church at Jaime's angry words.

Jessa felt her own anger rise. The scene was uncalled for.

"The last thing I am is stupid, and these bruises on my neck keep me very aware of what happened *to me!*" she snapped, her eyes glittering like glass as she reached up to jerk the collar of her blouse down.

The mumblings around the church increased in sound and fervor.

"You deserve that and more!" Jaime roared. Renee and Aria came forward to wrap their arms around her.

"Ohhh, look at the besties consoling the grieving wife," Jessa taunted, wanting to hurt her. "If only she was *truly* grieving. Right, Jaime?"

Jaime lurched for her.

Jessa smirked.

Suddenly, a strong male hand grabbed her arm and began dragging her out of the church. Bold, defiant, and feeling crucified, Jessa kept her eyes locked on the faces of her ex-friends even as she was escorted from the church and she felt the sweltering heat surround her like a wool blanket.

"Jessa, you knew better than to come here."

She looked up as the church doors were securely closed in her face. She was surprised to see Eric's father, Eric Sr., was the one to lead her out.

Jessa knew his parents well. They had even attended social functions at her house or she saw them at parties at Jaime and Eric's. She even imagined the days *she* would be their daughter-in-law.

Jessa nodded as she corrected her clothing. "I'm sorry that this whole ordeal ended in Eric's death. I just wanted to say good-bye to him, Mr. Hall. I honestly had no plans to say anything to anyone."

"Call me Eric," he said.

Jessa looked up in surprise at the warmth in his voice. She was a woman used to the ways and subtleties of a man and she recognized that tone. His desire and appreciation of her was evident. It both surprised and disturbed her.

As if I would really do a tag team on a father and son.

She arched a brow when the tall and silver-haired version of Eric tilted his head to the side to eye her legs.

What the hell? He's just as crazy as his son!

"Mr. Hall," Jessa said sharply.

He shifted his eyes up to meet hers.

"I'm sorry for the loss of your son and I apologize for the scene. Good-bye," she said, her voice stiff with indignation. She turned and walked away quickly on her heels.

Once Jessa reached her car and slid behind the wheel, she was glad to see that Eric Sr. had reentered the church. She closed her eyes and breathed deeply as she fought to calm her nerves, sooth her anger, and overcome her embarrassment.

"Oh Lord, help me to forgive Jaime," she prayed, squeezing her eyes shut as she raised her hands palms forward. "Help *me* to forgive *her,* and please forgive me for letting her push me to react to her, Lord. Amen, amen, amen, amen."

The chaplain at the hospital told her to turn to God and call on Him when she faced trials and tribulations. She definitely had felt the tribulations of being placed on trial as Jaime judged her.

"Ignorant ass," Jessa muttered.

"They trying me, Lord, they *trying* me," she said, pounding her fist on the steering wheel before she started her Jag and smoothly pulled out of her parking spot.

She saw the small press corps perk up as she neared the open gate. At first Jessa wished for any other way to get out and avoid them, but Jaime's accusations rung in her ears.

"You deserve that and more!"

More? Any more beyond being strangled into unconsciousness was death. Did Jaime, or even Renee and Aria, truly believe she deserved to die? Who else felt that way?

Jessa shook her head and tightened her grasp on the steering wheel until the brown skin over her knuckles stretched thin. She slowed her vehicle to a stop just outside the gate and opened her door. A microphone was immediately stuck in her face as she exited the car.

Jessa looked into the face of Maria Vargas, the local news reporter who was building her career on the back of Jessa's shame and near death. She reached up and pushed the microphone from being so close to her glossy mouth.

"Ms. Bell, I am Maria Vargas with WCBL—"

Jessa smoothly held up her hand to stop her. "Yes, Ms. Vargas, I'm very aware of who you are. I just want to make a brief statement because I believe the press—including you, Ms. Vargas—has played out the brutal attempt on my life as if it is fiction. As if my life and my feelings are not real," she said, reaching up to use one red-tipped finger to pull down the collar of her blouse. "These bruises are real. That night was real. I almost died. I made many mistakes. I am not a perfect woman, but I did nothing that was worthy of my death, and for people to say 'She brought this on herself' or 'You deserve that and more' is harsh and it's cruel. I was a mistress . . . *not* a murderer."

Jessa turned and faced the camera. "I am a victim in this whole crazy story you all are salivating over like a silly soap opera. For all of you out there wishing death on another person—on me—I'll pray for you. God has already forgiven me."

Jessa's heart was pounding as she turned and opened her car door.

"Has Mrs. Hall forgiven you, Ms. Bell?"

"Ms. Bell, were you hoping to attend the funeral of your ex-lover?"

"Were you turned away from the funeral, Ms. Bell?"

"Ms. Bell . . . Ms. Bell?"

Jessa ignored the rush of questions from the reporter and slammed her door shut, not caring if she took off a limb of one of the crew surrounding her car. She accelerated forward and pulled away, hating that her nerves and emotions still stirred inside her until she felt unsettled and unsure.

She hated that.

Jessa was a woman used to knowing—and getting—what she wanted. But her life had spiraled out of her control ever since she made the choice to have Eric as her man by any means necessary.

She thought of one of the Bible verses the hospital's chaplain gave her to read once she revealed all of her sins to him: *"If there be a controversy between men, and they come unto judgment, that the judges may judge them; then they shall justify the righteous, and condemn the wicked."*

Jessa had never been closely tied to church or religion, but she knew the basics, and that verse had scared her. She hadn't thought about pissing off God when she was fighting for her heart. She hadn't thought about anything but believing Eric, loving Eric, and above all, having Eric.

Be careful what you ask for.

Biting her bottom lip, Jessa released a heavy breath and steered her Jaguar toward the on-ramp for the Garden State Parkway. She used one hand to unbutton the collar of her blouse as she steered with the other.

She felt her face and chest heat in anger. *That bitch*

threw me out the church! That. Bitch. Threw. Me. Out. The. Church.

Jessa pounded her tightly balled fist against the steering wheel. Her stomach clenched in anger as she thought of the press adding that footnote to the already sordid details of her story.

I shoulda stormed the church and slapped her fake ass so hard that she spun into that casket with her crazy ass husband.

But Jessa had other plans for the bougie bitch. She wanted to—no, she was going to—remind her ex-friend that Jessa Bell was one bitch not to play so closely.

As she slowed to a stop at a red light, she reached into her bag and pulled out her cell phone. Using a bright red-painted thumbnail, she scrolled through her saved text messages. She entered a message quickly and hit Send. Before she could count to five, her phone vibrated in her hand with a response. A smile spread across her face like butter melting in the summer sun.

She would teach Jaime a lesson *and* have a little no strings attached sex. Killing two birds with one stone suddenly made her *very* happy. Jessa pressed her back against the soft leather of the driver's seat before she eased her knees wider apart. The move caused the hem of her skirt to inch up her thighs. She eased her hand up her thigh and raised her hips just enough to shift the lacy edge of her bikinis to the side to lightly stroke her clit as she laughed softly.

The sudden blare of a horn shook Jessa and she looked up to see a dusty white pickup truck parked beside her at the light and the white red-headed man looking down into her car. She raised her finger and sucked off the juices as she winked up at him just before she tooted her horn and accelerated forward, leaving him behind.

Dropping the cell phone onto the passenger seat, she

felt a little of her anxiety eased. Just a little, though. She rode in silence, wishing she could erase the scenes replaying in her mind like an old-school record that skipped:

The first time her husband, Marc, had invited Eric over to the house when he moved into Richmond Hills. *I honestly looked at him like a brother . . . back then.*

The moment that a look shared between them had changed everything between Jaime and Eric. *When Jaime thought Eric and I weren't to be trusted she had been so wrong because that moment came years later and it surprised us both.*

That first kiss they shared in Eric and Jaime's kitchen. *Once we crossed the line, there was no turning back.*

The first time they made love, said I love you, or planned to be together. *It felt like we were made to be.*

The moment she pressed Send on that text message to Aria, Renee, and Jaime. *They had stopped being my friends long before that. All of them.*

The moment she realized that Eric wasn't moving in with her, wasn't giving up his marriage, wasn't willing to make her his number one. *His betrayal shattered me and I thought it couldn't get worse.*

Until . . .

Eric had begun to stalk her. *I am a grown woman and his insistence didn't fool me into thinking that was love. It was pure craziness.*

And then the look in his eyes as Eric tried to kill her. Jessa shivered from that last memory as she reached up and lightly touched her neck. *Thank you, God, for letting me live.*

Jessa slowed her car as she neared the front gate of Richmond Hills. She slowed to a stop and lowered the window to enter her code into the keypad. The tall, black wrought-iron gate opened with ease and she drove forward, passing the glass-enclosed security booth and giving

Lucky, the red-faced portly security guard, a brief head nod before she zoomed forward around the curve leading to the clean streets lined with beautiful, stately homes that were worth three quarters of a million. Mostly more.

From behind her shades she ignored how the few neighbors not attending the funeral eyed her vehicle as she passed them. *Judging me,* she thought, fighting the childish urge to flip their condescending asses the bird.

Instead, she forced herself to slow down and do a slow roll through the subdivision. She refused to speed through. She refused to hide.

It takes two to tango, and Eric was right there dancing with me. And once I *ended the dance, he tried to kill me.*

Jessa's lips twisted as she eyed the large silk black wreath hanging on the front door of Jaime's house. And it was Jaime's house now. Eric's suicide left her to play the role of the grieving suffering widow.

A bunch of bullshit. Jaime was as full of shit as a stopped-up commode. She probably had her trick, the stripper with the dick for sale, on speed dial for a "good-bye to her husband fuck" once the last guest left her house after the repast.

Jessa knew *all* about Pleasure. Once Eric discovered that his perfect wife had cheated on him with the sexy stripper, he had Jaime investigated by a private detective. Eric had been more than willing to lay up in Jessa's bed and share every sneaky-deaky detail of the investigator's report with her. And the detective earned every red penny of his three thousand dollars. He dug it all up, including Jaime's secret trips to that strip cub for years . . . and the fact that the sexy Pleasure was serving up his dick at a price.

It took every trick I had to suck and fuck away the anger Eric felt from his wife making a fool out of him.

Jessa sucked air between her teeth and waved her hand dismissively as she pulled her Jaguar into the driveway of her brick and stone French country-styled structure. She paused a bit to see a large floral arrangement on her front doorstep. As she climbed from her car and tucked her clutch under her arm, she looked over her shoulder just as her next-door neighbor Mrs. Tuttle, Mr. Houston from across the street, and the Levys all turned away from staring at her. She felt the coldness of their shoulders even across the distance.

It was always easy to sweep at someone else's door. But the problem was there were no real secrets in Richmond Hills.

Mrs. Tuttle's gardener, Hector, was chopping down more than the bushes. Mr. Houston's wife had no clue that she couldn't get his dick as hard as Yuri around the corner. And the Levys? Word on the street was he'd backhand her like a pimp did his ho if she got out of line behind closed doors.

Everyone has secrets, yet everyone judges, casting stones and sweeping around the wrong doors.

She shifted her eyes to Renee's spacious and pristine brick Colonial and then Aria and Kingston's beautiful Mediterranean. *Humph. Everyone.*

Turning around, she continued up onto the porch, stooping to pluck the card from the flowers.

Jessa,

I'm very happy you're okay and I appreciate your gratitude for my help, but I can't accept flowers or pretend I approve of your role in the entire thing.

Best,
Mrs. Livingston

The flowers she sent Mrs. Livingston for saving her life had been returned and her thanks thrown back in her face. The weight of their judgment was bearing down on her shoulders and hindering her revival. Every attempt she made to do better and to be better was being rebuffed.

"Fuck all of you," she said aloud in her husky voice.

With one last look around Richmond Hills, with eyes filled with just as much condemnation as her neighbors had for her, Jessa used her key to enter her home, leaving the arrangement on her porch as she closed the wooden door securely behind her.

Chapter 2

In the hours that passed since the funeral, Jessa's anger had not cooled one bit, especially when she had been busy putting things into place to make sure Jaime regretted the stunt she pulled at the funeral. Visions of slapping the taste out of Jaime's, Renee's, and Aria's mouths haunted her as she kept replaying the embarrassing scene in her head, over and over. She sat soaking in her oversized porcelain floating tub and the hand lightly resting on her thigh closed into a fist.

"You deserve that and more!"

Jessa shook her head in disbelief as Jaime's cold words continued to echo around her.

Really, I deserve to die behind a dick? Bitch, please.

She closed her eyes as she lightly rested the back of her head on the smooth edge of the tub. She had tried to read her new leather-bound Bible to find solace, but that had not worked until she found the verse she took as a clear sign that Jaime deserved to get as good as she gave: "*Ye have heard that it hath been said, An eye for an eye, and a tooth for a tooth.*"

Okay, truthfully, she knew what she had planned for Jaime was hardly sanctioned by God, but Jessa couldn't let Jaime slide with embarrassing her like that. Jessa had never been one to be slapped and turn the other cheek. Never.

God, you will have to forgive me.

Just as the water in her porcelain floating bathtub began to cool, Jessa rose, letting the water run down and drip off the curves of her body as she reached for the plush white towel from the heated rack on the glass multicolor tiled wall. She moaned a bit at the feel of the warm cotton against her skin as she stepped out of the tub and buried her feet into the thick plush mat.

Looking around, she allowed herself a moment to enjoy her surroundings. Everything spoke of affluence. "So different from how I grew up," she whispered aloud, shifting her eyes up to take in her reflection in the oversized mirror.

Raising her hand, she lightly traced her face, remembering the sad little girl she used to be: afraid to hope; afraid to dream; afraid to love. Being abandoned by a mother had a way of doing that to a little girl.

In time, she learned to push down the sadness and shield it with emotions that made most think she was inherently sarcastic and insolent and vain. All the while she was a wounded child trying to make sense of it all.

Sighing, Jessa pushed aside the sadness and regrets, leaving her bathroom en suite to enter her spacious circular-shaped walk-in closet/dressing room. She paused at the marble island and dropped her towel to the hardwood floor. Atop the island she selected one of the thirty perfume bottles neatly organized alongside her various scented lotions and black suede jewelry displays.

Jessa smoothed lotion onto her body, sprayed her pulse points with perfume, and selected a racy sheer corseted bustier to wear with a matching ruffled bottom panty. When she stepped out of her dressing room/closet, her feet were cushioned in one of the hundred pair of heels lining the shelves on the far wall.

She was just closing her new leather-bound Bible and

sliding it inside the top drawer of her dresser when her doorbell rang. She licked her nude lips and gave herself one last look at her reflection before she left her bedroom and tightly closed the door behind her.

With each step she descended she kept her eyes locked on her closed front door. Mostly because she wanted to get to what awaited her on the other side, but also because she didn't dare chance a glance into her living room. Since she returned to her home yesterday, she pretended the room didn't exist. The room or the memories.

Jessa planned to call in her interior designer to gut the room and hopefully her memories of Eric trying to kill her along with it.

Stepping in front of the door, she fixed her face into a sultry smile, but then remembered there was no need for the pleasantries or even seduction. Not with a paid dick.

Opening the door, her eyes shifted up and her head tilted back a bit to take in the square and handsome face surrounded by jet black and thin dreadlocks. He was all things built for good sex: tall and muscular, rough and unpolished with black tattoos on his deeply bronzed caramel skin.

"Pleasure, I assume?" Jessa asked, reaching out to lightly wrap her hand around his wrist. She was surprised that she actually felt her pussy tingle at the sight of him. The feel of his smooth, oiled skin. The smell of his warm cologne. The way his eyes were taking in all of her own sex appeal in the naughty little getup she greeted him in.

Damn!

Looking down at his cell phone, he nodded his head as she pulled him inside. "You're Jessa Bell?" Pleasure asked, his voice that deep timbre that made you think of walls crumbling.

"The one and only," she said, pausing slightly when she wondered if he had seen her on the news. "Do you know me?"

"Not yet," he said with a lick of his smooth lips as he eyed the top of her full breasts and shifted down to her shapely legs. "But I will."

Jessa didn't know if he was lying or not and didn't care. Jaime didn't give two shits about Eric, but this man standing before her, ready to please, had been the woman's fixation for years. He was the man Jaime was fucking when her phone missed and dialed her husband, unknowingly filling his voice mail up with the sounds of her being fucked well by her lover.

Jessa stepped forward to look out the door and down the long and winding street. Sure enough, cars were lining the street outside of Jaime's home. The bitch was there.

But first things first.

Jessa stepped back in the house and closed the door behind her, turning to eye Pleasure as she leaned back against the wood.

"How did you get my number?" he asked.

Jessa's heart double-pumped, but she smiled smoothly. "You serviced one of my neighbors."

"Which one?" he asked.

Jessa lifted a brow before she pushed up off the door and turned slowly with her hands up in the air slightly. "No guns. No shields. No police here," she said with a laugh as she finished turning to face him.

Pleasure smiled as he pushed his hands into the pockets of the black oversized sweats he wore with a black wife beater T-shirt.

"But it was Jaime. Jaime Hall," she said, her eyes on him.

His eyes widened a bit before he frowned and licked his lips.

"She told me you were a good fuck well worth the price and I just had to see it for myself," Jessa added, walking up to him. "A thousand, right?"

Pleasure nodded before he freed his hands to grab her

waist and jerk her forward. He bent his head to press his mouth to hers, but Jessa turned her head slightly, causing his lips to land on her cheek instead. She cut her eyes up at him as he leaned back in surprise.

"No kissing," she told him softly but firmly. "I mean . . . really, though?"

Pleasure nodded in understanding as he stepped back from her. "No problem," he assured her, even though his eyes glinted just a bit.

Jessa knew her tone was slightly mocking, but she didn't care. She wasn't paying to placate him. She reached up and stroked his cheek and slid her hand down his bare muscled arm before she moved past him to take a seat on the stairs. "I don't think I'm in the mood for dick today. Eat me," Jessa said softly as she used her hands to press her knees apart. Wide.

Pleasure crossed his arms over his chest and looked down at her with an almost bored expression on his face. "I don't eat pussy," he countered, seeming to deliberately drag his tongue across his bottom lip.

Jessa leaned back and pressed her elbows onto the stairs behind her. "Yes, but I can pay *you* enough to eat me . . . but you can't pay *me* enough to kiss you."

"Don't be so sure."

Jessa nodded as if acknowledging a deft chess move before she raised her legs and raised her ass from the step to ease off her panties. She flexed her foot to toss the panties at him before spreading her legs wide again. "Five thousand dollars."

Pleasure eyed her as Jessa used her red-tipped fingers to spread her lips and expose her clit. She tingled and moaned in the back of her throat as she let her head fall back and her eyes closed.

She smiled in pleasure and pure satisfaction when she suddenly felt the energy of his presence near her, moments before his hands replaced hers.

Jessa's hips thrust up at the first touch of a man. This man. *Shit!*

"Five thousand," he whispered hotly against the pulsing flesh of her pussy.

Jessa licked her lips and nodded as she brought her hands up to cup the back of his head. "Humph. Everyone has a price," she moaned as she eased his head forward until she felt the first cool touch of his mouth to her clit.

Jessa's entire body seemed to melt. It had been so long since her sex drive shifted out of park.

Eric's compulsion for her had killed any desire to bring a new man into her life. She had worried that even the sight of her with another man would truly push him over the edge.

But now? Now Eric was in a place where he couldn't affect her. See her. Stop her.

Pleasure stroked his tongue around her throbbing clit before suckling it into his mouth.

Jessa cried out and arched her hips upward to do tiny and tight circles against his mouth. *No wonder Jaime couldn't get enough of this Negro,* she thought with a wince of enjoyment as he probed her core with a flicker of the tip of his tongue.

Damn.

Jessa released her grip on his dreads to massage her breasts and tease her taut nipples pointing up to the ceiling. "Oooh, eat my pussy. Oh shit. Eat my pussy. Oh my God," she moaned with a hiss as she allowed her mind to pretend that it was her deceased husband, Marc, pleasing her and not some stranger that she was paying. And that thought made her shiver more.

"You like that?" he asked.

Jessa looked at him to find his deep-set coal black eyes on her intently before he ran his tongue inside the moist fold of her pussy. "For five grand? I damn well better,"

Jessa said, her body still a mass of shivers as a fine sheen of sweat coated her body.

His skill and technique could not be denied. The man knew his way around and inside a pussy. Every move. Every suck. Every kiss. Even every heated bite. Everything had a purpose. Everything.

"Damn your pussy good."

Jessa arched her back and wrapped her legs around his waist as she felt the familiar rise of heat in her loins. She felt nervous and anxious as he licked, sucked, and stroked her closer and closer to an explosion. A nut that she needed.

"What do you want from me, Jessa?" Pleasure asked.

Jessa looked at him, surprised by his intensity. "What?" she asked dazed and brought out of a passion-filled fog that felt like fugue state.

"What do you want from me?" he asked again, his eyes locked on hers.

Jessa frowned, feeling like he was trying to draw her into a trance or some shit. *What the fuck?* "I want you to make me cum," she snapped, making a face like "duh."

Pleasure dipped his head to lick the cord nestled just above her plump clit.

Jessa's stance softened again as heat rose inside her pussy like an inferno. "Oh. My. What. Oh. Oooh. Oh. Yes. Yes. Yessssss," she moaned, her heart pounding.

"You want to cum?"

Jessa reached out her hands. One pressed against the wall and the other gripped one of the rods of the staircase. "Yes, make me cum all in your mouth," she told him, biting her bottom lip as she slowly rocked her hips back and forth against his mouth.

Oh Marc, she moaned in her head, enjoying both the reality and the fantasy.

"Say please."

"What?" Jessa asked, wishing he'd keep his mouth filled with her pussy and not words.

"Say please," Pleasure demanded, shifting his head to kiss her inner thigh.

Jessa sat up a bit. "*Please* give me my money's worth," she snapped.

"What's my name?"

Jessa laid back against the stairs and sighed, feeling her ardor cool. She said nothing, hoping he would shut the hell up. Giving herself a five count, she forced herself to relax and guided his mouth back to work. "Look here, playa. I'm not feeling this routine of yours, and maybe it works on lame-ass women like Jaime, but I don't need the sideshow. My focus is on the main arena . . . if you get my drift," she told him, looking down at her pussy as she flexed and opened it like a blooming rose.

He raised his hands and pushed her legs up high until her ass was up in the air. He blew a cool stream of air against her exposed asshole before he licked a wet trail from it up to the tippy-top of her clit.

Jessa's grip on the stairwell tightened until she thought she could tear that motherfucker free. There were no more words and she didn't need them.

Pleasure used his strong hands to ease the thick and moist lips of her pussy open wide until every bit of her was exposed to him. He dipped his head and suckled the pulsing cord above her clit again and Jessa cried out sharply.

Now this some new shit, Jessa thought, welcoming that familiar rise of intensity and anticipation as she felt her nut rising fast. She allowed herself to give in to the pleasure. To get lost . . . and somehow found all at once. And when she finally felt the first explosion, she enjoyed the ride. She felt some of the stress and tension of the last week leave her. She felt renewed—rejuvenated—and ready for war.

* * *

Ten minutes later, on legs still slightly wobbly, Jessa came downstairs with fifty crisp one hundred dollar bills in the pocket of the white velour suit she now wore. When she went upstairs to quickly change and to retrieve his fee, she had looked out her balcony to check the status of the repast at Jaime's house.

Her timing couldn't have been better.

Jessa tilted her head as she looked at him. "Another hundred for a sneak peak at the dick. I am *dying* with curiosity."

Pleasure smirked as he looked directly in her eyes and jerked his pants down. "No charge," he assured her with a smile.

Jessa's eyes shifted down to see one of the thickest and longest dicks she'd ever come across. Her eyes widened and she swallowed over a lump in her throat. "Ooh. Ummmm. And . . . and . . . and *that's* not even hard. Right?" she asked, completely unsure.

Eric was average sized, but Pleasure's dick made him look juvenile in comparison.

Pleasure chuckled as he bent down to ease his pants back up. "You got my number," he told her.

"Listen, I have to get the rest of your money," she lied, already walking to the door to open it wide. "You can walk with me right down the street if you're nervous I'm gonna skip out on you."

Pleasure shrugged and walked out of the house ahead of her. "I can wait at my truck for you to get back," he told her, laid back.

Jessa closed the door and smiled up at him. "Thanks. Be right back," she told him, hurrying off down the street.

The sun was just beginning to set and the skies were darkening. Jessa's heart was beating fast and she was glad that most of the residents on this block of Richmond Hills were at Jaime's house. Not a sole was outside to see her walk up onto the porch.

She could hear the mingled voices of the people filling the living room.

Smiling like a cat, Jessa pulled the small remote from her pocket and edged just close enough to the window to point it toward the DVD player. She hit Play and the large flat screen hung over the fireplace filled with the image of Jaime getting fucked—and well—by Pleasure in the back room of the strip club where he worked.

Eric's private detective was *damn* good for discovering that the owner of the club privately videotaped the activities in his back rooms. Money talks, and the detective walked away with the DVD.

Jessa knew making a copy of it would come in handy one day . . . just like sneaking into Jaime's house to load the DVD into her player while she was at the funeral playing the bereaved wife.

Bitch, please.

Jessa allowed herself one last peak as the voices and loud cries of surprise and shock echoed outside. The sight of Pleasure's big dick sliding in and out of Jaime from behind looked like hardcore porn on the screen.

Jessa laughed and dropped the remote she took earlier onto the porch as she turned and descended the steps to stand in the street outside Jaime's home. The front door opened and people began filing out like schoolchildren during a fire drill.

Embarrass me? Jessa thought. *No, bitch. Take that.*

Several people eyed her in shock, reprimand, and even anger. Women snatched their husband's arm and pulled them away from her like she could fuck them with her eyes.

Jessa ignored them and kept her eyes locked on the front door. *I ain't done yet.* She turned and motioned up the street for Pleasure to head her way. Seconds later, the headlights of his truck turned on and he backed out of her driveway.

"What the hell do you want, Jessa?"

She turned and looked up at Renee standing on the top step glaring down at her. Jessa briefly took in some of the neighbors standing in a crowd across the street before she turned and took in the tall and curvaceous frame of her one-time best friend, then rolled her eyes. "Save some of that anger for your husband's white baby mama," Jessa drawled sarcastically. "Or are you too drunk to realize that I'm not her."

Renee's eyes glittered with anger. "You don't want to fuck with me, Jessa," she warned, her voice hard.

Jessa spared her another bored glance. "I'd be careful with the threats; you're facing enough charges, aren't you?"

Renee's discovery that her husband of over twenty years had an affair with a woman who eventually had his child drove Renee to the bottle, and when the woman came to Richmond Hills to confront her, she almost drove her vehicle into the woman in a drunken stupor, landing herself in jail and with a court battle to fight. Renee was free, but Jackson wasn't back in their home, and so Jessa assumed the word on the street was correct that she wasn't going to forgive him and try to rebuild their marriage.

Who gives a flying fuck?

"What's going on, Renee?"

Jessa shifted her eyes to Aria as she stepped on the porch as well. Their gazes locked and Jessa didn't back down. They had been friends since college, but now it was clear they were enemies . . . and that was fine by Jessa.

Unlike Renee's, Aria's husband, Kingston, was back in his place as the king of the castle. Jessa's eyes darted down to Aria's stomach. She heard that Aria was pregnant. There was a time she probably would have been the godmother.

Fuck her and her whole crew, including the one she's breeding.

Jessa pulled her cell phone out when Aria came down a step. "Please don't violate your restraining order and get your happy-to-be-pregnant ass thrown in jail."

Aria balled her hands into fists and glared Jessa down before she climbed back up on the step. "You ain't shit," Aria said.

"Being married to a doctor don't change a damn thing about all that tricking you use to do, Miss Queen of Ain't Shit."

Jessa felt like she was on a roll. She loved putting these women in their place. When her husband died, every woman in Richmond Hills looked at her like she was the sexy widow on the loose looking to replace her dead husband . . . including her three friends. They never said it, but she could see the doubt in their eyes whenever they came upon her with their husband.

"Did y'all enjoy the show?" she asked, just as Pleasure finally pulled to a stop behind her.

Things couldn't get any sweeter when Jaime finally stepped out onto the porch. She didn't miss the way Jaime's eyes widened at the sight of Pleasure's truck.

"One second," Jessa said playfully, holding up her finger before she turned and handed the wad of money to Pleasure through the open passenger window.

He took the money and then looked beyond Jessa at Jaime.

"Thank you so much; it was worth every penny," Jessa said, her voice purposefully loud.

"That's the man in the video!" one of the neighbors exclaimed.

Pleasure frowned and looked out his open driver's side window at the people loitering in the streets still dressed in the funeral black. "What the fuck is going on?" he mumbled.

Jessa blew him a kiss and turned to face her enemies. "Looks like we have the same taste in men. He was worth

every cent for me. Was he worth it for you?" Jessa asked Jaime.

"Hey, don't call my phone no more," Pleasure said, raising his windows.

Jessa shrugged and waved her hand to dismiss him just before he pulled off with a squeal of his tires.

"You're pathetic, Jessa," Jaime said, her newly cut weave swinging just above her shoulder.

The weave addict is trying to kick cold turkey.

"No, I am not the one to play with. That's who I am," Jessa told her, before she turned to face their neighbors. "Still feeling sorry for the widow. Please don't be fooled."

One by one, the neighbors shook their head or waved their hands at her dismissively before turning to head back to their homes. Jessa's face filled with confusion. "Hypocrites!" Jessa yelled at them, the veins in her throat straining as her heart beat wildly. "All of you are nothing but hypocrites. To hell with you!"

One by one, the doors to homes opened and closed behind her neighbors. She whirled and Jaime's porch was clear.

Jessa was left alone in the street . . . like worthless trash.

Like the little girl left behind by her mother. A mother who never came back for her.

Tears of frustration filled her eyes as she stormed up the street to her home. She slammed the door hard enough to make her entire 3,000 square foot home shake. "Damn," she swore in a fierce whisper, sliding down the door until she sat on the floor and then pressed her knees to her chest.

Her gaze shifted about the beautiful grand foyer and inadvertently landed on the entrance to the living room.

Pow!

Memories of the night came flooding back to her. Jessa flinched and closed her eyes, but she couldn't erase the memory of all the blood or the sight of the back of Eric's head blown away.

Tears raced down her cheeks. She didn't feel any of the victory she thought she would claim. There was no redemption in her revenge, and everything she claimed that night in the hospital with the chaplain at her side had gone out of the window.

"God forgive me," Jessa whispered, her lips trembling as more tears fell and more emotions that she couldn't quite name welled up in her chest. "Lord, please . . . *please* don't give up on me."

Chapter 3

The sounds of construction from the first level of her home had forced Jessa to rise early and spend the majority of her morning on the large balcony surrounding her master suite. The noise was a major distraction, but ever stepping into her living room again with it looking like it did when she almost died was a definite no-no.

She'd even paid the hefty price for them to get started on the project on a Sunday. She couldn't go another day avoiding looking in or going near the room at all costs. In her mind, that room was nonexistent, but she knew that couldn't last forever. And since she had no intention of leaving Richmond Hills again, she had to make sure the home she loved *stayed* the home she loved.

Thus the contractors taking over her first floor. Her wish to have everything about that room changed was coming true. Money talked and Jessa paid her interior decorator, Keegan Connor, well enough to make sure bullshit walked. The room had been stripped bare—the flooring, the furnishings, the fireplace, and the fixtures. Everything. Gone. And hopefully the memories along with it. In a week the room would be completely redone.

Jessa sighed as she tried to focus her attention on the leather-bound Bible in her lap. She was trying to strengthen her ties to the Lord and believed that she *had* to turn to Him because she had no one else. No parents. No husband. Not even the man she thought she loved. No friends.

" 'Just me, myself, and I—that's all I got in the end,' " Jessa sang the Beyoncé hook softly.

But then her eyes fell on the Bible. *The chaplain said that God never leaves you.*

Biting her full lips, she shifted her eyes up to the skies. Jessa had never been one to mull over the lack or abundance of friends. Never. But she felt her desolation. She felt her vulnerability. She felt like a leper in her community. She had never been the type of woman—the type of person—to give a fuck.

Being six years old and standing there as your mother walked out of your life, climbed into a car with one of her men, and drove away never to be seen again had a way of hardening a heart. Top that with the inconsistent phone calls filled with lies of coming back for her and then the calls dwindling down to the point she stopped having hope it was her mother when her grandmother's phone would ring. She just wanted her to come and take her away from what she considered to be a nightmare.

When you lose your love for your own mother that you once cherished and almost worshipped, it was hard to give a flying fuck about anyone else. Especially when you're afraid to love. Afraid to have it taken away. Afraid to be betrayed by it.

Her mother left.

Her father made one brief appearance in her life.

Her grandmother passed away in her sleep, but she had never been overly affectionate of the grandchild she felt she got "stuck" with.

Marc, with his insistent love, his devotion, his affections, and his supportive ways had broken through her shell, and he was the first man—the first person—she had risked her heart on . . . and then he died. She was left again with a broken heart.

No one knew it, but his death pushed her right back to that place as a child when she had protected her heart and her feelings at all costs. Going back to truly not giving a fuck about anyone else had felt like home to her. It placed her feet on solid ground again.

Now almost dying had changed her again . . . and maybe not for the better.

Closing the Bible, Jessa rose to her feet and stood at the railing of the balcony with a nice summer breeze blowing her black silk robe against the curves of her body. She would give the world to have Marc here with her, at her side, his hand on her hip, his lips on her neck. Loving her. Loving her like nothing she had ever known before . . . or felt like she would know again.

Jessa lowered her head to her chin as the first feel of tears wet the front of her robe. She turned and rushed into her bedroom and then across, moving to her dressing room to drop her robe and quickly pull on a charcoal gray 1940s-inspired fitted dress with a severe A-line hem that came just below her knees. Light makeup. Jewelry. A subtle spray of perfume and then a quick twist of her jet-black hair up into a loose top knot. As the sound of construction continued around her, Jessa was glad to grab her shades, keys, and Birkin and flee the house.

Behind the wheel of her Jag, she drove out of the cul-de-sac, avoiding the sight of Aria and her handsome husband, Kingston, enjoying their Sunday morning on their porch together. The sight of them being affectionate in front of their sprawling home was the epitome of the American dream: love and success.

Things she would never have with Marc and foolishly thought she could re-create with Eric. She could admit now that in her jealousy of Aria's life, she wanted to destroy it. She wanted to peel back the lies in their relationship so that she didn't feel so lost without Marc. And that's part of the reasons she included Aria—the closest friend to her of all three—in that text. She wanted to shake Aria's happiness up because she couldn't stand to see her have it.

What kind of person am I, Lord? Just how fucked up—messed up—am I?

Jessa slowed the Jag as she waited for the electronic wrought-iron gate to open. She tapped her fingers against the steering wheel, anxious to be on her way. She turned on some music, glad when the sounds of a classic Luther Vandross song filled the interior of the car, because she was anxious to be free of her thoughts, free from self-reflection.

As soon as the gate opened, she zoomed ahead, forcing her body to relax as she drove. It took only two additional songs for her to reach the Heavenly Rest Cemetery. Jessa followed the curving path leading to a beautiful weeping willow tree. After parking, she climbed from the car and was careful not to walk directly over anyone's grave as she came up to her husband's plot.

She pressed a kiss to her fingertips before pressing them to his headstone. She smiled a bit as she looked down at his portrait etched onto the black granite. She moved to take a seat on the granite bench at the foot of his plot. There were many days after his death that she found solace sitting here in silence and remembering the goodness of him and his love for her.

But it had been years since her last visit. Trying to fill her life up with Eric had occupied her time.

Marc, I was a fool to think he could replace you.

Jessa licked her gloss-free lips as she wrung her hands together struggling to find the words. "One of the things that made me love you was how you believed in me. How you saw the good in me when I didn't even see it in myself. Everyone hates me and . . . I guess I understand, but do you hate me, Marc?" she asked, her voice breaking to even below a whisper as new tears fell.

"This is the most I've cried since you passed away," she admitted with a half laugh as she used the sides of her hands to wipe away her tears. "I don't know if it was Eric trying to send me to you up there or PMS or . . . or . . . hell, I don't know. I just know I'm sick of crying. Remember how it makes my eyes and face puffy, like I lost a round to a boxer."

Jessa fell silent and she wiped her hands on her dress as she eyed the sketch of him on the headstone. "I never allowed myself to think how you would feel about me getting involved with Eric. A piece of me was so pissed at you for leaving me. You know I *hated* those motorcycles. I gave every last one away after you died . . . but I guess you know that."

She blinked away more tears.

"I wasn't trying to hurt you—or even Jaime—back then. I just knew I wanted to be happy. I wanted not to be alone again. I wanted to be loved." Jessa dropped her head in her hands. "I'm sorry. I'm so sorry. Aw shit. I'm crying again."

She jumped to her feet and made sure to walk along the edge of his grave to press another kiss to her fingertips before pressing them to his lips on the picture. She turned and made her way back to her car with just one last look back at his grave over her shoulder before she climbed behind the wheel and drove away.

Jessa fingered the bruises that had all but disappeared from her neck. They had been bright and bold against her caramel complexion. Her own badge of shame similar to the scarlet letter pinned to the bodice of Hester Prynne.

Forcing her fingers away from her neck, she steered the

vehicle back toward Richmond Hills but passed the entrance to the subdivision to drive three blocks to turn into the gated parking lot of the church. Although Eric had been buried at his family's Catholic church, something about sitting in the parking lot in her car and watching the people enter the Methodist church reminded her too much of what happened just two days ago at the funeral.

What if they have seen my face and heard my story and don't even let me in?

What if the sermon is on wayward women who covet thy neighbor's husband?

Jessa gasped at an image of every woman in the church rising to their feet and pointing to her as they shouted, "Mistress," "Whore," "Jezebel!" Especially since a lot of the Richmond Hills community attended the church.

Jessa hated the fear she felt, and she hated even more when she steered her car out of the church's parking lot. The old Jessa would have walked in with her head held high and dared a soul to challenge her.

Not wanting to return to the house and the noise, Jessa steered her Jag toward the Terrace Room. She hadn't really eaten in the days since the attack. *Maybe the smell of food will make me hungry,* she thought as she pulled up to the valet station of the chateau-styled 1930s home that had been converted into a restaurant.

She hadn't been there since the day she met with Aria and got into the altercation that left her on the floor with a knot on her forehead from the cell phone the bitch threw at her. Climbing from the car with her Birkin, Jessa gave Andre, the valet, a warm smile that he returned before he climbed behind the wheel of the Jag and pulled off.

She eased her shades up onto the top of her head as she walked up the brick steps into the restaurant. Her steps faltered as the eyes of Kilpatrick, the restaurant's maître d', shifted from hers. Or rather he averted them from hers.

Jessa instantly felt regret for coming here. She was still being judged—and now by the staff that once respected her. Refusing to let him or anyone else see her sweat, she inched her chin higher and stepped up to the wooden podium where he stood.

"Table for one," Jessa said, her husky voice cool.

Kilpatrick nodded his bald head and retrieved a leather-bound menu. "Um, yes, ma'am. Right this way," he said, his usual cool composure gone as he appeared flustered in her presence. "Ms. Bell?"

Jessa looked up at him with her eyebrow cocked high. "Yes?"

Kilpatrick licked his thin lips and stepped closer to her. "There won't be any repeat altercation like your last visit?"

Jessa felt some of the tension leave her shoulders. The man was worried about an embarrassing scene and not the scandal called her life—well, not entirely. She just remembered that he had politely asked that both she and Aria refrain from having "a dining experience at the Terrace Room."

"I can assure you, Kilpatrick, no drama. Just breakfast," Jessa replied.

"No guests?"

"No, Kilpatrick," she stressed. "No guests."

He smiled at her and turned. "Right this way."

Jessa followed the tall and slender white man farther into the beautiful interior filled with the bright light streaming through the many windows and the French country décor that spoke of both comfort and elegance.

She spotted Councilman Weathers and his wife as she passed. Jessa had volunteered to work during his literacy campaign last year. She opened her mouth to speak, but when the councilman's wife frowned at her, Jessa almost ate her words.

"Hello, Councilman Weathers," Jessa said in a husky voice with a soft smile as she passed their table.

The tall and distinguished politician with silver-flecked hair nodded his hair at her. "How are you feeling, Ms. Bell? Ow!"

Jessa watched as his wife glared at him, and she knew from his grunt that the woman probably kicked him under the table. She kept her eyes locked on the back of Kilpatrick's head, ignoring the stares and whispers of those around her.

He held her seat for her and Jessa offered him a polite smile over her shoulder. "Thank you."

"Yes, ma'am," he said, handing her the menu. "And I'm glad to see you are doing well, ma'am. Truly."

"Thank you, Kilpatrick," she said, hating that even a moment of kindness from a maître d' mattered so much to her in that moment.

Jessa lowered her menu and found nearly five sets of eyes on her. They looked away as she met each of their gazes. The waiter came and she ordered an egg-white omelet with chicken sausage and fresh fruit on the side.

I need a diversion, Jessa thought.

She noticed a handsome man at the bar eyeing her before he raised his glass to her in a silent salute.

Not that *type of diversion,* she thought, giving him a polite smile.

The smile waned when a beautiful woman soon joined him with a kiss to his cheek before she took her seat. Jessa's eyes dropped down to take in that they both wore wedding bands. She rolled her eyes as she took a sip of the glass of ice water her waiter sat on the table.

Especially not that kind of diversion.

She was not playing the mistress anymore.

There is nothing about me built for second place.

Plus, the woman took all of the blame and the heat for

the man's indiscretion. She was left behind to deal with her role in the affair while death had seemed to elevate Eric beyond the fact that he disrespected *his* vows.

Bunch of prime-grade, stank-ass bullshit. Oh goodness, Lord, forgive me. It's a bunch of BS.

Releasing her desire to use profanity was becoming harder than her promise not to sleep or deal with another married man.

Sitting back in her chair to cross her legs and lightly fiddle with her utensils, she bit her bottom lip as she got lost in thought. She had a lot of idle time on her hands, and although Marc's death had left her a widow, she was a very wealthy one. The double indemnity clause on his life insurance had doubled the face value of his policy because of his accidental death and left her with three million dollars—not including all of their other assets.

Still, she wanted to do more than be the sexy wealthy widow with time and dimes to spare.

"Ms. Bell, can I get something straight with you?"

Jessa didn't move her stance one bit but shifted her eyes to take in Councilman Weathers's wife standing at her table, sighing and licking her lips slowly. "Mrs. Weathers, I don't know, so I can't even began to fathom what you and I have that needs to be straightened out," Jessa said, tilting her head to look past the woman's bulky frame at Councilman Weathers sitting at their table shaking his head as if to say, "Don't blame me for that."

"Your *services* will no longer be needed in any capacity dealing with my husband or his philanthropy efforts," Mrs. Weathers told her in a cold voice filled with reprimand.

Lord, see how these people test me?!

With a tight smile, Jessa tilted her head back and looked up at the woman. "Mrs. Weathers, I'm not sure what services you're trying to assume I was giving your husband . . . but I think it is quite clear looking at you and then looking at me that I am most certainly not his type. I would need thirty more years and forty more pounds to compete with you, darling."

The woman gasped as her birdlike eyes hardened.

Sorry, Lord, but she brought her ass over here for this.

"Listen here, you little *slut,* you stay the hell away from my husband," the older woman snapped.

Jessa started to toss her glass of water in the woman's face, but she saw Kilpatrick eyeing them nervously.

"Well, you listen here, you jealous little porker. Get yourself together so you can love yourself enough not to run around here insecure that your husband has his eyes on better-looking women. Don't put your insecurity onto me because my *shit* is together. Understand?" Jessa tossed her hair over her shoulder. "I don't want your husband and don't bother to thank me."

The woman's eyes were filled with distaste and venom. "No one wants you here."

Jessa smiled at her, taunting her. Mocking her. "If you and the rest of these insecure wives truly believed that *no one wanted me,* you wouldn't be over here. Now would you? You all are scared shitless that your husbands want me here. Again, I don't want them and you all can thank me later."

Mrs. Weathers turned and stormed away from the table, even bypassing her husband at their table to leave the restaurant. Again, Jessa felt all eyes on her. She just shook her head. *Another piece of scandal to add to the rest,* she thought, just as her waiter brought over her food.

"Someone left this message for you with the concierge, madam."

Jessa eyed the tiny white envelope in the waiter's hand like it was a skunk tooted up to spray her. "Just sit it there. Thank you."

As she ate her meal, she occasionally eyed the envelope. Her name was written in a bold and dark slashing that had to be that of a man. She knew that inside was an offer that perhaps they hoped, or thought or prayed, she couldn't resist. Long before—and after—Marc's death, men had clamored to be the one to find out just what it took to please a woman like her. She was no fool—especially with the man at the bar casting secretive looks in her direction whenever his wife wasn't paying attention.

Long after Jessa finished her meal, the note remained where the waiter sat it, and when she paid her bill and rose to her feet, she eyed the man as she tore the note into a hundred tiny pieces and then dumped the new confetti into the side pocket of her purse before walking out of the restaurant with her head held high.

Jessa decided to take the twenty-minute drive to treat herself to a mini-shopping excursion at Short Hills Mall. Mostly, she was killing time. Her decorator said the men would be finished for the day in a few hours and then the peace and serenity of her house would return . . . until tomorrow.

She had barely made it out of the parking lot of the Terrace Room before she felt the contents of her stomach rewind. She covered her mouth with her hands as she waited for the nausea to pass. She tried to breathe easy and deep, hoping the moment would pass.

It didn't.

Slamming on her brakes in the middle of traffic, Jessa barely made it out of her car before she emptied the contents of her stomach on the curb in front of a beautiful Victorian. She reached out for the hood of the car as her back arched with each expulsion until her throat hurt and she felt drained.

"Are you okay?"

Jessa covered her mouth as she looked up at an older white woman coming down the porch of the house and looking at her with concern. She nodded, hating the taste of her mouth. "I'm so sorry. I just got sick all of a sudden. I'm sorry about this," she said, waving her hand at the vomit she couldn't stand to look at. "It must have been something I ate."

The older woman smiled at her. "Perhaps," she said, turning as a tall silver-haired man came from the back of the house with a bucket.

Jessa looked at the woman oddly. "What do you mean?" she asked, stepping up onto the curve as he rinsed the vomit down the drain.

"Perhaps it was something you ate or perhaps you're pregnant, sweetie?"

Jessa's knees gave out as she shook her head voraciously. "No, it definitely was the egg whites or some bad chicken in my sausage or—"

"Or a bun in the oven," the woman said as the man Jessa assumed to be her husband headed back up the drive toward the back of his house with his empty bucket swinging at his side.

Pregnant? I can't be pregnant. I'm not pregnant. No. No. No!

Jessa stepped down off the sidewalk and made her way back to her car. "Um, sorry about the mess," she said over her shoulder before climbing into her car and closing the door behind her.

She pulled off like the driver of a getaway car in a bank robbery and almost drove into a car coming up on her left. "Shit!" she swore, her heart pounding even faster as her hands began to tremble.

The driver laid on his horn as he swerved to miss her as he passed.

Jessa pulled forward to the red light and took that moment to rest her head on the steering wheel as she breathed in and out deeply as she counted to ten. *I cannot be pregnant. I can't. Old people always assuming someone wants to be full up with child.*

Jessa looked up just as the traffic light turned green and she pulled forward, forcing herself to steer her Jag. She didn't want another vomiting incident in the high-end mall. It was obvious to her that she had caught a twenty-four-hour bug or had some bad meat or, God forbid, someone in the kitchen of the Terrace Room had skipped a hand wash and passed her a germ.

"Because I am *not* pregnant," Jessa said out loud with authority, smoothing her still shaky hand over her forehead. "Shee-it. No. Hell no."

She released a nervous laugh that ended in a drawn-out sigh.

After three consistent mornings of singing into the commode, Jessa threw on a pair of sweats and Uggs and drove like a bat out of hell to the local pharmacy. Thirty minutes later, she was sitting on her commode and looking down at the positive pregnancy test in her hand.

I'm pregnant.

I am pregnant.

I. AM. PREGNANT.

Me?

She had never considered having children. Years ago, she swore she never would, and not even in the haze of her delusional relationship with Eric did she contemplate children. Her dreams had been filled with a life of traveling and just enjoying the good life.

And now?

Jessa rose to her feet and studied her reflection. She looked and felt a mess. A hot mess.

"I am pregnant by the man who tried to kill me," she said, her voice sardonic. "Ain't that some shit."

She hadn't had sex with any other man except Eric . . . and the last time had been less than two months ago.

She dropped the pregnancy test into the sink and covered her face with her hands. "Damn," she whispered hoarsely.

Renee Clinton

My marriage is over and my life will never be the same again. Although that hurts me to my core, the same things that had the power to destroy me have made me stronger, and I am finally able to deal with every blow that fate has thrown at me.

And the walls of my marriage had begun to weaken and crumble at the edges long before that stupid text message Jessa Bell sent us all that day. My husband knew nothing about that text and he came home that night and admitted to me that not only had he had an affair, but some faceless woman was now pregnant with his child. See, the shit would have hit the fan regardless of Jessa sending the text or not. My husband wasn't the guilty one for that *injustice, but he had a couple of his own to reveal.*

Every day he begs to come home, but I have noticed that every day the plea is given with less and less conviction. Perhaps he is tired of asking for something I am denying him, or maybe he is becoming comfortable in his role in his new family with that white bitch and their bastard child.

There was no need to lie; I could care less about the bitch or their child. If I had stuck to my original goal that day I climbed behind the wheel of my car drunk with al-

cohol, jealousy, and mostly rage, she and her baby would be dead.

But then I would be facing murder charges instead of Driving Under the Influence, Criminal Mischief, and Misdemeanor Assault. When my trial date finally comes up, I could be facing up to three years in jail.

The goodness in all that?

Last month nothing but tequila could have gotten me through accepting the idea of that. But I am over thirty days sober and reconciled to doing the time for my crime.

I would have needed a shot—or several of them—to finally give my attorney the go-ahead to serve Jackson with the divorce papers in the morning.

I can't lie and say the thought of not spending the rest of my life with him doesn't tear me up, but I will never accept his affair or his child, and so it is time to move on and do what I have to do to rebuild my life . . . without him.

"Ma, you still up?"

I blinked away any hint of the tears that almost fell as I turned to see my son, Aaron, who is the exact replica of his father nearly thirty years ago, strolling in the kitchen where I sat at the large island under the lone light illuminating from the ornate ceiling fixture. "Yes, why are you roaming so late? It's after midnight, son."

"I wanted a snack," he said, pulling open the door to the pantry.

Renee ran her fingers through her soft and short natural curls. "Is your sister still mad I made her move back home from her grandmother's?" she asked, hating the bridge that had developed between them.

Kieran just didn't understand. She was angry at Jackson for his affair and outside child, but she was just as angry at me for not forgiving Jackson and trying to rebuild our family. The embarrassment of my arrests and the details surrounding it wasn't much help—especially for a teenager still in high school.

"She'll get over it, Mom; you have other stuff to worry about," Aaron said with a simplicity that was aged beyond his eighteen years.

I honestly didn't want to talk about my upcoming court case. For now, until the time drew closer, I just wanted to pretend it didn't exist.

"How are you doing about Darren moving to Atlanta?" I asked, my eyes intently on my son even as just a twinge of guilt nipped at me.

In the midst of the storm of Jessa's text and my husband's affair, I came home late one night to find my college intern, Darren, fucking the hell out of my son—whom I had no idea was gay. I was still dealing with that because I loved my child and nothing could make me turn my back on him. Nothing.

But I could not accept Darren being in my son's life when I almost slept with him last year. Although I threatened him to stay away from Aaron, my clueless son wrote me a letter begging me to understand that he loved Darren and wanted to be with him.

In the words of my friend Aria: no haps.

"If he cared about me, nothing should have made him leave," Aaron said, digging into a bag of chips.

I knew my son was hurting, but this was for the best and I made sure of it. Besides, if Darren truly loved my son, then it should have taken more than five thousand dollars to send him on his happy way.

Smiling, I reached across the table and stroked my son's hand. "You know you have to tell your father, Aaron," I said gently.

Aaron glanced up at me before focusing his attention back on the chips. "I thought you would have told him."

I shook my head and stood up to pull my son's head against my belly as I hugged him close. "It's not my business to tell, Aaron. I don't want to take this from you, and I know that I would have preferred to hear it from you.

Tell him," I stressed, wishing I could carry the weight for him. But I couldn't.

Aaron nodded. "I will. It won't be easy. But I will."

I smiled softly and bent to press a kiss to the top of his head."

"I'm going back to bed," he said. "Night, Ma."

I crossed the kitchen. "Night," I called behind him, opening the fridge to pull out a bottle of water.

Pulling the lightweight robe I wore closer around my curves, I made my way out the patio doors to the deck off the back of the house. I tipped my head back as I sipped the water.

I froze as a flash of color caught my eye. I turned my head and looked up. Across the distance, I saw Jessa on her balcony dressed in her own floor-length nightgown and robe.

Our houses were too far apart for me to see her expression, but I could tell from Jessa's stance, with her head almost lowered to her chest, that something was sitting heavy on her chest.

Maybe she regrets that stunt she pulled at the funeral, *I thought, squinting my eyes as I continued to watch Jessa as her shoulders started to shake and she raised her hands to wipe her face.*

"She's crying?" I couldn't help but shake my head in disbelief.

Jaime thought it was Jessa who loaded the DVD into her player. I had my doubts even though Jessa had now proved to us that she was the boldest of bitches. Where would she get the DVD from? Truly, I felt for the shame the DVD brought Jaime, but I had so much on my plate that I didn't have the time nor really the inclination to play "Guess Who Made an Ass out of Jaime."

Suddenly, Jessa looked down directly at me. My heart pounded with so many emotions. Surprise. Anger. Pity.

Jessa turned and stepped inside her house. I could hear the closing of her balcony doors echo into the night.

"Oh, what a tangled web you wove, Jessa," I said softly, before walking into my home without another thought spent on her or the reason for her tears.

Chapter 4

"I think you are going to love it, Ms. Bell."

Jessa gave Keegan Connor, her red-haired interior decorator, a Texas transplant who refused to let go of her Texas roots or accent, a smile as she continued down the stairs with an ease that was as fake as Keegan's hair color. Giving the banister one last firm clutch, Jessa stepped down off of the final step.

"You are really going to be amazed about what my team accomplished in two weeks, darling," Keegan said, lightly placing her hand on Jessa's back to steer her toward the living room.

Jessa fought the urge to touch her throat. The bruises were gone, but the memories remained. Wanting to be stronger, she took a deep breath and took long strides to walk into the living room. As she looked about the room, she didn't recognize it. Everything had changed as promised. The décor was now warm and inviting instead of her usual cool sophistication. Gone was Eric's blood staining her floors to be replaced by all new hardwoods that were nearly ebony in color. Even the windows were different, with metal bars arranged in large diamond shapes.

Jessa felt some of the tension in her shoulders ease. Some, but not all.

See, even with the room being flipped around with her

new plush leather furnishings separated into two seating areas, Jessa still knew the spot where Eric choked her and then shot himself. Her eyes went to the set of four armless chairs situated around a huge tufted ottoman.

That was the spot. She would never forget it.

Keegan came to stand beside her. "Taking it all in?" she asked.

Jessa cleared her throat as she crossed her arms over her chest in the sheer ivory blouse she wore. It took her a moment to realize that her fingertips were lightly stroking her slender throat. She eased her hand down.

"Yes, it is *amazing*. Thank you, Keegan," Jessa said warmly, turning her face to smile at the woman.

She was surprised when the woman lightly grabbed her arm. "I been where you're at. Keep your head up, sugar," Keegan told her softly, with a wink.

Jessa stiffened a little bit as she side-eyed the woman.

Keegan held up her hands and leaned back. "Not trying to offend—"

Jessa shook her head. "No, no, I'm sorry for trying to ignore the elephant in the room," she said.

Keegan nodded in understanding. "I understand it's not something you want to shout from the rooftop. Everyone hates the mistress, and the husband buys his wife some jewelry and kisses her butt for a few months and all is forgiven while they spend the rest of their life wishing the other woman to hell."

"Exactly," Jessa agreed as she watched Keegan move over to the sofa to make deeper dimples in the throw pillows with the sides of her hands.

"The man I was involved with took his wife on a month-long cruise around the world and I got blackballed out of Texas. No business. No friends. Nothing," Keegan said, shrugging as she walked back over to Jessa.

"Is that why you moved to the East Coast?" Jessa asked, intrigued by the conversation.

"Oh, yes, it was either move and start fresh or sit there like a crocodile about to be skinned for those bitch's shoes, darling," she said dryly.

Jessa shook her head. "Would you ever date a married man again?"

"No, no. I'm the *Mrs.* now, so I spend all my free time making sure karma doesn't bite me in the ass," Keegan said, her eyes taking on a serious turn before she looked away.

Jessa's eyebrows dipped as the moment became a little strained. She knew that Keegan truly did feel like her happiness had a time limit on it because of the wrongs of her past. "Tell me about this rug," she said, surprised when she eased her arm around Keegan's and tugged her forward wanting to distract her from her fears.

Keegan gave her a little smile before launching into a Vanna White description of the silk woven rug.

Jessa barely heard her, her thoughts were too occupied. Full. Ripe. Being bred with her own growing fear.

Were the sins of a mistress *ever* forgotten . . . or forgiven?

Jessa took a deep, steadying breath before she climbed the stairs to the house. She pressed a red-tipped finger to the bell and then stepped back to wait. She crossed her arms over her chest as she saw the peephole darken.

It took a full ten seconds or better before the door opened.

"What are you up to now, Jessa?" Renee asked, her face more tired and agitated than angry.

"Can I come in?" Jessa asked, pressing her hands into the pockets of the ivory slacks she wore.

Renee's square and pretty face became incredulous before she suddenly stepped back and waved her in.

Jessa couldn't deny that she was surprised as she entered the home of her ex-friend for the first time in months. Nothing about the stylishly country décor had changed except the lack of any alcohol on the bar that held little more than a glass holder now.

"What do you want, Jessa?"

She turned. "To apologize for sending that text. It was childish and spiteful and . . . and . . . I was wrong," Jessa said, leveling her eyes with the other woman to find them to be filled with suspicion.

"Why *did* you do it, Jessa?" Renee asked, finally stepping away from the closed front door. "Forget the affair. That's for you and Jaime to deal with. Why on earth would you send that text to all of us like this was a dumbass game and we were your pawns. We were friends. *Good* friends."

Jessa hated that she felt the weight of the guilt Renee was stacking on her shoulders. "Look, I'm not here to rehash it or be best friends again. I'm just apologizing for the text. That's it."

Renee tilted her head back and wiped her face with both of her hands. "Okay, you know what, I have so many other things on my plate. Um . . . yeah . . . so . . . good night, Jessa."

Dismissed.

Jessa had to press her lips together to keep from putting Renee in her place. She came looking for absolution from her sins, not to absolutely cuss Renee the fuck out.

Stay with me God, I'm trying . . .

"Okay," Jessa said, walking past Renee to open the front door.

"Jessa."

She stopped in the doorway but didn't turn.

"Aria told me that you thought we all turned and distrusted you and your motives with our husbands once Marc died," Rene said from behind. "But you were wrong. I never questioned you until the day you sent the text."

Jessa looked over her shoulder and arched her brow.

"And so none of you ever said I was a walking 'fuck me' sign?" she asked, her voice low and challenging.

Renee's eyes widened a bit.

"You three have to be careful of your little conversations when you think no one is around," Jessa said with a fake smile. Jessa paused and let that sink in before she said softly, "Good night, Renee."

She closed the door firmly, thinking back to the day she walked to Aria's house and decided to come up the driveway and around to the patio doors. Her friends were sitting around the island and her steps paused when she overheard Jaime say:

"*We need to set Jessa up on a blind date so she's not alone during our couples' excursions looking like a walking 'fuck me' sign.*"

"*Jessa would never do that. Would she?" Renee said.*

"*Especially to me . . . she knows I would whup that ass and good," Aria said.*

Jessa had stood there in the shadows and listened to her three friends laugh. She waited a few minutes and then entered with a fake smile on her face and all the while thinking that her best friends in the world didn't even trust her.

Pushing the memory away as she felt her anger stir, Jessa made her way to Aria's house. Honestly, Jessa didn't trust that Newark-bred bitch as far as she could throw her. Ever since they met in college, Jessa had noticed that Aria was smart and studious, but she definitely had an edge like she was always two seconds from either cursing someone out or slapping them.

Opening Aria and Kingston's mailbox, she took the folded envelope from her pocket and slid it inside before closing it. The front door opened and Kingston walked out on the porch. He said nothing as he jogged down the stairs, brushed past her, and snatched open the mailbox.

Jessa stepped back from him. "It's just a note apologizing to Aria for sending that text," she said calmly, as he turned to her with the letter balled in his hand.

Kingston shook his head as he eyed her. "If that's what this really is—and not you starting some more shit in my marriage—then it's still not enough," he said, his dark and handsome face tight with some emotion.

Jessa figured it to be anger. She understood that. "If you could just give the letter to Aria," she said before turning to walk away.

"No, Jessa. You owe me an apology as well and I want it."

She paused and turned. "What?" Jessa asked, her face showing the surprise she felt.

Kingston pointed his finger at her accusingly. "You lied on me and you caused major trouble in my marriage, Jessa. Hell, Eric was the one fucking you, and I'm sorry to say, but Jackson messed up his own marriage. Aria and I were just fine until you played your childish games."

Jessa arched her brow. "Are you talking about the text or the truth about your wife's past?" she asked. "You can't claim perfection when it's based on secrets and lies."

Kingston's jaw tightened.

Jessa dropped her head wishing she had swallowed back the snide remark alluding to his wife's tawdry teenaged past of sleeping with strange men and stealing their money as they slept. Less than a month ago, in anger, Jessa had shared with Kingston the secret her best friend had once shared with her.

"Look, Kingston, I apologize. Okay? I am regretting the things that I have done. Please, give Aria the letter," she finished before turning to cross the street to Jaime's house.

"You're not wanted here, Jessa. Can't you see that?" he called behind her.

She stepped up on the sidewalk and turned. "That is my home and I'm not leaving it. The only thing I have to offer any of you are my apologies and you can take it or leave it. I really don't give a damn."

Kingston waved his hand at her dismissively before turning to jog back up the stairs and into his home to slam the front door.

Wham!

Her patience was wearing thin. Truly, she wanted to go home, pour a glass of wine, and lounge on her deck toasting her second chance at life and saying a huge Cee Lo Green "Fuck You" to everyone.

Turning, she looked up at Jaime's home briefly before she continued up the stairs and rang the doorbell. *Last one,* she thought as she waited, hating the nerves she felt. Jessa had *never* been one to let anyone see her sweat.

The door swung open and Jaime stood there in a white all-in-one bodysuit with a white towel around her neck. Her face instantly filled with venom. "You have got to be the craziest bitch I have ever laid eyes on," she spat, her eyes flashing.

Jesse's back stiffened. *Be with me, Lord, for she knows not what she does . . . or what I want to do. Amen.*

"I wanted to apologize for my role in all this, Jaime. I wanted—"

"You wanted to get your ass whipped is what you must want, having the audacity to walk your scandalous, trifling, no-good, backstabbing ass up on my porch. Just who do you think you are, Jessa?" Jaime's newly cropped chin-length hair moved about her face as she did a full-on sistah-girl head bob.

Jessa sighed because she was bored. "Save the reality TV bad-girl crap for Aria. The role suits her better."

"You need your head checked, Jessa. Seriously. You need to have your oblivious ass on someone's couch," Jaime said.

Humph, I've had my ass up on your couch . . . while your husband ate my pussy.

Jessa looked up to the heavens. *Sorry, Lord, it slipped. I'm sorry. At least I thought it and didn't say it.*

"You were wrong for fucking Eric and stabbing me—*and Marc*—in the back. That was trifling enough in itself."

Jessa stiffened and her anger came in a flash. "Don't bring Marc into this, Jaime. And I am dead damn serious. I came to apologize to you, but don't cross the line."

Jaime stepped out onto the porch and pressed her nose to Jessa's. "Cross the line like you did fucking my husband, Jessa. Huh? And then sending that stupid text and planning to run away with him. Huh? And then telling that motherfucker about the money. Huh? How many lines did you cross?"

Jessa didn't back down. In fact, she arched a brow and tilted her head to the side to look at Jaime from head to toe. "If you think I am going to stand here like a classless hooligan and argue with you, you're mistaken. My shit is too together for that," she told the woman in a low voice that had to bounce off her face since they were so close.

Jaime raised her hands quickly and pushed Jessa.

As she stumbled back, caught off guard, Jessa's hand went to her belly as she tried to keep her body from falling back down the stairs. *My baby!* She fell back against one of the columns flanking the porch with an *umph!*

Jessa eyed the other woman as she stood there looking pleased with herself. She licked her lips as she stood up straight and pretended to dust herself off. "You really have to be more careful with how you handle a pregnant woman, Jaime. Eric would hate for something to happen to his unborn child," Jessa said, knowing she was completely wrong for the satisfaction she felt as Jaime's eyes got as big as half dollars and her mouth fell open in shock.

She hadn't meant to tell her like that. She really hadn't.

"Jaime, look, I really came to apologize and I didn't mean to tell you like that—"

"You're lying," Jaime spat.

Jessa shook her head. "No, Jaime. No, I'm not. I'm not lying," she said softly, feeling a stress headache beginning to pulse at the base of her neck. She turned and walked down the stairs.

"If you think you are going to pimp your bastard child off on Eric, you are mistaken. You tell Pleasure or whomever you were sleeping with that they have a baby on the way, but don't bring that bullshit on my front step, Jessa Bell! Do you hear me?" Jaime screamed at the top of her lungs.

"Hell, everyone can hear you," Jessa muttered as she just continued to walk away, not bothering to explain that she had no other lovers except Eric or even acknowledge Jaime still screaming at her like a fool.

"Do you hear me, Jessa? You and your bastard stay the hell away from me!"

Later that evening, Jessa dropped her robe and stood nude in front of the full-length mirror of her dressing room. She cocked her head to the side as she studied her body. Soon her breasts and belly would swell. *Oh God, and probably my nose,* Jessa thought, raising her hands to touch it as she twisted this way and that in the mirror.

She pressed her hand to her flat belly.

The day after she took the pregnancy test she had herself in her OB/GYN's office. Everything was all confirmed. She was two months along. There was a baby on the way singing, "Sign, Sealed, Delivered I'm Yours."

Jessa closed her eyes as she tilted her back and released a long, steady breath filled with all of her stresses. She hadn't even decided if she was going to have the baby yet—if she even deserved to have the baby—but today when Jaime pushed her and she thought she was going to tumble down the stairs, her first thought had been the baby. *Her* baby.

Her baby by the married man who killed himself after trying to kill her because she wanted to end their affair.

My life is a fucking soap opera.

Turning from the mirror, she quickly walked back into the bedroom and snatched up the deep purple sheer demibra and thong she had laid out earlier. She pulled on a fitted matte jersey dress, but then changed her mind and grabbed a pair of linen slacks and button-up white shirt to put on instead. The dress said vamp. Not the image she needed for where she was going.

It took her just twenty minutes to drive to the hospital and another five minutes to find the chaplain's office. It was late and it was hardly the spot for a confession, but Jessa knew she had to lay her burdens somewhere in order to make some hard decisions on what to do.

Taking just a moment to pause, Jessa knocked briefly on his door.

"Come in."

She entered and smiled a bit as the chaplain, Reverend Dobbins, rose from his seat and barely looked that much taller. He was a man of short stature with a pleasant round face and not a bit of neck. His scalp and cheeks were almost as red as his hair. But his presence that night had calmed her, and tonight she sought that same peace as she struggled with all of the repercussions of her affair with her best friend's husband.

"Hello, Reverend Dobbins," she said, strolling into the brightly lit office, and extended her hand to him.

He nodded and smiled, causing his cheeks to rise and nearly close his eyes. "How are you, Ms. Bell?" he asked, patting the back of her hand while he warmly shook it.

Jessa settled into the seat he offered with a wave of his hand. "You remember me?" she asked, setting her clutch in her lap as she crossed her ankles.

Reverend Dobbins nodded. "Of course, and I've been praying for you," he said, taking his seat. "Your story was quite unforgettable, Jessa."

"That's an understatement," she joked lightly, looking

down at her hands briefly. "And there's more." *More than I am even willing to acknowledge.*

"Okay."

Jessa sat back in the chair. "I truly want to be forgiven by God—"

"You have been," Revered Dobbins added gently. "Without question He forgave you as soon as you asked him to."

Jessa was confused. "And it's just that simple?" she asked.

"Absolutely."

"But how can he forgive me when I can't seem to forgive myself? I honestly believe that all of my sins were the reason I was almost killed a couple of weeks ago. You know? Karma, right?"

Reverend Dobbins shook his head. "The Lord doesn't punish us for our sins . . . and you can't continue to punish yourself. The only way to move forward and to feel better and to do better is to say I messed up, but I see where I went wrong and I won't do it again."

"But I am still dealing with my anger and I have done things since I was released from the hospital that were wrong, but in the moment it felt like I needed to pay back the people who hurt me." Jessa thought of Renee's dismissal, Kingston's anger, and Jaime's scorn.

"Again, you recognize your misstep, you pray for strength and guidance, and you make the correction. No one is perfect."

Jessa fell silent.

"Have you been reading your Bible, attending a church, or going to Bible study?" he asked.

She shook her head, feeling conflicted. She understood the anger everyone had for her, but she had never been one to let anyone talk to her or treat her any kind of way. "I tried to apologize to these people, Reverend, and everyone threw it back in my face. So why should I still feel guilty if I am saying I was wrong?"

"You have to be just as willing to forgive as you are to be forgiven."

Jessa hated the tears that filled her eyes. "But I feel like I am being punished for my sins and I don't want that on me."

Reverend Dobbins leaned forward and folded his pudgy hands on top of his desk. "Are you truly regretful of your actions, or are you doing what you think God wants you to do to be forgiven?"

"I want back in God's good graces," Jessa admitted with ease, blinking away her tears.

"But are you truly regretful of your actions?"

Was she? Jessa stood and paced in his small generic office. "This is not me. I do not feel like *me,*" she stressed.

"And so the change has to be with you, Jessa, and not with other people."

Jessa crossed her arms over her chest as she continued to pace back and forth. She stopped and faced the clergyman. "So I shouldn't think of this baby as another payback for *all* my secrets and sins?" she asked softly.

Reverend Dobbins's blue eyes filled with surprise. "You're pregnant?"

"By the man who tried to kill me," Jessa added before he even needed to ask. She felt overcome with emotions and tears filled her eyes. "All I can think about is this baby growing up and people pointing fingers or talking about all the scandal or that their mama was a mistress. I don't want that for this child."

Jessa dropped down into her chair and covered her mouth with her hands as she tried to breathe through the tightness in her chest as her tears flowed freely. "I don't want my sins on this baby," she whispered brokenly through her tears. "And there are things no one knows. Things I will carry to my grave. But why should this baby suffer? I don't deserve this baby."

And there was the truth.

Suddenly, Jessa felt Revered Dobbins's presence near her and she looked up as he took her hand in his and knelt.

"That baby, even in the midst of the darkness of your life, is a blessing. God has blessed you, Jessa, and only you can write the story of your life that will be told."

Jessa nodded, but her doubts nipped at her.

"I'm going to give you some Scriptures that I want you to read every day. But right now I want to pray with you, child. Can we pray?"

Jessa lowered her head and closed her eyes, tightening her grasp on Reverend Dobbins's hands as he began to pray for her strength and serenity in a low voice that was meant for just them and God to hear.

Jessa returned to her beautiful home in Richmond Hills, among the neighbors who scorned her, just as confused as ever. Was she ready to have this baby? Was she ready to take the walk to being saved? How often would her anger and need for revenge cause her to backslide? How many times could God truly forgive?

She pulled up to her mailbox and was surprised to find nothing but a business card when she reached her hand in for the mail. Frowning, she reached up to turn on the interior light as she looked down at it. "VINCENT GRANT. INSURANCE AGENT," Jessa read aloud.

Jessa tossed it onto her passenger seat, assuming a random insurance agent was going house to house to sell premiums. When she reached up to turn off the interior light, she noticed handwriting on the back of the card that had flipped over when she tossed it. Frowning again, she picked it up.

She read aloud again:

"Perhaps this time we could dine together at the Terrace Room. Call me."

She immediately thought of the man at the restaurant that day trying to get her attention before his wife, woman, or whatever walked up. She suspected he was also the one who sent the note to her that day. "And now he had his happy ass to my *house?*"

Jessa turned her car onto the driveway and grabbed her cell phone. She blocked her number and dialed his cell phone.

"Hello."

"Mr. Grant, this is Jessa Bell," she said, shutting off the Jag and climbing out of it to stride up the drive to her front door. "I don't know how in the hell you got inside Richmond Hills—"

"I live here. Me and my wife just moved in around the corner about a month ago," he said.

"What the fuck ever? Didn't you just say you were married, so why the hell are you dropping notes in my mailbox?" she snapped.

"Oh. I assumed you didn't care—"

"You assumed wrong," Jessa told him in a hard voice, her heart pounding just as hard.

"I just wanted to try some pussy that was good enough to make a nigga wanna kill you," he said. "Sheee-it."

Jessa pulled the phone from her face as she walked inside her house. "My patience is just as short as your penis, so stay the hell away from me, freak."

She ended the call and fought the urge to throw her phone against a wall.

You brought this on yourself. You made them think you are a serial mistress. The eternal side-chick.

Kicking off her heels, Jessa jumped a little when her landline phone rang suddenly, echoing inside the spacious house. She padded barefoot into the kitchen and grabbed the cordless from its base on the granite countertop. She looked down at it and didn't recognize the number but knew it was a New York area code.

Jessa answered it. "Hello."

"Hello, is this Jessa Bell?" a female voice asked.

"Yes . . . and you are?" Jessa asked coolly, her guard immediately up.

"My name is Myra Moseley and I am with Power Up Publicity," she began, her voice husky and refined but with a tinge of a street vibe around the edges.

Another Aria, Jessa thought. "I'm not sure why you would be calling me, Myra?" Jessa said, sounding and feeling tired. She just wanted to go bed—well, drink a glass of wine and go to bed, but that was a no-no now.

"Well, I have a friend at the news station in your hometown there in Jersey who sent me info on your story."

Jessa immediately tensed.

"And I thought the statement you made after you left the funeral really struck a chord with me, and I think there's an audience out there who can either relate to your story or learn something from it. You are absolutely right. Why on earth do you deserve to be brutally attacked in your home for ending an affair that everyone blames you for anyway."

Jessa remained quiet, still wary, but listening.

"With my connections, your story, and how well you come off on camera, I think we can really get you booked on talk shows across the country and give you a chance to tell your story. Give you a chance to put a spin on how your life is told."

Jessa licked her lips. "Why open myself up to more attention and speculation and judgment. For what reason?" she asked, turning to set her clutch and her keys on the counter before walking to her restaurant-quality refrigerator and grabbing a bottled water.

"I'm here to tell you, Jessa—can I call you Jessa?"

"Sure."

"Jessa, that local news station is already pushing this story to break nationally. It would be a big boost for them and that newscaster who is all over this. The only thing you can do is get out there and tell your own damn story . . . especially the ex-mistress who is regretting her decision to be the other woman."

Jessa thought the woman's words rung so close to her counsel from Reverend Dobbins.

"Only I can write the story of my life that will be told," she said softly, almost to herself as she remembered his words of advice as she pressed her hand to her belly.

"That's right, Jessa. *Only* you."

Chapter 5

Two weeks later

Jessa held up her hand to the makeup artist and yawned. "I'm sorry," she said. "I am so tired."

"That's okay. We'll be done soon," the young black woman said, her dreadlocks as thick as sausage links and long enough to reach her lower back.

Jessa shifted her eyes from the woman's face to her reflection in the lit mirror running above the long counter of the hair and makeup for *The Kerry Kay Show.*

Jessa was nervous, but she was determined to work this interview for everything it could bring her. Kerry Kay was no Jeremy Kyle or Jerry Springer with its edgy tone and rowdy audience. Kerry Kay was on the verge of becoming the next Oprah Winfrey or Barbara Walters.

"How you feeling?"

Jessa shifted her eyes up as Myra strolled into the room. Again, Jessa noted how the woman didn't resemble what she imagined on the phone. The short and petite woman with the big corn-fed smile was not the overly gorgeous, supremely confidant, diva in training. Myra said she loved to be underestimated.

"I'm fine," Jessa lied, refusing to show the nerves that had her stomach bundled in a tight knot.

Myra looked at her with eyes that could con a homeless person out of *their* last nickel. "Could I have a quick second with her?" she asked the makeup artist.

"Sure."

Jessa spun in the chair to face her publicist as the woman left the room. "What's up?" she asked, already knowing what was coming.

Myra smiled, big and bright. "Listen, I know you're Ms. Sophistication personified, but this whole cool exterior is going to put people off and alienate you."

Jessa crossed her legs. She knew Myra was good at what she did. Jessa did her homework and the woman handled some heavyweight New York clients. Certainly not A-list clients but was well-respected, and Jessa went with her because she was drinking the Kool-Aid the woman was pushing.

Myra had plans for her. Big plans. Jessa was on board.

But . . .

"I'm not going on television and crying like Jimmy Swaggart. I *am* apologetic. I *am* more enlightened since I almost died. I *am* willing to tell my story. I *am* not going to make an ass out of myself," Jessa stressed, her eyes showing no room for debate on that.

"But you can't come off like the cold-hearted side-chick on the come-up," Myra stressed back.

"Side-chick? Come-up?" Jessa said with a disgruntled eye. She knew exactly what the terms meant, she just refused to acknowledge them as part of her vocabulary. *Next I'll be head bobbing, chewing gum, and saying "Nigga, please" on the regular.*

"How about this? Just be real to how you feel and don't try to hide behind the cool façade," Myra suggested. "The point is to come off like the reformed mistress, not a spotlight-grabbing, money-hungry charlatan soaking up five minutes of fame like these reality TV chicks."

"Okay," Jessa agreed, just to end the conversation.

Thankfully, Myra left the subject alone after one last squeeze of Jessa's hands before she moved to the door to wave the makeup artist back in. Jessa felt a wave of nausea hit her. She closed her eyes and breathed deeply until the moment had passed.

Morning sickness was taking its toll on her. The doctor said it should get better in the next few weeks after she entered her second trimester and Jessa couldn't wait. She thought about the baby she was carrying. It all seemed unreal.

"Okay, all done."

Jessa opened her eyes and nodded in appreciation. The makeup was less dramatic than her normal bright red lipstick and heavily done eyes. Myra thought a more natural look was best. That and the wide-leg pantsuit she wore that was a far cry from the form-fitting, well-tailored designer dresses she preferred on her curvaceous shape.

Jessa actually thought she looked younger. *Humph, well, I'll be damned. Maybe less is more.*

One of the show's associate producers popped her head in. "We're ready for Jessa," she said to Myra.

Jessa rose to her feet, trying not to feel like one of those ass backward *Jerry Springer* guests waiting to air their person problems on the show.

The travel, accommodations, and personal car service had been far above anything she was sure most talk shows were doling out, but still, what was she opening herself up for?

"Jessa, they're ready for you," Myra said, standing in the doorway.

Jessa gave herself one last perusal in the mirror before leaving the room. *God, please strengthen me . . .*

* * *

"Jessa, you admit that you entered into an affair with a man who was married to one of your closest friends and ... ised husband?"

... looked across the small di- ... to her. She was an average ... ess skin and a beauty that ... en. She was pretty. She was ... was on target to fill the gap

... ly," Jessa finally admitted, ... zed club chair in which she

... ndreds of audience members ... eir murmurs rose. She looked ... ned one of the women jump- ... ng "Whore!" at her as she pointed.

"I think I chose to deal with the sudden death of my husband—whom I loved deeply—by turning what was a love between friends into something more . . . particularly when I noticed that his attention had changed. We shared a look and I knew that he looked at me different, and it nudged me to view him in the same way. I wish now that we never had that moment."

Kerry Kay eyed her. "Why specifically?" she asked as she settled her chin in her hand and leaned in to watch Jessa closely.

Jessa wanted to snap, "Get out of my face!" but instead she licked her lips.

"There were so many repercussions of the affair. I ended friendships because of it, and then when I told him that it was over and that I wasn't interested in the secrecy and the lying anymore, he became . . . different. He changed."

"He stalked you?" Kerry asserted.

Jessa nodded. "Yes, he still wanted his wife *and* me. He wasn't willing to take no and . . . and . . ."

Her words faltered as she was pulled back to that night. Eric's erratic behavior. His cruel words. His hands on her neck. The breath leaving her body. Unconsciousness . . .

She was surprised by the tear that raced down her cheek.

Kerry leaned over to press a soft tissue into her hand. "And what?" she gently urged.

"He strangled me. He blamed me for leaving. He blamed me for telling his wife and ruining their relationship. And he was obsessed with me. That was the scariest night of my life." Jessa lightly dabbed at her eyes, careful not to ruin her makeup.

Kerry Kay looked at her sympathetically before turning to face the camera. "We'll be back with more and Jessa will tell us about the scary night her married lover attempted to kill her before taking his own life."

Soft and sad music filled the studio audience.

A man with a headset on came up on the stage and Kerry turned to him in a low voice. Jessa heard something about the last segment running too long. Turning her head from them, her eyes happened to land on a small cluster of women sitting in the audience whispering together; then they all turned to eye her.

Jessa stiffened her back and met their stare. She felt their judgment. She turned her head and another woman's eyes pierced her as well.

"And we're back in five, four, three, two . . ."

Kerry Kay faced the camera again. "And we're back. We were just listening to the story of a former mistress who nearly died after trying to end the relationship," she said, before turning her head to look at Jessa. "Tell us about that night."

Jessa didn't see any compassion in the woman's eyes and she knew she wasn't getting her story told the right way. "Um, he had made promises that he didn't keep. He was very different with me than he was with his wife. I had no idea that once he discovered her affair that their relationship behind closed doors became very sadomasochistic. I didn't see that side of him until I attempted to end our relationship. His behavior was very erratic, very intense, very crazed. At one point when I refused to open the door to the home we were supposed to share, he stood outside and masturbated against my window."

"Were you afraid of him?" Kerry asked.

"Yes," Jessa asserted. "It seemed the more his wife pulled away from him or angered him, the more he wanted me to still be there for him, and when I wasn't, his anger and everything disturbing escalated to the night he forced himself into my home. He blamed me for destroying his life and he strangled me until I blacked out."

"Now, what happens after you lost consciousness has been chronicled in detail by the local news media in New Jersey. Let's take a look," Kerry said.

Jessa averted her eyes as a collage of all the news media clips played, detailing all of the sordid details of the love triangle that turned deadly.

"I noticed that you didn't watch the tape," Kerry said. "Are you embarrassed by this story taking on such life and exposing a lot of your dirty secrets?"

"Yes," Jessa said emphatically. "Most definitely."

"I've always believed everything in life happens for a reason and there is the ability to pull a lesson out of adversity. What is the lesson in all this for you, Jessa?"

"Even before the attempt on my life, I made the choice not to be his or any other man's mistress anymore, but the point has really hit home since I've seen all of the blame of the relationship laid at my door," Jessa said, locking eyes with her host. "I accept my role in it, but now it's as if his death has absolved him from any blame and to have people feel as if I deserved to die because I was a mistress. I ended the relationship, but my trial and persecutions never ended. I do wonder about that."

Myra nodded from her seat in the front row as Kerry reached over and lightly clasped Jessa's hand. Jessa had spoken with truth and with real emotions, but she did accept the small victory of drawing the woman—and perhaps many more—onto her side.

Her interview on *The Kerry Kay Show* wouldn't premiere for two weeks, but just the golden nugget of the taping—and the recent news of a high-profile murder-for-hire involving a mistress looking to be the wife—led to Myra booking Jessa on several of those cable entertainment news shows to speak about her own thoughts and wishes on the case as a "reformed mistress." Before they parted ways at Newark International Airport, Myra received a call finalizing Jessa's input in an article on the dangers of being a mistress by a major magazine publication.

As Jessa rode in the backseat of the black SUV of the car service, she felt adrenaline at the chance to increase her platform and get her story told. She wanted to change her image. *For my baby.*

I'm having this baby.

She didn't feel she ever deserved the right to bear a child, but Reverend Dobbins said that this pregnancy was a blessing from God.

An image of Eric's face distorted with all kinds of crazy suddenly filled her head. *Lord, please don't let that shit be hereditary.*

"Driver, do you have another appointment this afternoon?" Jessa asked, tilting her head to the side to eye the man.

His eyes shifted up to the mirror to eye her.

Jessa didn't miss the interest clear in his eyes. "I would like to go to the mall. I would pay you for the extended time," she told him.

"I could go off the clock and we could make it a date," he offered, his voice deep and nice. The kind to make you shiver when you heard it through a phone line or close to your ear.

Jessa noticed his handsome features when he first opened the rear door for her to climb into the SUV, but dick and everything it was attached to was the least of her concerns.

"I am pregnant and the only man I would even think of having sex with is the father. And since he's dead and burning in hell for all perpetuity, looks like I'm celibate for the next seven months or so. Still want that date or should we schedule ahead for the night after my six-week checkup?" she asked, the sweetness of her tone doing nothing to belie the sarcasm.

He chuckled. "Nah, I'm good."

Jessa smiled coldly. "Short Hills Mall, please."

She slid on her shades as she sighed and settled back against the plush leather of the seat. She knew she was a little too hard on the man, but it felt good to let a little of her normal bitchy self show. Her wit and snappy comebacks had always been a part of her charm. She felt a little like the old Jessa.

Bzzzzzzzzz.

She opened her bright orange Birkin and pulled out her cell phone. She frowned, not recognizing the number. "Hello?" she said, smoothing the deep waves of her hair behind her shoulder.

"Jessa, this is Jaime. I have Pleasure on the line—"

Jessa's head pounded at the sudden intrusion into her life. "I'm not his pimp and don't have to be privy to your business transaction of Dicks on a Dime," Jessa said smoothly, recovering quickly. *I'm on a roll today.*

"Real funny, Jessa. I thought you should tell Pleasure that you're claiming to be pregnant and he might be *one* of the candidates."

Jessa felt her anger rise, but she forced herself to smile as she saw the driver's shocked expression in the rearview mirror. "Pleasure, why not just tell Jaime that all you did was eat the hell out of my pussy—and thanks, by the way. Now, unless science has changed and you can get a woman pregnant with your clever little tongue—particularly two months before we even met—then there is no chance in hell that you my *babbydaddy,*" she said, meaning to add extra emphasis to the slang term.

"I just wanted to make sure you weren't telling people I got you pregnant" he said, his dark and deep voice suddenly filling the line.

"No offense, Pleasure, but as fine as you are, your dick has more miles on it than a thousand rental cars. I wouldn't raw you for a million dollars. So puh-leeze and bye-bye."

Click.

The SUV came to a stop and her driver turned in his seat to eye her.

Jessa rolled her eyes and removed her shades. "Poor, Jaime, but your attempt at a Maury Povich moment missed the mark . . . like that new hairdo of yours," she said smoothly.

"You are such a bitch, Jessa."

"How did you get my number?" she asked as she motioned for the driver to turn around and proceed ahead.

"Eric's death has made a substantial amount of resources available to me. Financial and otherwise."

"Well, you didn't need to waste it getting my private cell phone number when I live down the street from you. Now, don't blow all that money in one place, you don't have the resources or the work history to build it back up again," Jessa said, meaning to sound bored even as she quickly made a note to contact Eric's private detective to see if he sold her number to Jaime. She might have stumbled on the man's info in Eric's home office and contacted him.

"Jaime, why don't you go ahead and plan your evening of fun, fucking, and finances with your man-whore and I'll enjoy a little shopping trip to make sure your stepchild has a wonderful wardrobe when he or she arrives."

"That's if you're even pregnant, bitch . . . and if you are, your bastard child means nothing to me. Clear?"

Jessa's eyes glinted with fury and Jaime's words felt like a gut punch. That was the third time the woman had addressed her unborn baby as a bastard. The third damn time.

Lord, this double-life–living, trifling, backbone-lacking, confused, and unsure heifer is trying me. She is trying me.

"Ooh, good comeback. You always were the smart one in our little clique," Jessa said, her voice heavy with sarcasm as she let the slander of her baby pass . . . for now. "And ask Pleasure to do that little tongue trick just above the clit. If your pussy isn't numb from overuse, you should cum like crazy. I know I did."

Jessa ended the call and dropped her phone back into her bag before sliding her shades back into place.

"You're hell, huh?"

Jessa said nothing. Behind the cover of her shades, her eyes were filling with tears she refused to let fall.

"That's if you're even pregnant, bitch . . . and if you are, your bastard child means nothing to me. Clear?"

Jessa dismissed Jaime but not her words. Who else would call her child a bastard or even worse—behind his or her back or even more boldly to their face. A child shouldn't have to bear the sins of the parents.

Jessa fell silent with her thoughts as she looked out the window at the green trees lining the roads leading to Short Hills Mall. Day by day, the idea of having this child was settling with her. She would be happier if the baby wasn't Eric's, but there was no turning back on that now.

I am going to raise this child.

A soft smile lit up her face. But when she thought of her

own mother and how easily she had left her behind, the smile faded and sadness filled her eyes. With focus she could see her face in the tinted glass and she wondered if she would ever forgive or forget being left behind. Abandoned. Shelved. Forgotten.

And it had hurt all the more because she had been a little girl completely enamored of her mother . . .

"Ninety-eight, ninety-nine, one hundred," Jessa said, her voice slightly soft and husky even at the age of five. She ran her slender fingers through her mother's shoulder-length hair and thought it was just as soft and pretty as her Barbie dolls. She set the brush on the table where her mother said and came around her to bury her face in her lap.

"Move, Jessa," Darla Logan said, her voice filled with irritation as she brushed her daughter's head from her lap.

Jessa's eyes filled with tears and her bottom lip trembled as she stumbled back a bit.

Darla lit a cigarette and took a deep drag of it, her bright red lipstick staining the butt. She used her free hand to fluff the soft waves of her face before she finally glanced over at her daughter. She sighed as she turned in her chair. "Look, Jessa, your mama has a date. I'm trying to find you a new daddy," she said, her eyes already showing the effects of whatever she kept sipping from the glass.

"Where my daddy?" Jessa asked, easing back over to the table to pick up her mama's bottle of perfume. She inhaled deeply of it.

"No one knows that but him and God," Darla snapped, as she took the perfume bottle from her daughter's hand.

"But I thought Cary was gonna be daddy?" Jessa said, standing on the tips of her bare feet to pick up her mama's lipstick tube. "I heard you call him Daddy when he spent the night."

Darla took the lipstick tube and lightly grabbed her daughter's chin. She kindly smiled as she undid the tube and put a little of the bright red lipstick onto Jessa's lips. "Look, you get your coat and I'm gonna take you to Grandma's house," she said, her breath filling Jessa's nostrils.

The little girl frowned at the sour smell of liquor. "I'm staying the night?" she asked, her words garbled from the back-and-forth motion of the lipstick on her lips.

"Um, no, I'll come and get you as soon as my date over. Okay?"

Jessa nodded and turned to look at her reflection in the mirror. "Everybody say I look just like you, Mama," she said, smiling as she turned this way and that.

Darla stood up. Her bright red bra and panties looked even brighter against her deep bronzed complexion. Jessa watched as her mama picked her pocketbook up from the foot of the bed and took something from it that she slid into her mouth.

"Can I have some, Ma?" she asked, her hand already extending.

Darla looked down at her daughter with sad eyes. "Trust me, you don't want none of this shit," she said before turning to pull on the clothes laid out on her pretty white lace-covered bed.

Jessa ran to her room and grabbed her pink coat with the bunny ears on the top of the hood. She settled down on her knees in front of her television. Soon she was giggling from the colorful cartoons, actually ending her laughter with a sigh filled with content.

It wasn't until the show went to a commercial that she jumped up and ran into her mama's bedroom.

"Mama," Jessa called out as she stood at the bedroom door and saw her mother leaning forward as she sat on the edge of the bed.

Jessa frowned as her mother fell forward off the bed and onto the floor. She rushed to her side as Darla struggled to rise to her feet. "You okay?"

Darla brushed her daughter's hand away. "I'm fine, Jessa. Get off me!" she snapped.

Again the tears came and the bottom lip trembled. Her mother was her everything and she hated to make her angry.

Darla stumbled into the adjoining bath.

Soon Jessa heard the water running as she sniffed and wiped her tears with her sleeve. "I'm sorry, Mama," she said when Darla reappeared.

"Okay, Jessa. Thank you," she snapped, her words slurring, as she tugged on the wool coat that matched the dress she wore.

Darla was known for her style and fashion, and Jessa loved to play with her makeup, clothes, and jewelry.

"Let's go."

Her mother grabbed up her hand and pulled Jessa behind her through the modest-sized home and out the door. Jessa felt like she was running to keep up with her mother's stride.

Her grandmother lived just down the street and they were climbing the stairs to the big brick house in no time. Jessa pulled off her coat as soon as they stepped inside. "Grandma," she called out.

"I'm in the kitchen," her grandmother called back.

Jessa made to run in that direction, but Darla reached out to grab her arm. "Hey, give Mama a big hug," she said, her eyes glazed.

Jessa was more than happy to oblige as she wrapped her arms around her mama's neck.

"Tell Grandma I'll be back to get you tonight. Okay?" she said, pressing a kiss to Jessa's cheek.

"Okay, Mama."

Darla smiled a little as she looked at her daughter. "You

do look just like me," she said softly before standing up and walking out the door.

Jessa moved to the window and pulled the curtain to watch her mother stumble back down the street to their house. She hoped her mother would turn and look back, but she didn't. Something didn't feel right.

Jessa was still standing there a little while later when a flashy red car pulled up in front of their house and her mother came outside with a suitcase in her hand. A man got out of the driver's seat and took the suitcase to put it in the trunk before he got back in the car. They pulled away.

Jessa was still standing there when her grandmother walked out of her kitchen.

"Where your Mama?" she asked.

"She said she'll be back," Jessa said, her nose pressed to the cold window as her breath fanned out on it and then evaporated.

That was a lie. It was one of many her mother told her in the days after she left Jessa behind with her grandmother. Until the calls stopped all together.

Jessa shook her head as she remembered pressing her face to the car window anytime they would pass the house where she had lived all her life with her mother. Her grandmother owned the home, and once her mother ran away with the man in the bright red car, they eventually rented it out to a new family.

Jessa never laid eyes on her mother again. Not even at her grandmother's funeral years later. It was as if she never had a mother and her mother never had a child.

Jessa pressed her hand to her belly and closed her eyes. *I'll do better by you. I swear.*

Chapter 6

Two weeks later

Jessa was just finishing one final lap around the large pond that made up the center of the Richmond Hills subdivision. Stationed around the water were the clubhouse with an indoor heated pool, a tennis court, a playground area, and a small dog park.

She came to a stop and bent over to press her hands above her knees as she inhaled and exhaled slowly as she waited for her heartbeat to slow down. It had been so long since she ventured from her cul-de-sac to take advantage of the amenities offered by the high-end subdivision.

Standing tall, she placed her hands on her hips in the form-fitting unitard she wore as she looked at the ducks in the pond. It was many Sunday afternoons that she and Marc would finally pull themselves from bed or from lounging around the house to sit by the pond and just read or talk or sightsee their neighbors.

She shifted her eyes over to the playground and envisioned a small girl of about six with pigtails and colorful bows laughing and running around with the other children. Her daughter.

Lord, I am grateful for this blessing, but I can't help but wish this was Marc's child and not Eric's.

And that was the truth.

She would have to decide whether to even tell Eric's parents eventually, and Jessa wasn't looking forward to their intrusion into her life. Unless . . .

Jessa shook her head. It would be ungodly to never tell them that their dead son had fathered a child before his death. She was trying her best to redeem herself, and how could she if she pulled another of her "old Jessa Bell" stunts like that? That would open the door to even more karma, and Jessa felt her plate was full.

But it sure would make life more simple.

Sighing, she moved over to take a seat on one of the black wrought-iron benches. Summer was finally drawing to an end and the breeze she felt had just a tinge of coolness to it. It felt good. She closed her eyes and tilted her head back to enjoy it.

"A neck made for . . . kissing."

Jessa stiffened and frowned in distaste before she opened her eyes. Vincent Grant was standing in front of the bench next to her, pretending to stretch. Jessa just released a heavy breath and eyed this silly Negro trying to beg for pussy on the sneak.

"I haven't seen you in a while," he said as he raised his arms high above his head.

Jessa fought the urge to stand up and push him hard enough to send him tumbling down the small embankment and into the pond. *Maybe a little dip will cool his perverted horny ass off.*

Or maybe something else will . . .

Jessa pulled her cell phone from where she had it snug and secure inside her sports bra. It was a little sweaty as she pretended to make a quick call but instead turned on her video camera. She pretended to put her arms over the back of the bench with the camera in the hand closest to him.

"I really wish you would let me take you out," Vincent

said, now sitting down on the bench and retying his already tied sneakers.

"And I wish you would understand that I am not interested in you and you're harassing me," Jessa said, being sure to tape him.

"I can't stop thinking about fucking you," he said, turning his head to gaze at her like he wanted her to see how serious he was.

And so Jessa eyed him as well. "And if you don't leave me the hell alone, you pervert, I will take out a restraining order and then everyone—including your wife—will know that you dream of fucking me, you perverted ass."

Vincent sat up straight. "Who would believe you?" he asked with a smirk.

Jessa stood up. "Probably no one," she said before walking away. If the man approached her again, she would threaten to show it to his wife; then it was their problem to fix. She really wanted him and any other man looking for a quick fuck with a sexy woman to leave her the hell alone.

The next man to be blessed with my body will be my husband. And that's all to it, she said to herself, just before she spotted the woman who had been in the restaurant with Vincent that day walking up as she pushed a stroller.

Is this God's way of telling me to show her the video now? she wondered.

Jessa's steps faltered as the woman neared. She was tired of being treated like she was the spider trapping men in her web.

"How you doing today?" the woman said in a polite and friendly voice as she passed Jessa.

"Good, and you?" Jessa responded, her words stumbling a bit because she was surprised by the woman's kindness.

She looked down at her phone. The still image of him was on the screen. Was she a nice woman completely clueless to her husband's philandering? Was it Jessa's job to give the woman a clue?

She looked over her shoulder as the woman picked their baby up from the stroller and handed it to Vincent with a warm smile. If she didn't know any better, she would think they looked like the perfect suburban family.

Looks can be deceiving.

Jessa turned and pushed her cell phone back into her sports bra, deciding not to ruin the woman's day with her husband's foolishness.

But shouldn't she know?

Would she rather know?

Not in the gloating way she had texted Jaime, Renee, and Aria, but to truly let the woman know her husband was not to be trusted. Just a heads-up, woman-to-woman.

It was so much easier to be bad, because trying to do right, live right, and be right was a constant struggle. Still, Jessa was determined for the sake of her child to get her shit straight.

Thankfully, the nightmares about that night had faded along with the scars on her neck. She still didn't use her beautiful living room as much as she had in the past, but every day things were getting better to deal with. Reverend Dobbins said she had only God's presence in her life to thank for that.

Her interview on *The Kerry Kay Show* was scheduled to air Monday. In just twenty-four hours her story would shift from local drama to national news. Myra, her publicist, had already lined her up for several small speaking engagements and interviews. That day she even scheduled Jessa for a full photo session for professional head shots.

"With your looks and your story of survival and redemption, this could be big," Myra kept telling her. "Just hold on and enjoy your ride through fifteen minutes of fame—and if we work it right, that fifteen could stretch much farther. Trust me."

Jessa didn't have much trust in anything. Never had. But she was going to use the platform . . . and see where this road was going to lead.

She looked up just as a golf cart came on the trail toward her. She recognized the bright pink colors as Aria's. It slowed down as it neared her, and for a moment she could picture Aria revving the gas and running her ass off the road. All Aria did was pass her by with her head straight as if Jessa didn't exist in that moment or in her life.

Jessa chuckled as she continued on her way. She wasn't looking to be friends with any of the ladies again. She just regretted the way she ended their friendship. But the end was coming anyway . . . and so fuck her. Being friends with Jaime, Aria, or Renee was not going to get her into heaven, but apologizing for what she did to them could.

That was all she was concerned with, and if they didn't know, they needed to know.

Reverend Dobbins said God had forgiven her and would always forgive her, but when would she be able to forgive herself? That's what she was working on. And there was more to be forgiven. More than Jessa even liked to admit to herself. Something she never told anyone.

But God knew.

God knew everything.

All of our sins and griefs to bear . . .

Jessa pushed her hair behind her ear as she took notes in her freshman math finance class. She still couldn't believe she was a student at such a prestigious university. Her hard work in school had gotten her the grades to get in, and a few scholarships plus the college fund her grandmother set up for her in her will was paying the bills. She would graduate without one school loan to tie her down.

Although her grandmother had never been overly affec-

tionate and at times acted like raising her grandchild had been a burden, Jessa was thankful for the trust fund and grateful for the chance to build her own legacy outside of being the little girl betrayed by her father and left behind by her mother.

"Miss Logan . . . Miss Logan?"

Jessa looked up at her professor staring at her from where he sat his tall and lanky frame on the edge of his desk at the front of the class. Every eye in the class was on her and her heart pounded. "Yes?"

Just then the class began to stir and Jessa looked down at her watch. Their hour-and-fifteen-minute class was over.

"Don't forget your reports are due Monday. Enjoy your weekend," Professor Reign said, turning to begin placing papers in his worn leather briefcase.

Jessa rose and began gathering her things into her book bag. She walked over to the door behind one of her classmates, but instead of walking out the door behind him, she stepped back and closed the door before locking it. She dropped her bag to the floor and turned to eye her professor.

He dropped his head as he massaged his beard. "Jessa—"

"What, Jon?" she asked, eyeing the tall man with the type of skin tone that made his race ambiguous.

He was mixed. His mother was Latino and his father was a mix of Pakistani and Black. He was tall, well over six feet, and his frame was rail thin, but he was strong. He was handsome and had this kind of laid-back air that was nothing like Jessa had ever seen before.

She had made the choice to fuck the professor, and once she set her mind to it, he hadn't been able to resist her stunts. Just like he wouldn't be able to resist her now.

She smiled as she walked over to where he stood. "So

you don't want this pussy anymore?" Jessa asked, grabbing his hands and pulling them behind her to press against her buttocks in the jean dress she wore.

He snatched his hands away and lightly grabbed her upper arm to guide her toward the door of the classroom. "I told you I don't want to do this anymore. My wife is suspicious," he said, pushing her hands away as Jessa tried to unbutton the jeans he wore.

"Fuck your wife," Jessa said, meaning it. In her world, it was all about her. Caring about what other people wanted or felt left her open to getting hurt, getting disappointed, getting left behind. "As a matter of fact, Jon, fuck me.*"*

He stepped away from her and Jessa stepped back just enough to lift the edge of her dress and pull her panties off to toss over at him. "Smell it."

He caught her panties with one hand and eyed her before pressing his face against the black lace.

Jessa stroked the inside of her pussy with her finger and drew it up to her mouth to suck. She saw his dark eyes take in the move.

"I'm not going to lose my wife behind this," Jon said, even as he stepped closer to her and pressed his large and warm hand between her thighs.

Jessa pursed her lips as she hissed in pleasure. "I want your dick not your heart," she told him truthfully, reaching out to unzip his jeans and release every bit of his long and thick inches. His dick was darker than the rest of him and damn near bigger than the rest of him too.

Jessa felt her clit throb with life. "I don't have much time. I got another class," she told him, turning to press her hands to the door as she wiggled her bare ass at him.

"This is the last time, Jessa," he told her seconds before he spread her ass cheeks and slid his dick inside her wetness.

Jessa gasped at the feel of his hot hardness against her

rigid walls. Her fingernails dug into the wood of the door as each stroke seemed to cause a vacuum inside her before filling her again.

His hands came around to unzip her dress and free her breasts from the bra. As he teased her nipples with his fingers and stroked his dick inside of her, Jessa bit her bottom lip to keep from crying out. Wanting control and wanting to please him, so that he would continue to be her secret lover, she rose up on her toes in her shoes and then bent her legs to work her hips to pull downward on his dick.

"Shit," he cried out, bringing one hand up to tightly grasp a handful of her hair to jerk her head back and the other to ease around her body to lightly massage her clit.

Jessa cried out in pleasure as every pulse point on her body raced.

Knock-knock.

Someone knocked at the door. They didn't stop. Jessa didn't stop. She felt the vibrations of the door against her face as they knocked, but the feel of his dick inside her and his fingers titillating her clit was racing her toward an explosive nut that she wanted more than anything. More than whomever or whatever they wanted on the other side of the door.

Knock-knock.

The door handle rattled as someone tried to open the door.

Jessa looked over her shoulder. "You better not stop," she whispered back to him, enjoying the feel of his nuts swinging lightly between his thighs and slapping against her.

"Jon," a woman called through the door before turning the handle again.

Now he froze.

Jessa widened her eyes in a rush of anger and disappointment.

"That's my wife," he mouthed to her, motioning for her to stay still.

Jessa felt her nut drifting from her. "Fuck me," she mouthed to him, pulling his hand back down onto her clit.

He waited to see if she would knock again. Many moments passed and she didn't, but his face remained conflicted before he stepped back from Jessa and freed his dick from her.

"I can't do this anymore, Jessa," he said, pushing his sticky dick back inside his jeans before zipping them up.

"I'm gonna get me," she said as she turned to press her back to the door, then slid her hand down to lightly circle her clit with her index and middle fingers.

She closed her eyes and tilted her head back as she bent her legs and circled her hips with a moan.

Suddenly, her professor grabbed her and Jessa opened her eyes just in time to see him turn her over one of the desks. He slid his dick into her with one hard swoop and pounded away inside her pussy like he was trying to prove a point.

His fingers dug into her ass deeply as he fucked her. "This the last time, Jessa," he swore as she reached out blindly to grip the edge of the desk as she came with a force that made her feel as if her heart would burst.

She took and again used her hips to pull down on his dick as she felt it stiffen inside of her before each delicious jerk filled her with his cum. She didn't stop until she felt him go limp inside of her.

Soon he freed himself from her and moved away without saying another word.

Jessa picked up her book bag and used the package of wet wipes she brought to clean up a bit before she caught the panties he tossed at her from across the room. She straightened her clothes and pulled her book bag up onto her shoulder. "See you Monday, Professor . . . if not sooner," she said, already bold and confident at just eighteen.

She unlocked the door and stepped out of the classroom, pulling the door closed behind her.

"I thought so."

Jessa looked up in surprise as a slender light-skinned woman with freckles and a wild and curly natural stepped into her path. She recognized her from the pictures in their home. It was the professor's wife. Jessa sidestepped her, but the woman sidestepped as well to stay in her path.

Jessa's eyes flashed even as her heart pounded. "Excuse me," she snapped.

His wife leaned forward and inhaled briefly before she finally walked past Jessa. "Next time don't wear so much of that body spray if you're going to fuck a man in the bed he shares with his wife," she said in a low voice.

Jessa turned and eyed the woman over her shoulder before she watched her enter the classroom and gently close the door behind her with a soft click.

Her short affair with the sexy professor came to an immediate end that day and Jessa was transferred out of his class. Back then, her only regret was that they got caught and the dick was no longer accessible to her. Her boldness with him came back to bite her on the ass.

Married men were too much work and she had steered clear of them . . . until Eric.

He hadn't been my first affair, but he was most definitely my last, Jessa promised herself that as she walked back to her section of the Richmond Hills subdivision with a lot on her mind. The pregnancy. The talk show. The death of Eric. Her almost death at the hands of Eric. The hatred so many people had for her. Her journey to redeem herself with God.

Sometimes it was all just too much to bear.

Jessa quickened her steps as she felt all of the emotions and fears and regret choking her. She fought not to let a tear fall, rapidly blinking her eyes as each step got her closer to home. She would never let these people see her break down. Never.

"Wow, don't you look pretty, darling."

Jessa smiled as she took her seat across from Keegan at the table at Morty's, a popular steakhouse restaurant in Livingston. "I was at a photo shoot when you called and invited me to dinner. I came straight from there."

"A photo shoot?" Keegan asked,

"My publicist hired a makeup team, stylist, and photographer to take head shots of me today, believe it or not," Jessa said.

Keegan smiled a little. "I think she's on to something. The stories about you, even in the local media, have changed. There's less cries of 'kill the backstabber' to "okay, maybe she's a victim in this too.' Maria Vargas has a lot less to suck her fangs into."

Jessa nodded as the waiter came over to the table to remove the bottle of wine from the bucket to pour her a glass. She quickly placed her hand over the wineglass. "No, thank you. I'll have lemonade please."

Keegan arched a bright red brow. "No wine?" she asked as the waiter took his leave.

"No," Jessa said simply, still not a hundred percent trustworthy of the friendship the woman was trying to forge with her. It was all about motivation and Jessa wondered about Keegan's.

"Well, thank you for meeting me, sugar," the other woman said, taking a deep sip of the red wine filling her goblet. "I couldn't take another night around that house alone."

Jessa eyed her. "Alone? Your husband out of town or something?" she asked, opening her menu as she felt her hunger rise. It had been a long day at the photo shoot and her nerves to the new surroundings had killed her appetite all day.

"Or something, darling," Keegan said, her Texan accent thick. "My husband left me for another woman."

"Damn," Jessa said.

"Damn is right," she drawled. "I guess karma is a bitch, huh?"

Jessa shifted her eyes away from her. *The same karma that led to Eric almost killing me? The karma she prayed didn't affect the life of her baby?*

Jessa shook his head. "That's not karma, Keegan, that's *his* issues, just like it was Eric's issues that he was crazy as hell," she asserted.

"Humph, didn't stop his bitch of an ex-wife from calling me to gloat about it." Keegan sighed as she motioned for the waiter.

"Is she psychic? How does she know already?"

"Damn good question."

"Are you okay?" Jessa asked, not sure of what else to say.

"The blow doesn't land so hard when you're waiting for it to fall," Keegan said, motioning for the waiter to refill her wineglass.

"I'm ready to order," Jessa said. "Are you on more than a liquid diet?"

Keegan shifted her eyes up to the waiter as she smoothly flipped her red hair over her shoulder. "What I'm hungry for isn't on the menu," she said, letting her eyes fall eye level to his crotch.

Jessa leaned back a bit with a slight frown, wondering if Keegan was feeding into the hype of the big dick brotha, as she watched the woman lick her lips as the waiter smiled like he had just won the lottery. "Maybe you two should get a room?" Jessa said, slightly sarcastic. "*After* you take my order for the short ribs, please."

"I'm sorry," he apologized, his eyes still on Keegan. "And what can I get for you?"

Keegan shook her head in regret as she looked away from him. "Just a house salad," she said.

"You sure?" he asked.

Jessa cut her eyes up at him. "Yes, she is sure. Thank you."

Something in Jessa's tone or the look in her eye made him double step from their table. Keegan's eyes followed his walk away.

"If it wasn't for the fact that I plan to annihilate my husband in court and sit back pretty on his money, then I would've chanced a ride on that pole," Keegan said, directing her eyes back to Jessa.

Jessa did smile at that. "So you're going for the jugular, huh?" she asked, taking a deep sip of her water.

Keegan's eyes sharpened. "Oh, yes, sugar. His first wife got half and now I'll take half of that half and let his new bitch ponder living on just a quarter of his worth. And he best be happy as a pig in slop that we didn't have children, because I would have *made sure* my babies got their birthright."

Jessa's eyebrows arched a bit as she leaned back in the chair and crossed her long legs. She thought of the baby growing inside of her. Although she was capable of providing a good lifestyle for her baby, so could Eric *if* he had lived.

"Eric's death has made a substantial amount of resources available to me. Financial and otherwise."

Eric's resources. Eric's finances.

And I am carrying his one and only heir.

Does Eric escape his responsibilities through death, or was it her job as a mother to make sure her baby received his or her birthright?

"Excuse me, Keegan," Jessa said, easing her cell phone

from her purse as she rose from her chair and walked to the restroom.

She checked to make sure each stall was empty as she dialed. Her call went straight to voice mail. It was after business hours and she expected that.

"Lincoln, this is Jessa Bell, and I need for you to call me first thing in the morning. I am curious to see if I have any legal standing to contest a will on behalf of my unborn child as the sole heir—"

"Hello, Ms. Bell?"

She turned and gazed at her reflection as her attorney's voice suddenly filled the line. "Hello, Lincoln."

"I'm in the office working late in preparation of a trial tomorrow," he said. "Now, what was this about contesting a will?"

Jessa leaned against the wall and studied her reflection as she rearranged her hair with her fingertips in the mirror as she coolly explained her pregnancy, the death of her child's father, and her child's right to any inheritance.

The line was quiet for a few seconds. "And the father did not know about the pregnancy?"

Jessa shook her head. "No, he passed away before I even knew. So no provisions were made in the will. I'm not sure I want to pursue this, I'm just curious if it's even possible."

"And his widow has no children?"

"No," Jessa said simply, her eyes narrowing as she remembered Jaime calling her child a bastard. Jessa felt a sharp pierce of anger.

"How far along are you?" he asked.

Jessa could tell he was taking notes. "Three months."

"It's too risky for a paternity test."

"That's if you're even pregnant, bitch . . . and if you are, your bastard child means nothing to me. Clear?"

Jessa hated that Jaime's words echoed inside her head—

and pierced her heart. "You know what, Lincoln, I want to pursue this. I want to fight for what belongs to my baby. Be it a dollar or five figures. I want it and I don't want to give his widow a chance to spend what doesn't belong to her," Jessa said, her voice cold as she made her decision.

"This is going to be a little bit of a battle."

Jessa shrugged. "No problem. It'll make the win all the more better. I'll be in your office first thing in the morning and I want those papers served to his widow before close of business tomorrow."

"I have to be in court by nine," her attorney said.

"Then I will be to your office by seven, or I should I look for more legal representation?" she asked as she swung the bathroom door open wide and strutted out like she owned the world.

Lincoln laughed. "Now, we go too far back for that type of chess move," he said.

Jessa felt some of her tension ease. Lincoln had been her lawyer for years, and they were always straight up and straight shooting with each other. They had even dated very briefly when she first graduated from college. They had no chemistry and a friendship had been forged. "See you at seven?" she asked with the hint of a smile in her husky tones.

"See you at seven," he agreed, sounding more like an agreeable older brother than anything else.

Jessa ended the call and made her way back to their table. Keegan sat with her chin in her hand as she gazed out the window at something. Or maybe nothing.

She looked up at Jessa as she retook her seat. "Everything okay, honey?"

Jessa nodded. "Just handling some business," she said, unable to deny that bit of excitement she felt as she pictured the look on Jaime's face when she got served those papers.

Aria Livewell

Writer's block was a bitch.

It was true and real and kicking my ass. Again.

But they were the highs and lows and ebbs and flows of being a writer. And that's what I am. It's what I was born to be. Be it short stories, poems, news articles, blog entries, or celebrity interviews for major news publications, words were my life. I was rarely at a loss for them.

God meant for me to be a writer. Well, that and Kingston's wife.

I know after everything we have overcome and fought for that God meant him for me. I just thank Him every day that we made it back. My jealousy and insecurities and fears about men because of my own shady-ass past had made me afraid to trust him. Afraid to discover that he was just as low as those men my cousin Jontae and I used to seduce and then rob when I was a teenager.

That dumb-ass stunt by Jessa Bell's tricking ass had just poured salt on the wounds, and I believed her words and doubted my husband. She was my friend since college, but she revealed the secrecy of my infertility to my husband out of spite? Jealousy? Hatred?

I don't know her reasons. I didn't really give a fuck. I just know that I could never forgive her.

Even though that no-good bitch's stunt actually made my life better after the initial storm. She pulled the Band-Aid off of wounds that were festering and needed to be healed. She tried to destroy my happiness, and instead her betrayal of our friendship had led to us fighting even harder for our love.

But I could never forgive her.

Even though her revelations actually led us to therapy, and in time our foundation was strengthened even more than before.

Even though I discovered that God was still handing out miracles and I was blessed with a pregnancy even though I had two abortions all those years ago and even more years of never getting pregnant.

Even though my husband was at my side at the hospital, just as happy as I was to hear about the pregnancy, and anxious to return to our home with me.

Even though my therapist, Dr. Kellee, was still guiding me through the layers of pain and guilt and shame I had about the bullshit I pulled in my teens. The same guilt and shame that kept me from believing in my husband.

My and Kingston's love was better than ever. The shit little girls dream about. The kind of stories told in romance novels.

But that was not Jessa's intention.

I pushed back a bit from my desk and opened the top drawer to find the crumpled envelope with my name on the front in Jessa's familiar handwriting.

Kingston had set the letter on my desk a couple of weeks ago and told me about it when I got home from doing an interview with a rapper just released from prison for drug trafficking.

"I caught Jessa leaving a letter in the mailbox," he said after meeting me at the door to take my suitcase from me.

"What now?" I asked, hating the nerves set off inside me.

Kingston pressed a kiss to my temples, my cheek, and then my lips before he shrugged. "She claims it's an apology," he said. "I didn't open it. It's on your desk.

"I don't have time for Jessa's bullshit," I said, before kicking off my heels, grabbing my husband's hand, and leading him back to the couch to snuggle up close together. Soon any thoughts about Jessa were lost in the heat of our passion.

But in the weeks since she sent the letter, my mind ran across it.

Especially when Kingston, Renee, and even Jaime said the bitch apologized to them. That surprised me.

Jessa Bell apologetic? Shocker.

And now she was claiming to be pregnant by Eric.

More drama.

So even if Jessa didn't have the restraining order against me for bopping her upside her head with her own cell phone in the Terrace Room, I couldn't beat the bitch's ass if she might be pregnant.

Or was this another Jessa Bell stunt?

Or . . . was my ex-best friend and I pregnant at the same time?

I picked up the letter and stared at it before dropping it back into my desk and closing the drawer.

I couldn't spare another moment on Jessa Bell . . . but I couldn't bring myself to throw the letter away either. One day curiosity would kill the cat, although I highly doubted that scandalous trick could say anything *to make me forgive her.*

Sighing, I tried my best to focus my thoughts and type the first word onto the computer for my article on the impact of reality TV on bullying among girls. But the words wouldn't come.

As my stomach grumbled loudly in protest, I pushed back, away from the desk, and made my way downstairs to the kitchen. I used the remote to turn on the small flat screen on the granite countertop next to the professional-grade refrigerator. Pushing loose strands of hair off my face, I grabbed a tiny container of Ben & Jerry's strawberry cheesecake ice cream and a spoon before sitting at the large island in the center of the kitchen.

> "Today on *The Kerry Kay Show* we are bringing some of the most scandalous news stories across the country into the forefront. And first we'll be talking with Jessa Bell—"

I almost choked on my ice cream as I looked at Jessa Bell sitting on stage next to Kerry Kay. I grabbed the remote to turn up the volume. "No, this bitch is not doing interviews. *What the fuck?"*

> "She is a former mistress who almost lost her life recently when she attempted to end the affair with her married lover . . ."

I sat for the next twenty-five minutes in stunned silence as I watched Jessa Bell play with the sympathies of both the studio and television audience. I shook my head at the tears, the sad face, the pensive sighs.

"I didn't know this crazy bitch could act," I said, feeling my anger for Jessa rise, particularly when she brought up that her lover's wife had had her own affair. She said no names, but it wouldn't be hard for anyone to research and discover Jaime's identity.

"You slick bitch," I said in a low voice before I turned and jogged up the stairs to enter her office. I snatched open that top drawer and grabbed the letter from Jessa to press into the small shredder next to her wooden desk with a shake of her head.

Chapter 7

"*Welcome back to SQN's Hardline News. I am your host Nunzio Gonzalez, and we are breaking down and exploring every horrific detail of the brutal murder of the unsuspecting wife of a mega-church minister by his mistress.*"

Jessa tensed from her seat in the news station of one of SQN's affiliate stations in New Jersey. She listened to the fiery and controversial host of the cable news show introduce his entire panel that included attorneys, a popular minister of a mega-church, and her. *God be with me*, she prayed as the light over the camera that she faced lit up.

She remembered to keep her face neutral as she listened to the two attorneys go back and forth with each other and the host for the next two segments on the upcoming trial.

"I want to take another look at this case, at the events leading up to this mistress actually planning and then going forward with her decision to brutally shoot the wife of her minister lover. Let's bring in a former mistress whose attempt to end the affair ended with her lover attempting to kill her before he shot himself in the head. Jessa Bell—and, no, the irony of her name is not lost on us—why do you think there seems to be such violence attached to affairs in the headlines?" Nunzio asked.

Jessa forced herself to relax in her chair. "I'm not trying to say that my experience makes me an expert on this subject, but I think history shows this is not a new phenomenon. Um, in my case, I wasn't aware of the issues that the man I was dealing with had. I had no clue that he was in a mental situation to snap and become violent with me. He had never been that way before. And so for me, this is more than just a mistress done wrong or a mistress no longer wanting to be second place, the capability or ability to murder someone is just ruthlessness in an individual regardless of what situation they're in. Although I will admit that at one time I did want him to leave his wife for me, but that I can't fathom murdering her or anyone else for that matter."

"Is there a ruthlessness to admittedly being the other woman?" Nunzio asked in his hard, pull-no-shorts voice meant to titillate his viewers.

"Of course, and that's why I have made the choice not to enter into that type of relationship again, but I will say I think a lot of the blame for the affair is placed entirely on the mistress. This minister is just as culpable for the affair and maybe even for not seeing that the person he brought into his life and his relationship was dangerous. But the focus is on the woman, as if she made the man overlook the marriage vows that he made, particularly in Reverend Franks's case as a man of the cloth."

"True," Nunzio said with a nod of his head.

"I think about one of my neighbor's husbands who is pursuing me to no end and the pervert is intrigued that the triangle I was in ended in violence—"

Nunzio slammed his hand down on the desk and his mouth fell open emphatically. "What kind of sick neighborhood are you living in?"

Jessa laughed. "Seriously, the man said to me—after

telling him in no uncertain terms that I am *not* interested—that he wanted to try some 'bleep' that was good enough to make a man want to kill me. That is crazy, and that to me is a clear sign that he is a fruit loop ready to flip."

Nunzio frowned in distaste.

"I considered telling his wife. I feel like she should know who she is married to. I feel like I should tell her, but then I don't want to destroy her either because it could be perceived as spite. I've done spiteful things in the past, but this time I just really want to warn her to get away from this man."

"Touchy situation," Nunzio said, tapping his pen on the desk.

Jessa nodded. "It really is."

Nunzio shifted papers on his lit desk before he looked back up at the camera with his lean and hard features. "Now, Reverend Franks has not been legally implicated in the murder of his wife. Do you believe he is still responsible for her death?"

Jessa shrugged as she turned her lips downward. "I believe that he is wholly responsible for the affair. I don't know enough about the case to say he plotted with his mistress to have his wife murdered. I have faith in the judicial system that if they cleared him of any wrongdoing, then his responsibility ends at the affair. To me, even if this man promised to divorce his wife and run away with this woman and then backed away from that promise, there is never a reason for someone to kill someone else. Never. To me, it completely lies at her feet for her actions. Having been someone in this type of secret—and at times exciting—relationship where he made promises to me that he didn't keep, I ended the relationship with him and tried to move on, but murder never entered my mind. So that's her crazy that could've manifested in *any* situation. She is just capable of murder. Period. Not because she's a mistress who was wronged, but because she's *crazy*. Period, point blank," she finished with emphasis and a look like "Right?"

Nunzio chuckled as he picked up a few sheets of paper and swiveled in his chair to push them in a drawer. "True, Jessa Bell. Very true," he said. "Before we say good-bye to you, what about this name of yours. It's hard to miss that if you say it three times fast, it sounds like the infamous Jezebel."

Jessa smiled a little, feeling more comfortable in front of the camera. "Yes, I know. But I married and became a Bell, so that wasn't a mark on me my whole life or me living up to my name or anything like that. It is just a coincidence. Because of being almost killed, I am truly trying to make amends and correct my life, and it's just a name, Nunzio," she said with a soft smile. "I'm thinking of adding my maiden name back to it to break it up. It'll be Jessa Logan-Bell."

Nunzio laughed. "I think that's a good idea."

"Me too," Jessa said with a nod of her head.

Nunzio faced the camera. "This is *Hardline News* and we'll be back to continue our in-depth look into 'The Murder of the Minister's Wife.' "

The light over the camera darkened and one of the crew stepped forward to remove her microphone. "Thank you," Jessa told him, as Myra stepped forward looking like she wanted to do a cheer as if she were on the sidelines of a football game where a winning touchdown was just scored.

"You are a natural. You are a star, Jessa. You did *g-r-r-r-eat*," she gushed.

"Who are you, Tony the Tiger now?" Jessa teased, accepting from Myra the oversized snakeskin clutch that perfectly suited the soft ivory linen dress she wore.

Myra just laughed.

Jessa felt tired. This was actually her second cable news show that week discussing "The Murder of the Minister's

Wife," which she thought sounded more like a horrible title of a mystery book than an actual news story headline.

Myra opened her iPad as they walked off the set. "Don't forget you have the interview for the magazine tomorrow. They wanted to do it in your home and take actual pictures of the room where the murder-suicide attempt happened—"

Jessa shook her head. "No, definitely not."

Myra held up one hand. "I already handled that and told them you completely redid the room so there was nothing to see anyway. The interview will happen at the Terrace Room restaurant tomorrow at three. Do you know where it is?" she asked.

Jessa smiled. "I think I can find it," she said as they exited the studio and then climbed into the back of a waiting blacked-out SUV.

Jessa's cell phone rang. "Excuse me," she said, interrupting Myra as she pulled it from her clutch and answered the call without checking her caller ID.

"Hello."

"You trifling, worthless, waste of skin and bones. Are you kidding me suing Eric's estate on behalf on your bastard child?"

Jessa sighed and settled back against the plush leather seat. "This call is as pointless as your behavior, Jaime. You're a college-educated woman and everything is laid out in the papers. Take them to your attorney and have your people contact my people. And what will happen is that same little baby that you keep calling a bastard will be recognized, will be respected, and will receive its inheritance. Your mouth wrote a check your ass is going to sign . . . over to me."

Jessa ended the call and powered the phone off before easing it back into her clutch with calm. She had already expected the call because her attorney let her know the papers were being served today.

Contesting Eric's will was more about getting what rightfully belonged to her child than thumbing her nose at Jaime, but Jessa had to admit—and she could only pray to God for forgiveness—that it felt damn good to put the bitch in her place.

Eric had been a successful man and Jaime had filed for divorce from him. His death occurred before the divorce was finalized, and suddenly the runaway bride was the well-off widow.

Well, she won't spend this baby's inheritance buying up Pleasure's dick.

"Umm . . . Jessa. Are you pregnant?"

Jessa shifted her eyes over to Myra. "Yes, I am."

"And it's by Eric?" she asked with the type of wariness a person had around a rabid animal.

"Yes, Myra," Jessa said coolly as she looked down at her stainless-steel watch with diamond accents.

"And you're suing his widow to contest the will?" Myra asked again, her tone still careful.

"Why, Myra?"

Myra's eyes widened as big as half-dollar coins. "Because this changes *everything,*" she said in exasperation, her fingertips flying over her iPad.

Jessa eyed her for a second before she turned and looked out the window at the passing scenery. She knew the news of the lawsuit was about to hit and she didn't care.

She was pregnant.

She was suing the estate of the baby's deceased father.

She had served her ex-friend and his widow with papers.

The truth was the truth and Jessa wasn't living lies anymore.

After lunch with Myra in the city, Jessa felt completely exhausted and ready to go home for an afternoon siesta.

Between the morning sickness and feeling tired as all get out, Jessa found herself sleeping more and more. *I'm not a young spring chicken,* she thought, as the SUV pulled up to the gate of Richmond Hills.

Lucky, the portly red-faced security guard stepped out of his glass booth. Jessa lowered the rear passenger window and leaned her head out. "Hello, Lucky," she said.

He looked at her and smiled politely. "Hello, Ms. Bell," he said, before entering a code onto the keypad to open the gate.

Jessa leaned back and started to raise the window via the power button on the door console.

"I saw you on *Hardline* this afternoon," Lucky said.

Jessa pressed a stiff smile on her face as she sat forward again. "How was I?" she asked, even as she felt her fatigue in her eyes and shoulders.

"You made some good points and you looked really pretty," he said.

"Thank you, Lucky." Jessa nodded and upped the window as she settled back against the seat.

Lucky suddenly placed his hand on the window.

Jessa frowned a bit as she looked at him.

He looked apologetic. "I just wanted to warn you that a few of your neighbors—the wives—they saw it, too, and they're pretty riled up to find out which one you were talking about?" Lucky said, looking bashful.

Jessa's face filled with confusion.

"Um, you know, the part about the neighbor's husband that's not taking no for an answer," he reminded her gently.

"Ooh," Jessa said in sudden understanding. "Well, they'll be okay. And so will I. Thanks, Lucky."

She successfully raised the window this time and motioned with her hand for the driver to go. She felt fearless as the SUV cruised through the street leading to the cul-de-sac where her home sat. Jessa wasn't in the mood for a bunch of cronies with insecurities.

Yes, she played the cruel game of "Guess Who" with her friends about a possible philandering husband, but she wasn't in the mood for the bullshit now.

But her eyes widened in surprise at the large amount of women gathered on her front door. *What the fuck?* "Slow down, driver," she requested, quickly counting more than fifteen women surrounding her house like this was the night of the crime scene. Black, White, Asian, Latino. Young, old, middle-aged.

Do all of these women suspect their husbands of approaching her for an affair? And all of them are honestly seeking out the truth of their marriage from her? What the hell?

It hadn't been Jessa's intention to have the wives of Richmond Hills shaking in their Louboutin pumps about their husbands. She had been making a point about the equal guilt of the husbands in beginning affairs.

The women parted like the Red Sea as the SUV turned into the drive leading to her two-car garage. Jessa gathered her purse and shades as the driver left the SUV to come around and open the passenger door. He helped her down out of the SUV and securely held her arms as he guided her through the women who immediately began shouting at her.

"Which husband is it, Jessa Bell?"

"Call her what she is . . . a jezebel!"

"Is it my Frank?"

"Or my Ryan?"

"Who is it, Jessa?"

"It's all your fault!"

"My husband better not be begging you!"

"Who is it, Jessa?"

"Why don't you move?"

"Yeah, nobody wants you here."

Jessa felt a thin hand push against her shoulder and she stumbled forward a few steps. Her hand went to her belly as her anger came in a rush and she whirled around with rage in her eyes. Most of the women stepped back. "You have until the count of twenty to get off my property before the sprinklers come on and the police are called," she said calmly but coldly, even as her eyes continued to flash.

She turned and finished her walk up to the front door. "Thank you," she told the driver before she unlocked her front door and entered her home even as they resumed hurling questions and accusations at her.

"Are those heifers crazy?" she asked aloud, shaking her head as she made her way into the kitchen to a bottled water. She looked out the window as the women moved to stand in the street in front of her home. Still wondering. Still suspicious of their husbands. "Now why don't they get the hell off of my property and go home and talk to their damn husbands. If they are that nervous he's not acting right, they don't need me to confirm a damn thing."

But maybe they do. Maybe women wanted to know for sure if the man they married was deserving of their trust.

Jessa poured the bottled water into a glass as she looked out at the women still hovering around her home and discussing their fears and suspicions with each other.

She thought of the video she had on her cell phone implicating one woman's husband of pursuing her. Her eyes scanned each face of the women. She didn't see her among the crowd.

No, if she were one of the women in search of the truth, I would tell her. I won't volunteer the info, but if she appears and asks me, his perverted ass is grass.

Jessa sipped from her glass of water and politely walked over to the control box on the wall of her spacious pantry. With a few pushes of the buttons on the keypad, Jessa turned on her sprinklers and increased their velocity to full blasts.

As she left the kitchen and began to climb the stairs,

Jessa chuckled into her glass at the high-pitched and surprised screams of the women who were suddenly all wet.

"There has been a very bizarre and shocking twist in the story of a local woman, Jessa Bell, who was the victim of an apparent suicide-murder attempt at the hands of her married lover, who was successful in his attempt to kill himself.

"I have here in my hands copies of court documents that were served to the wife of her married lover detailing her attempt to contest the will on behalf on her unborn child that Bell claims was fathered by her married lover, Eric Hall, nearly a month before his suicide.

"In recent weeks after the violent attempt on Bell's life she has been very vocal on many news outlets, including the nationally syndicated Kerry Kay Show, speaking out about her ordeal and her decision to never enter into an affair again. Although she has been very outspoken of late, calls to Jessa Bell or her reps have not been returned. We will definitely continue to watch and report on this story as more develops . . . and I definitely believe we have all not heard the last of his story. This is Maria Vargas reporting for WCBL."

"Well, the shit has officially hit the fan," Jessa said the next morning with a sigh as she placed the television on mute with her remote as she lay back against the many soft and plush pillows on her bed. She picked up her iPad and did a search on her name. Hundreds of links to articles about her interview on *Kerry Kay,* the attempt on her life, and the lawsuit against Eric's estate flooded the page.

Jessa didn't bother to read any of the articles. She didn't need her story told to her by someone else. No one knew it better than her-especially without the salacious lies and assumptions.

Rising from the bed, she slipped her feet into her flat satin slippers and pulled a short silk robe over the lace teddy she slept in. After quickly going through her routine of washing her face, brushing her teeth, and combing her hair, Jessa made her way downstairs. She paused midway down the steps to listen to the quiet of her house and her life. The irony? The quiet was so loud, so noticeable. So unbearable.

But soon this baby will bring life to my life. A second chance to make everything *right,* she thought with a wishful smile as she continued down the stairs and into the kitchen to start preparing her new morning ritual of breakfast, a glass of milk and her prenatal vitamin.

Her OB/GYN stressed the need for her to eat small meals throughout the day. Now that Jessa had decided to have and raise this baby, she was determined to do everything right.

She started a small pot of oatmeal just as her landline started to ring. Without a blink of an eye, she reached over and cut the ringer off, just as she had her cordless phone upstairs. The news of the lawsuit had opened the floodgates to reporters and bloggers wanting a statement from her. She was just grateful the gates of Richmond Hills kept anyone from showing up to her front door.

Ding-dong.

Jessa arched a brow as she pulled the pot of oatmeal off the stove and made her way out of the kitchen and to the front door. She eased up on her toes to look out the peephole and sighed to see Jaime, Renee, and Aria sanding there. Sighing, she opened the door. "I see more of you three now than when we were friends," she said dryly as she eyed all three.

"You've shown us we were all never friends," Aria snapped.

Jessa raised her hands and pretended to play a violin. "Sing me another sad song, that one's played out," Jessa said coolly.

"Jessa, are you serious about suing Jaime for a part of Eric's estate?" Renee asked, her face incredulous.

"Legal papers are pretty serious," she responded.

"So trading your sins for money wasn't bad enough. Now you want Eric's money," Aria snapped. "Now you're making your scandalous life into a business. Some kind of Mistress, Incorporated or some bullshit."

Jessa eyed her. "Isn't your restraining order still in place?" she asked, motioning with her hand for Aria to back up from her. "Give me fifty feet."

"Look, you crazy bitch, you are not going to get away with this," Jaime spat as she held up papers bunched in her hand.

Jessa frowned as she eyed her. "It's enough of this anger and bitterness bull. I don't like the energy around my baby," she said. "Do not come near my home again. Anything you and I have to say to each other can be done through the lawyers."

Jaime took a step forward.

Jessa stiffened her back.

Renee stepped in between them.

"I tried to apologize to all of you and you didn't want it, so I'm not trying anymore. I'm not kissing any of your asses. God has forgiven me and that's all I need," Jessa said.

"You think anyone believes that bullshit about you getting saved and wanting to change. Bitch, please!" Aria called from the street.

"Isn't the fact that you betrayed a friend, lied on innocent men, and almost got yourself killed enough. Do you have to be on television making her relive everything you did?" Renee asked.

Jessa laughed bitterly. "Everything *I* did. Just me. I

raped Eric. I stuck my hand up his ass and played the ventriloquist to the lies he told me. I caused all of this . . . including that lunatic trying to kill me."

"But you want the lunatic's money, though?" Jaime snapped from behind Renee's broad shoulder.

"And you don't?" Jessa countered, locking eyes with her. "You didn't love Eric and it had nothing to do with his involvement with me. You were paying Pleasure to fuck you long before then, and then was dumb enough to accidentally dial your husband in the middle of it all. That didn't have shit to do with me. You were cheating on him long before he started anything with me. So save the sob story for someone who doesn't know."

Jaime threw her hands up in the air.

"What I am doing is for the baby we made together, and if I could change it all I would, but the fact remains that I am pregnant with Eric's child and we both know he would have taken care of this child." Jessa pressed her hand to her belly.

"To hell with you, Jessa. But please know I will fight you every step of the way," Jaime swore.

Jessa shook her head slowly. "You will fight me to make sure Eric's child doesn't get one red cent of what would have been his inheritance if Eric didn't kill himself before he knew about the baby," she said with reproach and judgment.

"What baby?" Jaime snapped in disgust, waving her hand dismissively before turning to walk away. "Ain't no *damn* baby."

Jessa turned to face Renee. "And so, Renee, you wouldn't stand up for your kids? You wouldn't fight for their inheritance from Jackson if it was withheld from them. Huh?" Jessa asked.

Renee closed her eyes and pressed her fingertips to her lips. "But I understand how I would feel if Jackson's mistress sued me for it."

Jessa opened her mouth to speak but closed her mouth momentarily before she decided to forge ahead. "Is the child to blame for that? Does it lessen the fact that—and I'm sorry to say this—but the child by his mistress has just as much right as your children, Renee. I'm sorry, but it's true," Jessa stressed.

Renee's eyes filled with pain. "You're one mean bitch, Jessa Bell."

"I'm not a mistress trying to hurt the wife. I'm a mother taking care of my child. Just like you." Jessa leaned past her to eye Aria. "The baby you're carrying, if Kingston didn't help you take care of it, you wouldn't sue for child support. Huh?"

"I'm Kingston's wife. Not his whore!" Aria screamed back.

Jessa stepped back and started to close her door. "You're both hypocrites and I'll pray for you," she said softly before closing her door and locking it securely.

Chapter 8

Jessa let the tears that filled her eyes fall freely down her face as she knelt at the prayer bench and silently asked God to guide her steps on the right path to salvation. Reverend Dobbins moved down and stood before her, lightly placing his hand on her shoulder. His gentle touch really struck a chord within her. It was the touch of an older man who cared and was concerned about her. That was something Jessa had never known before.

The reverend moved on to the next of his kneeling parishioners and Jessa felt the loss of his touch. She rose to her feet and turned to press her crocodile Kate Spade's into the carpet as she made her way back to her seat on the rear pew of Reverend Dobbins's nondenominational church. She picked up her Bible and stroked it as her head hung to her chest. Soon her tears fell on the cover.

Jessa hated the weakness and uncertainty she felt. She hated how her secrets and sins haunted her. She hated the guilt she felt about being happy for this baby. She hated that although her intentions were good, no one believed that she regretted her affair with Eric. No one believed she wanted to change.

And she did. *For myself and for this baby.*

"God, I thank you for your presence in my life and I thank you for not leaving me when I stumble on this path to living right. I thank you for forgiving me when people push me to do things I know I shouldn't," she continued to pray silently.

And people were truly trying her by walking her last nerve with their judgment and reprimands. *I'm sick of their fucking bullshit,* she thought, wanting to choke nearly each and every one of her neighbors.

She rolled her eyes in exasperation as she caught her cuss-filled thoughts. "Sorry, God," Jessa mouthed, rising to her feet with everyone else as Revered Dobbins brought church service to an end.

Jessa was one of the first to leave the church. She was all for going to church every Sunday and even catching a night of Bible study once every other week, but she had yet to get accustomed to the whole ritual of the church members gathering outside and looking to converse.

Jessa was interested in getting the word, feeling a little closer to her Jesus, and going home. She wasn't looking to make friends or pretend to listen to the ramblings of nonministers who felt they were Christian soldiers.

Before she got into her Jag, she removed the feathery fascinator that perfectly matched the dark blue fitted dress she wore.

"Sister Bell."

Jessa made a face of annoyance as she heard her name called. She forced on a smile and turned just as one of the men from the church stepped in front of her. "Yes?" she said politely, tilting her head back to look up into his face. The man had to be close to six foot five.

"I just wondered if you were coming back for the program?" he asked. "All of the groups coming in to sing are really good. I thought you might enjoy it."

Jessa opened her car door. "No, thank you. I have other plans," she said.

"I was hoping to see you there actually," he said, stepping forward to hold her door.

Jessa's eyebrows rose in surprise as she looked at his large hands and then up to his face.

"I thought maybe we could have coffee afterward," he said.

Jessa stiffened. "I can't even come to church without getting hit on by married men? What the hell?" she muttered. "Look—"

He held up his hands. "I'm not married," he said. "If I was, I wouldn't have approached you. I'm a man of honor."

Jessa laughed bitterly. "Are there any more left?"

"Yes, plenty," he said with the utmost seriousness. "But I get it. I find myself asking that about women as well."

"And that's why you are 'approaching' a former mistress who is now pregnant with the baby of her married lover who tried to kill her before killing himself. And might I add, who is also suing the estate of her dead lover. That all just screams honor."

The man slid his hands into the pockets of his slacks in the tailored suit he wore. "Sounds to me as if you're judging yourself. Not me."

Jessa leaned back against her car as she gave him a serious eye. Although he was as tall—and almost as wide—as a tree, he had the kind of big-man good looks that reminded you of Gerald Levert. The deep bronzed skin, the smooth black hair and goatee, the bright eyes and warm smile.

Not the athletic type she was used to, but handsome. Still . . .

"Listen, I am just trying to get my life together and the last thing I need is someone else to answer to or worry about," she told him with honesty.

He smiled.

Jessa's mouth fell open a little bit at the sight of twin dimples as deep as wells.

"I just wanted to go have dinner and talk a little bit. I wasn't looking to propose," he told her, raising his arms to cross over his chest. "Reverend Dobbins thought we had similar stories to share."

Jessa eyed him.

"You're not the only human being with sins."

"What's your name?" she asked.

"Henry Lyons."

Jessa held out her hand. "It was nice meeting you," she said.

He undid his arms to take her slender hand in his. "Nice meeting you, too," he said.

"I guess I'll see you in church next Sunday." Jessa slid her hand out of his and climbed behind the wheel of her car.

He eased a card from his pocket and reached around her still-open door to hand it to her. "If you just want someone to talk to or to pray with or lay some burdens on . . . call me," he offered.

Jessa took the card with a smile and closed her car door. As she started the car and pulled away, she noticed a lot of the churchgoers had made their way out the doors and were watching them closely. She fought the urge to make a face at them all as she drove off the church grounds, leaving all thoughts of Brother Lyons and a prayer circle behind.

Or at least she hoped she would.

Love and everything it was or wasn't for her changed so many times over the years of her life. Through her family and her relationships and friendships, the definitions or expectations of love had shifted.

Running her fingers through the soft tendrils at her nape, Jessa steered her car toward Heavenly Rest Cemetery. But this time she made her way toward the rear of the property to Eric's resting place. As she stood at the foot of his plot, she let all of the emotions she felt wash over her and flow freely from her and her mouth.

"I hate you, Eric," she began. "But I hate myself more

for making myself believe that what we shared wasn't the biggest mistake we both made. I truly believed that I loved you and I deserved you and we would make each other happy. But I was wrong. What we shared wasn't love. But now I'm pregnant with your child, and what type of legacy have we created?"

Jessa looked down at the metal marker of his dirt-covered grave. His headstone had not been delivered yet. Either Jaime wasn't bothering with one or she ordered one custom. "I damn you to hell for trying to kill me. For making me this mess that doesn't know if she's coming or going. That could be me in the grave right now instead of you. I still can't believe you wanted me dead, Eric."

She felt her heels sink into the grass surrounding his fresh grave and she shifted her feet. "But I won't spend my life bashing you to our child. And that's not because of you. It's because I don't want to bring a child up spoon-fed on hating you. I know how it feels, and I wouldn't put any child through that."

Jessa sighed as she looked around at the gravesite. "Really, your widow could have chosen a better spot for you," she said, looking over her shoulder as a car sped by on the road just beyond the wrought-iron gate. "You tried to kill me and I wouldn't have stuck you back here in the hood."

"I know you are spinning in that grave because you didn't have the foresight to change your will once she filed for divorce." Jessa pouted her lips. "Tsk, tsk, tsk. You're usually smarter than that, Eric . . . but then again I would have thought you were too smart to kill yourself."

Jessa released another heavy breath. "She wouldn't let me say good-bye to you at the funeral and so I'm saying it now. Good-bye, Eric. I know you are burning in hell and I am doing everything in my power to make sure I don't join you there when my time comes," she said in finality. "I will never forgive you for trying to take my life, but I do thank you for teaching me about lust and love and how to know the difference between the two."

With one last glance at his grave, Jessa made her way back to her car. With her free hand, she loosened the tight bun at the base of her neck, running her fingers through the loose waves of her jet-black hair as she steered her Jag toward home. Summer was coming to an end, and although Jessa loved the fall best, she lowered the windows of the Jag and let the summer breeze blow against her face as she drove.

The last couple of weeks of her life had been chaotic. The press had just begun to leave her alone about the lawsuit. She was so tired of seeing Maria Vargas and her cameraman at random places she visited that Jessa didn't know what to do.

She remembered her grandmother saying once that the emotions of a pregnant woman manifested in the baby. And if that was true, Jessa was planning to give birth to a crying bundle filled with stress, anxiety, and anger. She didn't want that.

Jessa reached for her cell phone and dialed Myra's number. It rang three times and went to voice mail. "Myra, this is Jessa. Listen, I need a vacation. I know you have a busy week for me. But I need time away from everything. I need a break. No, no, I am taking a break. Just fix it. Fix all of it."

She hung up the phone and tossed it over onto her driver's seat with her oversized tote.

Maybe she would drive down to Pennsylvania to their cabin. She thought about all the grass and dirt and wildlife and frowned. The beautiful log cabin was deliciously delightful in the winter when everything was covered by snow. In the summer? Not so much.

Okay, maybe a quick flight to Antigua? Jessa quickly

pushed that thought away. Who wanted to do a beautiful romantic locale like that . . . alone? *Not me.*

Maybe a nice weekend in the Hamptons or Martha's Vineyard?

It really didn't matter where. It just mattered to get away from Richmond Hills. The old Jessa reveled in the discomfort she brought to the lives of her ex-friends and neighbors by her very presence. But day by day, more of the old Jessa was disappearing and it was leaving her raw and exposed like the little girl who couldn't understand why her mother left. She hated it.

As she turned her Jag into Richmond Hills, she was surprised to see Keegan's bright red hair poking out of the driver's side window of a green convertible Volvo.

Jessa actually felt happy to see the lively redhead. "Hey, Keegan," she called out.

She turned and spotted Jessa behind her before she climbed out of her Volvo and walked back to her in a deep purple jumpsuit and gold wedges. "Hey, sugar, I was just dropping by to check on you."

"I'm fine. . . . As a matter of fact, I'm in the mood for a mini-vacay. You game?" Jessa asked, following an impulse.

"Am I ready to sleep somewhere besides the big empty bed my dog of a husband left me to rot in? Hell yeah. Let's ride, Thelma. Louise is ready."

The very next day, Jessa and Keegan were in their bikinis and lounging on the deck of the small yacht they chartered to cruise around the Hamptons. The sun was beaming brightly. The smell of the ocean was refreshing. And Jessa felt good about being away from Richmond Hills.

"I really needed this getaway," Jessa sighed, stretching her limbs above her head to accept the crystal flute glass of apple juice spritzer the waiter presented her on a tray.

Keegan smiled at him as she took her flute of champagne. "You have to remember to put that baby first. Plenty rest. Less stress."

"I know."

Keegan sat up on the lounge chair and eyed Jessa over the rim. "You must have a clit on you bigger than a set of balls to sue that estate, though."

Jessa shifted her head on the lounge chair to eye her from behind her oversized shades. "If Marc and Eric were alive and I tried to force Marc to take care of a child that I knew belonged to Eric, then I would be wrong. Why is it different because they're dead?"

"Oh, look here, honey, I agree with you. I just don't know with all the press you're getting if I would have the nerve to do it," Keegan said, reaching over with her flute. "Cheers to you, darling."

Jessa touched her flute lightly to Keegan's before taking a deep sip.

"Good afternoon, ladies."

Both ladies turned their heads and then lifted them to look up at the tall and broad-shouldered man standing above them in all white. He was the owner and captain of the chartered yacht. Tyson Hearst.

Keegan pressed her full bosom forward as she smiled. "Hello, Captain."

He smiled as he shifted his eyes over to Jessa, who remained quiet. "Just call me Tyson."

"Nice strong name. Tyson," Keegan said, seeming to let it drip off her tongue.

"I just wanted to check on you and make sure you were enjoying the ride," he said, again his eyes shifting to Jessa.

From behind the cover of her shades she did watch him. He was just at six feet, but his frame was solid. His fairly light complexion reminded her of Marc, but it was there the similarities ended. His features seemed to be carved from stone. Everything except his mouth, which was sinfully soft and begging to be kissed.

By a woman looking for that, Jessa added, turning away to gaze up at the sun.

Suddenly, the brightness and the heat of the sun were blocked from her body. She licked her lips as she looked up at Tyson, who had moved to stand by her lounge chair.

"And you, Ms. Bell, are you enjoying yourself?" he asked.

Jessa raised her hand to shift her shades up on top of her head. "Trust me, if I wasn't, you would know," she told him, lowering her shades.

He chuckled. "Enjoy the rest of the trip," he said, before finally walking away.

"He wants you and he wants you bad," Keegan said, turning her head to watch him walk away.

"Since I don't want random men nutting on the head of my baby, I don't really give a damn who wants me," she said with honesty, adjusting her strapless bikini top.

"Darling, they haven't made the dick big enough to breach a cervix," Keegan drawled, finally settling back against her lounge chair. "If so, I wants no parts of it. Trust me."

Jessa just laughed.

"Don't you get horny?" Keegan leaned over to ask. "I mean, you have like six months to go and then another six weeks. Jesus, you're gonna be a born-again virgin."

Jessa leaned over to dig in her straw tote. She pulled out a satin-lined velvet bag and tossed it onto Keegan's lap. "I don't leave home without it."

Keegan's mouth fell open as she pulled out the glass dildo. "Oh my Lord," she said in wonder. "It's so *smooth.*"

Jessa laughed as she leaned over to take it back. "And the Lord doesn't mind me using it one bit," she said, turning the base to make it vibrate.

Bzzzzzzzzzzzzzzzzzzzzzzzzzzzzzzzzzzzzzzzzzzzzzz.

"Oh my word. I need one of those in my life. ASAP!" Keegan roared.

The ladies burst into laughter.

"Ooh, I have to tinkle," Jessa said, turning the vibrator off and slipping it into its sac before easing it back into her bag.

"You sure you want to leave me behind with that thing," Keegan asked, before sipping her champagne and arching her eyebrow.

Jessa just padded across the deck barefoot and headed down below to her stateroom. Tyson was coming up the stairs and they met halfway.

His eyes took in her curves in the low-riding bikini.

Jessa figured she better enjoy her shape before the baby spread her like a weather balloon in the upcoming weeks. She already had a small, barely noticeable curve to her belly. "Excuse me, Captain."

He smiled—or smirked—as he pressed his back to the wall of the stairwell to allow her to pass.

"If you're in need of the real thing, I can help you out with that," he called behind her.

Jessa paused and turned to face him. "Excuse me?"

"Your little toy," he offered.

Jessa felt herself flush with warmth, but she refused to show it. "I would have assumed your eyes would be on the path of this boat and not watching what your guests are doing," she told him coolly as she walked back up to him.

"You make it pretty hard not to watch what you're doing," Tyson countered.

"If you're looking for a fling, I can hook you up with my friend. She's in the market. I'm not."

"I like my coffee black with no cream. No offense to your friend," Tyson said, coming down two steps to look down at her.

Jessa twisted her hair up into a loose top knot. "Well,

again, I'm not in the market," she said, turning away from him.

"Are you married? Engaged? Taken? What?" he called behind her.

Jessa turned again. "Are you conceited? Caught up in yourself? Unable to comprehend that someone's not attracted to you? What?" she countered, placing her hands on her hips as she admittedly enjoyed the verbal back and forth.

Tyson laughed as he came down the stairs quickly and backed her against the wall outside her stateroom. His eyes half-lowered as he watched her and then pressed his hands to her bare hips to lift her up.

Jessa felt breathless from the chemistry between them. His hands were hot against her skin. She felt the bud of her pussy flutter to life and her nipples harden in a rush until they ached.

Tyson brought his head down. "If you ask me to kiss you, I will," he taunted.

Jessa's eyes dropped down to his lips and she fought the primal urge to suck his whole mouth. Swallowing over a lump in her throat, she felt her heart race.

She hadn't felt this kind of heat since Eric.

And the thought of Eric cooled her ardor as she remembered the child she carried.

"I would take you in that room and make you beg me for this pussy . . . if I wasn't pregnant and saved," she whispered against his mouth, enjoying when the look of passion in his eyes was replaced by confusion.

He released her and stepped back.

Jessa raised her hand to close his open mouth by pushing up on his chin. "And that's why the only dick going inside of me is my toy. Bye-bye, Captain," she said sweetly, before finally entering her stateroom and leaving him standing there with his penis as hard as time.

Jessa quickly used the bathroom and made her way back up on deck. There was no sign of the sexy captain with the raw edge and she was glad. Fiery chemistry like that got her in trouble.

Keegan had removed her bikini top and was sunbathing nude.

Jessa eyed her and decided that any nipples on large breasts that pointed up to the heavens were fake. "You're putting on quite a show for the crew," Jessa drawled.

"I know," Keegan purred. "Your cell phone was ringing."

Jessa dug her cell out of her tote. She had two missed calls from Myra. She dialed her back as she moved to the railing.

"Jessa! Thank God. You are not going to believe this, but I'm saving the best for last," Myra said, her voice filled with excitement. "We got an offer for you to be on a popular reality show that I'm still getting details on because I know how you feel about those. A modeling agency for fuller-figured models is interested in seeing some test shots. A ton of interview requests have come in since the news of the lawsuit. But that's nothing. Are you sitting?"

Jessa's head was already flooded with everything Myra dropped on her. She barely had time to process any of it. "Actually, I'm standing by the rail of a beautiful yacht overlooking the Hamptons," she said, trying to put a speed bump in Myra's path.

"Well, sit your pregnant ass down before you fall overboard."

Jessa turned and spotted the captain watching her with his arms crossed over his strong chest. She turned her back on him as she sat down on the lounge chair. "Go, Myra."

"Several major publishers have contacted our firm about you doing a book, and we're talking a six-figure advance or better."

A book? Saying what? Who would read it?

Jessa shook her head to clear it. Speaking engagements? Interviews? Modeling? Reality TV? Books?

"Myra, this all is more than I was looking for," Jessa said, feeling nervous about her new fame for the first time.

"I told you that I had big plans for you and I wasn't kidding," she said. "So you enjoy the night in the Hamptons and you get back to Jersey, because we got business to take care of. Big business."

Click.

Was Aria right? Had this all become nothing but big business. Her own Mistress, Inc. or some shit? And if it was a fabulous by-product on her road to salvation, was it wrong?

Chapter 9

It was very early in the morning, before the sunset, as Jessa lay quiet and reflective in the middle of her bed with her eyes cast out the window at the full moon, when she felt her baby move for the first time. She gasped a little in surprise as her body went still and she waited—and wanted—to feel something again.

"Maybe it was gas," she said into the quiet as she raised her silk pajama top and pressed her hands to her bared belly. Her baby bump was noticeable and she had begun buying new clothes one size bigger and looser flowing, but she had yet to really feel the baby move. At just under sixteen weeks, the doctor assured her all was well and she had plenty of movement she probably thought was gas, but she had been waiting for this moment. And so she lay silently waiting to feel that flutter again.

Moments later, she felt regret and a little stupid that she missed such a big milestone in her pregnancy or overestimated a gas bubble shooting through her intestines. All was well with the pregnancy, and Keegan was anxious to change one of the smaller bedrooms across from her suite into a beautiful nursery—once Jessa was safely out of her second trimester. She didn't want to jinx the pregnancy.

Jessa Bell was sure with every passing day that she wanted this baby more than anything. Her life was going to change, but she was determined to maintain some normalcy. She refused to become one of the stained sweat suit, sneakers, and ponytail-wearing moms who smelled of nothing but Similac and dirty diapers.

Jessa planned to show all these biddies how to do Glamorous Mommy . . . or die trying. She wanted to do this herself. She wanted to prove she could do it for this baby. Well, with a *little* assistance from a reputable nanny when business called her away from home.

"I promise I will be there for you and I will *destroy* anyone who tries to hurt you," she swore into the cool darkness of the room as she turned over onto her side and pulled her knees up as far as she could.

She looked up to the skies. "I'm sorry, God, but I'm just being honest. If someone messes with this baby, then vengeance will be *mine.*"

She was ready now to be a mother. To wear the stylish flats to make sure she didn't trip once her body defied balance at eight or nine months. To give birth. Jessa frowned deeply. *Okay, I'm almost ready for that.*

To bathe her baby. Coo to her babe. To smell her baby's neck and plant kisses on its belly. To see every moment and milestone of their life as they grew. To do hair. Cook dinner. Help with homework. Pluck the heads of any bullies and stand strong to fight any parent. First dates. First heartbreaks. First jobs and first cars.

Jessa's eyes filled with tears that were made up of happiness and past regrets.

And she wouldn't have men in and out of her life. Jessa couldn't count how many of her mother's boyfriends had flittered in and out of her life. Some names she remembered. Some faces she forgot.

And the baby was already affecting her love life—or at least her sex life.

Jessa stretched her limbs in the satin pajamas she wore as she thought about the sexy captain. She bit her bottom lip and smiled as she remembered the heat of his hands on her body. His dick would have been just as hard and hot inside of her. *And he wanted this pussy too,* she thought. She remembered how his eyes had followed her for the rest of their day on the yacht.

If she hadn't been pregnant—and promised the Lord she wouldn't have sex until she married *of course*—Jessa would have pushed him down onto the nearest chair, step, or bed and rode him hard.

Hmmm. He said he could put my glass dildo to shame.

Jessa had always had a healthy sexual appetite. She was in tune to her body's needs and wants. And right now she felt like she needed and wanted to cum. Sighing in frustration, and fighting the urge to lube up her glass dick, Jessa kicked off the covers and walked across the room to her balcony.

She wrapped her arms around herself because of the little bit of coolness in the air. She shifted her eyes about the many backyards of Richmond Hills. Nothing stirred. Nothing looked awry.

It was the epitome of upwardly mobile, high-end suburbia. Perfection . . . to those who didn't know any better. Jessa smirked and shook her head. The gossip mill was filled with stories of wives torturing their husbands because of their fears that sexy widow Jessa Bell had one or more of their husbands caught by the dick hairs.

Those dumb, insecure bitches didn't have a clue.

She wasn't looking for a man.

Not the warmth and security of a man like Henry from church.

Not the passion and promise of a powerful penis like Tyson the captain.

And definitely no married men.

Maybe once she had the baby and settled into motherhood, she would start to date and contemplate falling in love, but for now? None of these suburban saps had to worry. *Not about me anyway.*

That Friday was the annual Black & White Charity Ball benefiting the several charities the Richmond Hills community supported as a whole. Jessa had forgotten all about it until her tickets arrived last week. They could have saved the trees. She had no intention of breaking bread with people who hated or suspected her.

Aria, Renee, and Jaime glaring at her all night? Jessa felt like she'd rather fuck a tree root.

Sighing, she settled down onto the chair and crossed her legs just as she spotted a dark shadow exiting the Grayson's home across from hers. She squinted her eyes and rose back to her feet as she watched the male figure cross the backyard. Tall trees and bushes blocked the figure from her sight, but Jessa—who was thoroughly enjoying the early-morning shenanigans that reminded her of Eric sneaking from her house back in the day—shifted her eyes to the break in the trees. Sure enough, the shadowy figured reappeared and entered the wooden fence surrounding the Regan's backyard before scurrying across the yard and into the house through the patio doors.

So, Mr. Regan is fucking Mrs. Grayson. Hmmm.

Hypocrites. Cari Regan and Halle Grayson were some of the main women in Richmond Hills to make sure Jessa felt their cold shoulders.

"You know what. I'm going to kill two dumb birds and a cock with one stone," she muttered, entering her bedroom and picking up her cordless phone. She quickly dialed the Regan's number.

It rang twice. "Hello," Cari Regan snapped.

"Cari, hi, this is Jessa. Your neighbor around the corner—"

"Do you know what time it is?" she snapped.

Jessa strolled out onto her balcony again and watched as a light on the second floor of the Regan's home suddenly came on. "Certainly too early—or maybe too late—for your husband to be sneaking from Halle Grayson's home, especially since her husband is overseas on business," Jessa told her with way too much pleasure.

"What?" Cari snapped.

"See, you're so busy watching me that you are completely missing that he is definitely banging out Halle in her husband's absence," Jessa drawled, smirking as another light on the second level suddenly illuminated.

"Cari, what's wrong?" Hunter Regan's voice suddenly filled the phone line.

Were the Regans sleeping in separate bedrooms? Or was that his home office and he was pulling the whole "I worked late into the night and didn't want to disturb you" bit?

"I don't know what you are trying to prove calling me with this bullshit—"

"I bet his slippers are muddy, and if you walk out your back door and follow the footsteps from where they came, they lead straight to the back door of Halle Grayson," Jessa said. "Oh, and you're welcome."

Beep.

She held the phone as she eased down onto the chair. Moments later, the Regan's kitchen light came on and then Cari flew out the door looking down at the ground as she descended the steps of their deck and walked across the backyard to the door in the fence.

"You lying fuck, you!" she screamed as she turned and pointed her finger.

"Umph, umph, umph. Lookey here, lookey here." Jessa's eyes followed her line of vision and saw Hunter standing on the deck in his pajamas.

"Cari, come inside," he said.

"Go to hell or, matter of fact, go back to bed with your whore," she spat.

Jessa felt like she was watching a movie. *And I'm the director.*

She dialed Halle Grayson's number. It rang four times before she answered with a heavy and groggy voice. "Oh please, you're not sleeping, and if you look out one of your back windows, the Regans are putting on quite a show about you . . . and Hunter," Jessa said, as she watched Cari take off one of her slippers and begin to slap Hunter with it.

"Who is this?"

"Jessa. Jessa Bell," she said, before hanging up.

She locked her eyes on the rear of the Grayson house and barely saw the curtain of one of the second-floor windows move.

"Hey, Cari," Jessa called out.

Both of the Regans swiveled their heads in her direction.

Jessa pointed to the Grayson house. "Third window from the right. Second floor," she called to them in the distance.

Cari's head swung like the remake of the exorcist.

The curtain fluttered close.

Hunter gave Jessa the international hand sign for "fuck you."

Jessa's mouth fell open as Cari stormed through the opening in the fence and into the Graysons' backyard. "Oh shit," she muttered, as Cari tore off up the stairs to enter the Graysons' home through the same door her husband snuck out of.

What if they fought?

What if one hurt the other?

What the fuck have I done?

"Oh shit," she muttered, anxiously watching the Grayson house. She didn't think either woman had the clit to confront the other.

Hunter rushed into the house. Lights came on. Voices were raised. Insults hurled. Something glass crashed.

"Oooooh shit," Jessa moaned like she was sick, regretting her rash decision to dip into other people's lives.

She could just see the image of Reverend Dobbins floating above her and shaking his head in shame.

Jessa rose to her feet as the door flew open and Hunter walked out carrying his wife in his arms. She was still fussing and fighting. Halle stepped out onto her back porch.

"I'm *so* sorry," Jessa called behind them.

How dare *they* judge *her*.

"Judge not for yet ye be judged," she said. "Or something like that."

Jessa felt relief. The whole situation could have gone to the left like the night her ex-lover tried to kill her. If anything, she should have known better than to play with fire.

This whole getting right by the Lord thing was 24/7 and Jessa felt like she was always praying for forgiveness.

She went into the house, closing her balcony doors, before she dropped to her knees and prayed. "At this rate, I'll have knees as black as asphalt," she mused, before lowering her head for yet another talk with God.

Later that afternoon, Jessa was sitting at the island of her kitchen flipping through several glossy magazines that Myra sent her overnight. She was featured in each one—her inclusion in the interview on the emotional and physical dangers of being a mistress, and two articles detailing her scandalous story with little mention of her attempts at redemption.

Myra warned her that they couldn't completely control the way the story—her story—was spun.

Next week, she was headed into the city for talks with the producers of the still unnamed reality TV show and to meet with the literary agent Myra secured to broker her book deal. Because of her pregnancy, she turned down the offer to model, but the agency owners still wanted to take her out to dinner while she was in the city.

But first, she had some business in Jersey to handle. Jessa and her attorney were meeting with Jaime and her lawyers for a preliminary hearing about Eric's estate.

Ding-dong.

Jessa took another sip of her steaming cup of raspberry tea and closed the glossy magazine before she made her way out the kitchen and to her front door. In the days of old, she would have swung her door open wide, but now with The Furious Three (her three ex-friends) and The Insecure Ones (the suspicious wives) running around, the check of the peephole was mandatory.

Jessa hadn't really seen much of any of her neighbors since she was so busy traveling with her new business ventures. She was surprised to see the wife of the perverted insurance agent standing on her doorstep holding a covered dish. "What the hell is this all about?" she wondered out loud.

Smoothing the deep green silk jumpsuit she wore over her figure, she opened the door and stepped back. "Yes?" Jessa said in greeting.

"Hi, I'm Dina. I live in Richmond Hills with . . . I . . . we're neighbors . . . and . . . well, I," the woman stumbled, looking very stylish in the wide-leg slacks she wore with patent-leather flats and a silk fitted tank.

"How can I help you?" Jessa stressed with just a tinge of irritation in her voice. The woman was stumbling like a village idiot.

"Can I come in?" she asked. "I brought you some homemade blueberry crumb muffins."

Jessa stepped back and waved her in before closing the door and leading the woman to the kitchen. "I'll be honest with you, I'm not really sure what you could want from me," she said.

Dina sat the bowl on the island before she reached out and pulled one of the magazines to her. "You're very pretty," she said.

"Thank you," Jessa said, still wary.

Dina looked up at her and there was sadness in her eyes. "I . . . uh, know this sounds crazy, but I figured who do I know that would know better than you about this type of thing."

Jessa said nothing else as she raised her cup and sipped her tea, watching the woman silently over the rim.

"How does a wife know when their husband is . . . is . . . seeing someone else?" she asked, looking as if she had to push the words out of herself with force.

Oh shit. Well, I'll be damned. Jessa's hands tightened on the cup and she sat it down to keep from snapping the delicate handle.

"I really love my husband and I want to trust him, but things are so different, so forced with us lately. He travels more and stays out later. He hardly talks to me when he's home, and even then it's more arguing than anything. He's so secretive about his phone calls," she said in a rush. "And if he is cheating, I want to know. I want to move on with my life. I want to kick his doggish ass to the curb."

Jessa sighed and cut her eyes upward. She remembered thinking if the woman asked she would tell her, and here she was.

"I wanted to know if I offered you a fee, money, could you—"

Jessa's mouth turned downward and perfectly arched brows met in the middle.

Dina held up her hands. "I'm sorry, I didn't mean to offend you. I just—You're so pretty and I could tell he thinks so because I caught him looking at one of your magazine articles when he was in the bathroom."

That fucking perv! Jessa could just picture what his freaky ass was doing in that bathroom. He was a jerk off who jacked off.

Jessa walked over to her fridge and pulled out a bottle of white wine. She set it and a crystal goblet in front of Dina. "Sit down, sweetie," she said, then paused at how much she sounded like Keegan. Jessa poured a full glass of white wine before coming back around the island to pick up her cell phone.

"Aren't you pregnant?" Dina asked.

"It's not for me."

Dina's eyes dropped down to the phone before she picked up the wine goblet with both hands and took a deep swig.

Jessa pulled up the video of her husband begging for her "killer pussy" and then handed the woman the phone.

"I really wish you would let me take you out," Vincent said.

"And I wish you would understand that I am not interested in you and you're harassing me," Jessa replied.

"I can't stop thinking about fucking you."

Dina gasped deeply in shock, using shaking hands to push her auburn hair behind her ears as her eyes widened.

"And if you don't leave me the hell alone, you pervert, I will take out a restraining order and then

everyone—including your wife—will know that you dream of fucking me, you perverted ass."
"Who would believe you?"

A tear rolled down the woman's cheek and onto the screen of Jessa's cell phone. Jessa closed her eyes; unlike the early-morning shenanigans she exposed, she took no pleasure in the pain she saw on the woman's face.

Dina took another deep sip of the wine. "So my husband was the one you were talking about during that interview?" she asked.

Jessa nodded, "Yes."

"I didn't even consider him," she admitted with a sappy grin.

"Do you feel better knowing?" Jessa asked.

"Yup," Dina said with a nod.

"Are you okay?"

"Nope."

Jessa didn't know what to do. Hug her? Pour her more wine? Walk her to the door? She didn't know this woman but knew the thing felt hella awkward. She watched the woman as she stood looking off into the distance and sipping on the wine.

Jessa dropped down onto one of the high chairs surrounding the island. Her cell phone rang and Jessa lifted up in the chair to reach for it.

Myra.

Jessa let the call go to voice mail and set the phone back down.

"Can you send me that video?" Dina asked, lifting the bottle to pour more wine into the goblet.

"Um, sure," Jessa said, picking up the phone again.

Suddenly an image of Eric's face contorted in crazy rage flashed before her.

Jessa side-eyed the woman. "I'm going to be honest

with you, I believe your husband is crazy on the low. Maybe I should have stayed out of this. I really don't need another psycho trying to kill me for ruining his marriage."

Dina shook her head. "Vincent isn't violent," she assured her.

Jessa arched a brow. "Neither was Eric . . . until the night he almost choked me to death."

"Vincent isn't like that," Dina insisted.

"No one but a lunatic would say he wanted to try some of that pussy that was good enough to make a nigger want to kill me," Jessa stressed.

Dina frowned. "He said that."

Jessa nodded.

"Having that video doesn't change the fact that I saw it," Dina admitted, looking weak and sad and tired as she picked up her phone. "I'm going home to my baby and to pack my husband's shit."

Jessa followed her to the door.

"Thanks, Jessa," Dina said, before walking away.

Jessa stood there for a minute and watched the woman make her way down the street and eventually around the corner.

"I can't believe I let you talk me into this," Jessa said to Keegan as they walked down the lit hall of the subdivision's glass clubhouse.

"And I can't believe you wore red to a black and white ball," Keegan drawled, giving Jessa's strapless red silk dress the side-eye. The pregnancy had increased the size of her breasts and the strapless gown was barely doing its job. "If you cough hard you are going to have a Janet Jackson moment."

Jessa shrugged, pulling her side-swept hair over one shoulder. "Just giving them what they expect from me," she said.

"I'm glad I haven't pissed you off," Keegan joked, adjusting her own strapless dress of brilliant white over her breasts.

"Hello, Jessa Bell. I didn't think you were coming," Gladys Hornsby said, reaching over to politely air kiss Jessa's cheeks.

"Really, the RSVP didn't clue you in or my thousand dollar check that the committee deposited," Jessa quipped with a tinge of sarcasm she didn't try to hide.

"Enjoy," Gladys said stiffly.

Jessa walked into the clubhouse and paused at the doorway as she looked around. She spotted Jaime in a short black sequined dress by the bar. Aria and Kingston were both dressed in white and seated at a table near the dance floor. Renee looked really pretty and striking in a black-and-white-striped strapless dress with a wide belt and long flowing skirt that circled around her legs as she danced with one of their neighbors.

Jessa wondered momentarily if Renee had slipped off the wagon.

She eyed the Graysons and the Regans on opposite sides of the room. *That's for the best,* she thought, turning away from the drama she revealed.

But she turned right into the faces of Dina and Vincent looking perfectly happy together in black. Vincent's eyes were angry and Dina avoided looking at Jessa altogether.

They were sticking it out.

Jessa stepped out of the couple's path and waved them in.

"Isn't that the man from the video you showed me?" Keegan whispered to her.

Jessa turned and looked again at all of the people whose lives she affected. It was a graveyard of lives shattered by Jessa Bell.

"I can't do this," Jessa said. "I thought I could get a

good chuckle looking at how uncomfortable I made these people, but it is just a reminder of things I want to forget."

Keegan stopped a waiter and took two glasses of champagne. She downed both of them. "Then we are outta here, darling," she said with a wink.

With one last look over her shoulder and finding several sets of eyes on her, Jessa turned and left the party.

Jaime Pine-Hall

I can't believe the gall of that bitch.

As I sipped on my glass of Veuve Clicquot, I eyed that bitch's back as she left the party with Keegan Connor, the current go-to interior designer. I had plans in the works to put my own bachelor's degree in interior design to good use and change that.

But my focus wasn't on breaking out of the mold of being Eric's perfect Stepford wife. Not when I wanted to break Jessa's neck.

Finish the job Eric couldn't man up to get done.

First, she sleeps with my husband behind my back. Taunts me and the girls about it in a text message. Tells Eric about my secret bank account, after I made the choice to leave, which the bastard closed, leaving me penniless. Then she bum-rushes the funeral. Goes on the Slut American TV tour. Announces she's pregnant by my sadistic husband. Sues me to contest the will.

My grip on the stem of the flute nearly snapped it in half.

Thankfully her press hadn't increased my profile. And anytime someone did try to approach me for a comment or rebuttal, I sicced my attorney on their ass. Soon all the calls stopped and the limelight was left for Jessa's pathetic ass.

I caught Aria and Kingston's eyes on me. I fixed my face with a smile and raised my glass in a toast to them before I moved into the crowd.

For so long my life had been about control—or the lack of it. My mother controlled me with her opinions. My father controlled me with his money. My husband controlled me with his title. Pleasure controlled me with his dick.

To be honest, before Jessa sent that text, I didn't know if I was coming or going. I had no clue who the fuck I really was. Everything was about the perfect image and the perfect life. Humph, the perfect lie.

The whole time my husband punished me for my affair with cruel sex and cold treatment behind closed doors, I smiled and pretended that our shit didn't stink and everyone else in the world should want to be us.

I had already made the choice not to be anyone's puppet anymore, and Eric's death and subsequent will made sure that I wouldn't have to buckle to anyone's will for survival anymore. I was already in talks with a small coalition of his former employees who wanted to pool their funds and purchase his architectural firm. The man I once loved and respected I had grown to hate. His money hadn't changed that fact.

I just thank God his obsession with Jessa Bell had made the usually meticulous man take his eyes off the prize—his will. First when he caught me cheating and then when I served him divorce papers, I assumed he would've made sure my name was stricken off of everything. The only reasoning I could make of it was his need to always present the façade of a happy marriage. Divorce was the last thing the he or his Catholic religion dictated and maybe that played a role as well in his decision not to change his will. I could only guess. The only thing that I knew for sure was that he, his parents, and the church got their wish. Only death did us part.

Good riddance, motherfucker.

*Several swats with a riding crop and a man—*your husband*—calling you his whore as he forced you to gag on his dick had a way of hardening a woman's heart.*

I wandered outside on the patio and watched my neighbors dancing on the Plexiglas-covered pool with lighting that made them all look as if they floated on water. I played in the new shorter lengths of my wavy weave-free hair as I watched the many couples sharing touches and looks that seemed to be the setup for a night of hot sex once they got home.

It just reminded me that I hadn't enjoyed the comforts of a hard dick since my last day at the townhouse I rented when I left my husband. That was my last go 'round with the infamous—and far too popular—Pleasure. It had felt good to fuck him, nut, and then leave his dick wet and hard and wanting more.

Fuck him.

That male trick picked an older woman to fuck over me one night because she had cash. Oh, I missed the dick and the mind games, but that Negro *was a no-go. Knowing he screwed or ate or did whatever to Jessa's community pussy just sealed the deal that Pleasure would* NEVER *see, touch, sniff, lick, or fuck my pussy again.*

Still, he created a need in me that was making me run through batteries for my vibrator. And sometimes the rabbit just couldn't get the job done. Not when you wanted the heat of a body on yours, the strength of a man's arms around you, the pulse of dick inside you, the thrill of his tongue on your nipples as he stroked away.

A vibrator made me cum, but a man made me feel alive.

Still, a hired dick could still be useful—especially when a grieving widow didn't want to piss off the parents of her deceased husband by flaunting a new man around town when their son's grave was still fresh.

I gulped down the last of my champagne and walked out to my brand-new silver convertible Bentley to retrieve my cell phone. I hit "6" on my speed dial and a picture of Pleasure's dick filled the screen. The "6" was for sex.

It rang four times and went to voice mail.

I cleared my throat and waited. Moments later, my phone rang in my hand and the picture of his dick filled the screen again. "Busy?" I asked, watching many of my neighbors just arriving to the event. I could have walked to the clubhouse, but I wanted my flashy new car on display.

"Not really. Whassup?"

Even though the sound of his voice was pure sex to me, I said, "I wonder if you would do me a favor."

He chuckled. "What's that?"

"I wondered if you could pass on the contact info for one your coworkers who delivers like you or better than you or almost as good as you."

The line remained silent.

"Pleasure? You there?" I asked, taking my own pleasure that I completely caught that cocky, big-dick motherfucker off guard.

"You calling me to set you up with one of my boys?" he asked, his voice hard.

"Yes. Who do you think is worth the money more . . . that light-skin dude King or the dark-skinned dude named Ecstasy?" I asked with innocence. "Do they sell dick on the side too?"

"Oh, so you really don't want this dick no more?" he asked.

"No, definitely not."

"Fuck you, Jaime, find your own dick."

Click.

I laughed as I dropped my phone back on the driver's seat and closed the driver's door.

"Jaime?"

I turned in surprise to see Eric's parents walking up to

me. "I didn't know you were coming to the ball," I said, kissing both of their cheeks.

"It was a charity Eric supported every year and we wanted to donate ten thousand dollars in his memory," Eric Sr. said. "It was supposed to be a surprise . . . but now that you're aware of our gift, I'm sure you'll want to double the amount."

My back stiffened, but I smiled. His parents knew Eric and me had separated and were headed for divorce. Like my parents, they participated in a divorce intervention at the Terrace Room, hoping to see us reconcile.

The scandal surrounding Eric's death and Jessa's attempted murder by him had been embarrassing and shocking for people who—like most parents—saw their son as perfect. Like my parents, they were too refined and polite to speak of anything improper. It was all about the front.

"Of course," I agreed as we all walked into the clubhouse.

I fought the urge to tell them about Jessa's pregnancy and the chance of a lawsuit, but I held back. It was all over the news locally and nationally, but they hadn't asked me about it and I wanted proof the bitch was even pregnant before I raised their hopes of a grandchild by their deceased son.

"Nice car," his mother said.

"Eric ordered it before he passed," I lied with ease. "I'm not sure I'm going to keep it."

They said nothing more about it.

I just thanked God they didn't follow the news or didn't feel it warranted conversation. Either way, Jessa's pregnancy—or any further talks on the car—was a discussion I didn't want to have.

Chapter 10

Jessa rose to her feet and turned as her attorney, Lincoln Manning, strode into his Manhattan corner office. She smiled at him. "Lincoln Manning is never late," she teased, as he paused long enough in her path to kiss her cheek before taking his seat behind his leather-topped desk.

He smoothed his tie as he walked his chair up closer to his desk. "Actually, I was on a phone conference with my paralegal and one of the firm's partners and an attorney who is highly skilled in estate law," he said.

Jessa tilted her head to the side as she eyed the man.

"Your chances of this even making it to court are slim to none," Lincoln said, picking up his pen to work between his fingers as he leaned back in his chair. "The absence of a will would have made the estate intestate and it would have been handled by the probate court, and once the heir was born you would have had a better chance of halting the probate proceedings until the lawsuit was resolved."

Jessa eyed her attorney and friend. "So what's the bottom line?"

Lincoln leaned forward and locked his eyes with hers. "If—and it's a big if—it made it before a judge, the cost of the legal fees would not be sufficient for the amount you may or may not recover from his estate, which is sizable but hardly seven figures."

Jessa uncrossed one leg and crossed the other. "How long have we been friends, Lincoln?" she asked.

He smiled broadly. "So long that I barely remember how long."

"And do you think I give up so easily on *anything* I want?" Jessa asked in her husky voice.

Lincoln eyed her for a long time.

Jessa never flinched.

"Can I assume you really only wanted a lawyer and friend, and that's why you gave up so easily on me?" he asked.

Jessa closed her eyes, shook her head, and threw her hands up to the ceiling. "Do you know I have been hit on, propositioned, and offered amazing things more now than any other time in my life. And the really jacked-up part about it? I am not looking for love or sex or affairs or flings or anything . . . not even with a cute lawyer who is a cool-ass friend," she finished softly.

Lincoln patted his hands against his desktop. "The offer is on the table."

"Duly noted, counselor," she flirted.

Lincoln made a serious face. "Don't do that," he said sternly.

Jessa flung her head back and laughed.

They fell into a comfortable silence.

"Jessa," Lincoln said, leaning back in his chair again. "Let this go. Have your baby. Be happy. Collect social security. Tell his parents so they can help you and your child. Just move on," he advised.

Jessa was shaking her head before he even finished. "People want me dead for loving a married man who eventually tried to kill me because I ended it. That woman has called my child a bastard every chance she gets. She cheated on him first and filed for divorce, and now she's sitting pretty on her ass counting everything he left behind. If he had enough balls not to kill himself and he knew about this baby, he would have made sure that this child was taken care of. I know that and she knows that. *Fuck* her."

Jessa paused and licked the gloss from her lips. "I won't push this until I'm broke or I look a fool, but I'm not giving up yet. She's not going to win this easy."

"You may need to pull his parents into this on your side," he said.

Jessa truly didn't want the involvement of Eric's parents and had barely considered them once she decided to have the baby. "They helped to shape Eric into the lunatic that tried to kill me," she told him. "I don't want their influence on this child," she insisted.

"But you may need them to help establish paternity," Lincoln explained. "It would be easier to do it through them than exhuming the body."

Jessa eyes widened. "You mean they would pull his dead ass out of the grave?" she asked in astonishment.

"Yes, ma'am, and it ain't cheap," he assured her.

She frowned. Deeply.

Lincoln held up his hands. "I will handle the deposition today, but we have to bring an estate lawyer on to the case to make sure you get the best representation possible," he said, looking down at his leather Piaget watch. "They should be in the conference room by now. Ready?"

Jessa rose just as Lincoln stood up and came around his desk with leather folders in his hands. "Question is: Are they ready for me?" she asked smoothly before she preceded him out of the office.

Jessa and Jaime stared each other down from across the conference table as their attorneys volleyed back and forth about the validity of a lawsuit and the lack of precedent.

Jessa had to bite her bottom lip to keep from snarling at her ex-friend as she remembered the wench calling her child a bastard. She once asked the woman for forgiveness, but now Jessa could care less about Jaime. *Fuck her and fuck everybody in her world.*

Jaime's eyes said, "I hate you."

Jessa prayed her eyes conveyed, "You're late, bitch."

"Why are we even going through all this drama when there's no proof she's even pregnant?" Jaime asked, her eyes still locked with Jessa as she reached down into her bag on the floor and slapped a pregnancy kit on the table before sliding it across the table to Jessa with plenty of force.

Jessa smirked as she easily shifted and allowed the box to go spinning off the table to the floor behind her. "Silly bitch," Jessa mouthed, making sure the other woman could read her lips.

Jaime jumped up to her feet, but her attorney reached his hand out to steer her back down into her seat.

Jessa never flinched. She absolutely refused to let her enemy see her sweat even if her entire body was a riot of nerves.

"Ms. Hall, your attorney has a copy of the medical report confirming that Ms. Bell is indeed pregnant," Lincoln told her. "You do agree that the time frame matches up to the time that you discovered Ms. Bell was involved in an intimate relationship with your husband?"

Jaime's lawyer whispered something in Jaime's ear before she said, "Yes, Mrs. Bell made sure to alert me to the fact that she was sleeping with my husband."

"What were your husband's thoughts on having children?" Lincoln asked, making notes on his legal pad.

"We were waiting to have children. Our life was mapped out and kids wasn't on the schedule for a few years," Jaime said, looking and sounding belligerent.

"But you do believe that your husband wanted children?"

"With *me?* Yes," she stressed. "With a mistress? No."

Jessa fought the urge to throw out a snide remark.

"Do you think if your husband was aware of the child that he would have made provisions for the baby in the will?" Lincoln asked.

Jaime smirked and shook her head. "I can't speak for a dead man who didn't make the best decisions . . . obviously."

Lincoln reached for Jessa's hand under the table and patted it reassuringly. It was balled into a fist with her red lacquered nails nearly piercing the flesh of her palm. His small show of comfort evoked emotions in her that caused tears to fill her eyes. She blinked them away.

"But you do acknowledge that there is a possibility that Eric Hall is the father of Jessa Bell's baby?" Lincoln asked, redirecting his line of questioning.

"What I acknowledge is that I cannot believe a woman I called friend is so low and so slack to actually sue me behind this bullshit, as if fucking my husband behind my back wasn't enough?" Jaime chewed out, her eyes blazing as she glared at Jessa. "Are you obsessed with me? Do you want to be me, Jessa? First Eric, then Pleasure, and now you want the inheritance my husband left me."

Jessa laughed at her. A good rich, belly laugh that was completely mocking and definitely letting Jaime know just how foolish Jessa Bell thought she was. "Jaime, please, you don't even know who you are or what you want, so who can mimic you—a grown woman in her thirties going through the self-discovery that most women make in their late teens. Please, don't be silly."

"Ladies, please," Jaime's attorney said. "The sooner we finish this deposition the better, so that you two can return to your corners."

"I agree," Lincoln said before leaning over to whisper in Jaime's ear.

"Just keep cool, Jessa, this is almost over," he said.

She nodded.

"If you are truly interested in continuing with this matter, I think that not only proof of pregnancy is necessary but also proof of paternity," Jaime's lawyer said.

"Postnatal, not prenatal; there are too many risks to the pregnancy," Lincoln insisted.

"You expect us to wait all those months until she gives birth . . . then she should have waited to bring this matter up at all," Jaime's attorney scoffed. "I am sorry, but if you continue forward with this, we will request a court-approved paternity test as soon as possible."

"So that means your client is willing to give permission for exhuming the body?" Lincoln countered.

"No, I am not," Jaime stressed. "Why am I taking on the burden of my husband's bastard?"

Jessa jumped to her feet and picked up her glass of water to throw in Jaime's face in one swift movement that the woman didn't see coming until her face and hair were all wet.

Jaime gasped and then knocked her glass of water across the table to send water splashing against some of Lincoln's papers and Jessa's black pencil skirt.

"All right, counselor, that's it. Let's go, Jaime." Her attorney gathered his papers into his briefcase and grabbed Jaime's elbow to escort her out of the conference room.

"Jessa, you two cannot act like this during a professional meeting," Lincoln scolded her as he used a napkin to absorb some of the moisture from his papers. "Come on. Throwing water? You're a grown-ass woman. What you been watching, *Basketball Wives?*"

"I apologize, Lincoln," she told him truthfully as she dropped back down into her chair. "She brings out the worst in me."

"I thought you told me you're going to church and reading the Bible and trying to get saved?" Lincoln sat down in the chair next to her again. "I've seen all the contracts and know about the money—the good money—you're making recently. I know about the insurance policy Marc left. These people want you to risk a miscarriage to prove the paternity. Man, let this shit go."

Jessa said nothing as she turned her head to look out the window.

Soon Lincoln gathered up his papers and walked to the door. "Stay as long as you want; they don't need this conference room until after lunch," he said before leaving.

Once Jessa finally took her leave from Lincoln's office she headed straight home and spent the rest of the day in bed. She felt like she needed to rejuvenate mentally and physically. She didn't spare one thought on Jaime and the impending lawsuit. She gave herself a vacation from it.

The next morning she packed her bag and waited for her car service to arrive to drive her into New York for her week of business meetings and promotions. Leaving her bags by the door, she made herself a small bowl of cinnamon and brown sugar oatmeal with lots of walnuts as she took her prenatal vitamin. That reminded her to pack it, and she was just sticking the bottle into her purse when her cell phone rang.

Jessa pulled it out and answered the call. "Morning, Keegan," she said, looking through the large window over her sink at Aria walking Kingston to his car. Her belly was round in the robe she wore as Kingston kissed her neck intimately before bending to kiss her belly as well, then climbing into his car and reversing out of the driveway. Aria stood there and watched his car until it was out of sight before she turned and made her way back up the stairs and into her house.

They were the picture of happily ever after. A team. When she gave birth he would be there to support her, coach her, and love her through it.

Who will be there for me?

"Can you believe that Viagra addict is denying his affair!"

Jessa leaned back from the phone as Keegan screeched in anger. "Whoa! What happened?"

"My shitty ex-husband is saying he left the marriage because I was no longer satisfying him in any aspect and he is denying having an affair." Keegan sniffed and Jessa knew she was crying. "He is trying not to pay me major alimony. That lying, limp-dick, cheating son of a bitch."

Jessa made a face. "I'm sorry, Keegan. What are you going to do?" she asked, tucking the phone between her ear and shoulder as she emptied the steaming oatmeal from the small pot and into a bowl. "Do you have proof he cheated?"

Jessa paused at the hilarity of the conversation for a moment. A former mistress advises an ex-mistress turned wife on how to prove the existence of her husband's mistress. If she wasn't in the middle of the conversation, she would side-eye herself.

"No, but I wish I did, sugar drop," Keegan sighed. "That bastard just left here—"

"Huh?" Jessa asked. "He just left there? It's not even eight o'clock. In your words, *dah-ling,* something in the milk ain't clean."

"I was horny and he came by last night and a piece of me wanted him to stay the night and make that bitch wonder where he was."

"So you play yourself by fucking the limp-dick, cheating son of a bitch and then he got up this morning and denied he ever cheated?" Jessa asked her before taking a big bite of oatmeal.

Keegan sighed heavily. "It doesn't feel good getting screwed twice," she drawled, sounding Texan.

"Maybe he's not with that particular woman anymore but still wants the divorce," Jessa offered around a sip of tea.

"Or he's with someone new."

"Or open to someone new," Jessa countered, sprinkling more nuts over her oatmeal.

"I can't believe him and I still got the taste of his cum in my mouth!"

Jessa frowned and gagged a little before pushing the oatmeal away. "Damn, how horny were you?"

"Horny *and* out to prove a point."

"Not a good combo."

"Sure ain't."

"Listen, I'm headed into New York and my car service should be on the way," Jessa told her, rising to empty her bowl and wash it. She also was bored with the convo and ready to focus on her own worries. "Hire a private detective. If you need a referral I can e-mail you the contact info of the guy I use."

"Send it and enjoy New York."

Jessa nodded. "I will. Oh, and keep your legs—and your mouth—closed to his dick."

Keegan just laughed before hanging up.

Jessa's landline rang. She scooped up her cordless. "Yes, Lucky."

"Acclaimed Car Service is here."

"Let him up."

Jessa turned off the lights in the kitchen and walked in her sequined flats to the front door. As soon as she opened the door she was glad for jeans she normally avoided and a black cashmere wrap as she felt the slight chill in the air. The black SUV came up the street and turned into her empty driveway. She had parked her Jag in her garage. Jessa set her bags on the step and locked her door before securing the alarm with the new key code. It wasn't until recently that she remembered Aria knew her passcode.

The driver opened the rear door of the SUV and helped her in before getting her bags. Soon they were rolling out of Richmond Hills and Jessa looked around wondering if maybe it wasn't truly time to say good-bye to it for good.

Jessa loved the fast-paced vibe and energy of New York. As soon as she settled into her suite at the W Hotel on Park Avenue South she took a long shower and changed into a long-sleeve stretch silk blouse and a pair of wide-leg trousers, both in a soft lilac. There wasn't much more she had to do to prepare for her meeting with Myra and her new literary agent.

Locking her valuables into the safe, Jessa grabbed her oversized clutch, tucked it under her arm, and left her suite. She was riding down on the elevator when it glided to a stop on the fifth floor. She looked up and her face filled with surprise to see the captain of the yacht she chartered in the Hamptons step on. He looked handsome in a navy tailored suit and crisp white shirt open at the neck.

Jessa's clit throbbed with new life.

"Tsk, tsk, tsk. Not a walk of shame is it, Captain?" she asked with teasing in her soft husky tones.

He smiled as the elevator door closed behind him. "Surprise, surprise," he said.

Jessa's heart beat rapidly, but she played it cool. "Yes, it is. Yes, it is."

"No walk of shame," he said. "I had a meeting with someone wanting to buy one of my boats."

"I hope it went well," she told him, the smell of his cologne just enough to tease the senses and make you want to bury your face in his neck and get lost. "I have a meeting downstairs as well."

Tyson smiled. "I hope that goes well."

Jessa held up crossed fingers.

"Maybe we can go to dinner to celebrate . . . or commiserate," he offered as the elevator door opened up into the elaborately decorated lobby.

Jessa stepped off the elevator and looked up at him.

"It's just dinner."

"Yes, but why if it's not going anywhere?" she asked.

"Because you look damn good in and out of a bikini."

Jessa arched a brow. "That is true," she joked.

"Just dinner," he offered again.

Jessa couldn't lie that she was used to the company of a man and missed it. Not for sex entirely but also the flirtation. The banter. The enjoyment. Just dinner.

"How about the restaurant here at eight?" she said.

"See you at eight."

With one last smile, Jessa turned and quickly made her way to Olive's, the two-story restaurant located in the hotel. She spotted Myra rising to her feet and the maître d' led her to the table where the New York sun gleamed through the windows. That and running into Tyson elevated her mood.

"Hello, ladies," she said, setting her clutch on the empty chair before taking the seat the maître d' held for her.

"Jesse Bell, this is Olivia Young. Olivia, this is Jessa Bell, your new client," Myra said, her eyes excited and bright behind her spectacles.

Jessa shook hands with the tall and plump woman who was dark, lovely, and fashionable with hair that was shiny, wavy, and pulled up into a top knot that emphasized her wide-set eyes. Very Angie Stone.

"It's nice to finally meet you in person," Jessa said, admitting to herself that she was nervous. Everything about her life was so new and foreign to her. She was using every minute to learn and readjust.

"You as well . . . and we have some celebrating to do,"

Olivia said as their waitress came to their table. "Two mimosas with Veuve Clicquot and a sparkling cider."

Jessa felt anxious. Good news.

"We have three offers on the table, and all three publishing houses are very eager and aggressive in acquiring your book, Jessa," Olivia said. "Now, they all want the full story, though. Everything leading up to the affair, the stalking, the attempted murder, the pregnancy and the lawsuit, and details on how you have turned it all around and found God. But for all those wonderful details we are looking at a high six-figure advance."

Jessa's heart pounded as their waitress brought their drinks. Jessa hurried to take a deep gulp of hers. A book deal? A six-figure book deal? What in the fuck was the world coming to?

"Now you're making your scandalous life into a business. Some kind of Mistress, Incorporated or some bullshit."

Fuck you, Aria, she thought, raising her glass in toast to the women.

Mistress, Inc. was sounding real good right about now.

Jessa gasped hotly as she felt her climax cause the walls of her pussy to vibrate and pulse against the length of Tyson's condom-covered dick as he pressed a heated kiss to her neck. Her entire body tingled even as she felt herself free-falling back to reality.

She breathed through pursed lips as Tyson rolled over onto his back trying to catch his own breath. *Oh shit. Oh shit. Oh shit.*

"Damn," he swore, his hand over his heart.

"Are you okay?" Jessa asked.

She did not need a chapter in her life—or her book—dedicated to giving a man a heart attack after she swore she was saved and trying to live right. *Just my damn luck.*

"I'm good" he said, still breathing heavy.

Jessa sat up in bed and pulled the sheet up to cover her sweat-soaked breasts. "Listen, Tyson. Thank you, but I really need to get some sleep now. So if you could gather your things and . . ."

"Take my walk of shame?" he asked.

Jessa smiled bashfully. "Look, dinner was good. Conversation was nice. The flirting was fun. But this is not what I had planned for the night. As good as it was—and it was good—the night is over."

Tyson nodded and kicked the covers back. "Just use me up and toss me away, Jessa Bell," he said jokingly, standing up and walking naked across the room to pick up his pile of clothes from by the door.

Jessa had stripped him as soon as they shut the door. She dropped her head into her hands at the heated memory. She hadn't had a one-night stand since college.

God's just shaking his head right now. . . .

Jessa kicked back the sheet and walked naked across the room to the bathroom. She locked the door and immediately dropped down to her knees.

"Oh God, I am *so* sorry."

Jessa's eyes were closed tight and her hands were folded under her chin as she pressed her knees against the cold tile. "I will fast. I will read an extra chapter in the Bible every night and sign up for Joel Osteen's daily word and donate a portion of the proceeds of my book to charity. I will pay my tithes," she prayed vehemently. "Please, just forgive me for going back on my word to stay celibate until I marry. God, please, you know me and you know I am trying."

By the time Jessa finished her prayers and finally climbed from her knees with a heavy breath, ten minutes had passed and Tyson was gone.

"What the hell am I doing?" she asked herself out loud

as she dropped down on the side of the bed. "I'm pregnant, for God's sake."

Jessa spotted the note on the nightstand. She picked it up and read it out loud:

> *"The only way to get over the horror of a one-night stand is to do it all over again. Call me. 973-555-0987. P.S. Did I top the glass one?"*

Jessa just shook her head and let the note drop to the floor.

Chapter 11

Jessa spent the next morning deep into retail therapy. She hit all her favorites from Gucci and Prada to a full tour around Saks Fifth Avenue. But out of all the shoes, clothes, and jewelry she splurged on, the purchase she loved the best was the jumbo-sized plush vanilla teddy bear she bought and had shipped to her house. Everything about it screamed nursery, and she could see it snuggled in the corner of the crib or on the floor for her child to play and climb on once they began to toddle.

And so the teddy bear and all the warm feelings it evoked pushed Jessa to call Keegan to ride into the city to meet her.

"I can't believe you're ready to decorate your nursery," Keegan said, quickly using her iPad to pull up clear photos of fabric swatches that she had on stock in her showroom.

Jessa touched her stomach, enjoying the feel of its slight roundness as she imagined hearing a child call her "Mother."

"Even though I'm just four months, I'm ready to see it finished and have it sitting ready for when the baby and I come home."

"I hear you, sugar. I'm not going to turn down the business . . . especially with that slicky-tricky ex-dicky of mine."

Jessa smiled. "How's the private detective working out?"

Keegan side-eyed her. "I think his little side-boo kicked his ass to the curb or he's on his best behavior until the divorce is final."

"No more ex-sex. Right?"

Keegan shook her head, sending her red hair flowing back and forth. "No, no more. I'm good for a while. But as soon as this divorce is final, I am going to find the youngest man with the biggest—"

"Keegan!" Jessa said sharply even as she laughed.

"I just wish there was some way to catch the son of a bitch."

Jessa thought about the mob of women outside her house and her surprise visit from Dina, the wife of her perverted neighbor. "When I was married, I never doubted Marc for a second; but if I did, I think I would want to know for sure. I think I would even set up his ass to catch him in the act."

"And trust me, honey bee, plenty of women—and some men—would. Including me." Keegan winked at her.

"Would you ever go on that show *Cheaters?* You ever seen that?" Jessa asked, honestly curious.

"Hell no. Being on *Cheaters* would lead to me being on *Snapped?*"

"What's *Snapped?*"

"It's all about women being pushed to the edge and killing their husbands," Keegan explained. "The whole way that show is set up is meant to escalate the anger because you're on TV and you're embarrassed. You almost have to act a fool."

"That's true."

"Oh, I would love to catch my ex, but something televised for anyone to see . . . in repeats . . . and online? No, ain't no dick worth that shame, darling."

"I'm beginning to think most dick isn't worth a lot of things."

"Now I'm not anti-dick, sweetie. As a matter of fact, you need some dick in your life before you get cobwebs or produce dust." Keegan pointed between Jessa's thighs.

I'm good, Jessa thought with a shiver as she remembered Tyson's skills. The man was built for sex.

"Finally getting rid of that crazy no sex 'til after the baby rule?" Keegan asked. "You know that's gonna make giving birth even harder."

"That's not true," Jessa said, purposefully avoiding telling her about her night of sin-filled passion with the captain. *If Keegan wants to tell me ALL her business, then that's her business. And my business will stay MY business.*

Keegan just shrugged.

Jessa fell silent as she allowed herself to remember clutching the back of Tyson's head as his lips suckled deeply on her clit like it was ambrosia for the gods. And he hadn't stopped until she came; then he dipped down to lick up every drop as he pressed his thumb to her clit and kept her juices flowing.

Jessa grunted softly as she fanned herself with her clutch as she felt all her pulse points tingle.

"How's all your meetings and stuff going?"

"Good. Thanks." Jessa turned in her seat. "How much time do we have to browse and kind of get an idea of what direction we want to go in for the nursery."

"Which room are you going to use?" Keegan asked, turning on the seat to look over at Jessa.

"In a perfect world I would convert my dressing room/closet into the nursery, but—"

"You ain't giving up that closet," Keegan finished for her.

"No, I am not giving up my closet," Jessa agreed. "So maybe the guest bedroom directly across from me for when the baby gets a little older; but initially I want a basinet or smaller crib for my bedroom that matches the décor."

Keegan took notes.

"Since my bed is pretty close to the fireplace we may have to reconfigure the room." Jessa opened up her cell phone. "I want the nursery very neutral for now because I don't know if it's a girl or boy, but I definitely want everything centered around this bear."

Keegan leaned over to look at the picture. She nodded. "Forward that to me."

Jessa did. "I definitely want for the nursery one of those large round cribs. Very royal for this prince or princess."

"I know exactly where to go. Driver, Seventh Avenue please." Keegan made more notes on her iPad. "I'm thinking a really creamy rich vanilla as the base color and then we can always bring in blues and greens for a boy or lots of soft pink and yellows for a girl."

"Or leave the whole thing creamy vanilla," Jessa said, picturing the room. "On that side of the house there's a lot of natural light and the vanilla would brighten the room."

"I thought I was the designer," Keegan joked.

"One thing my mother gave me for sure, besides my looks, was damn good taste."

The ladies laughed.

Jessa successfully avoided Tyson for the rest of her week in New York. She never returned the messages he left, she returned the beautiful lilies he sent, and she scheduled any further appointments away from the hotel. On the day she checked out, she left early and wore oversized shades and a hat big enough to cover the moon until she climbed into the back of the car.

Still, she avoided the man, but the memories of that night replayed at the oddest moments and left her flushed and hot and wanting more. It reminded her of the heat and naughty passion she shared with Eric back in the beginning of their affair. And that for her spelled T-R-O-U-B-L-E.

Jessa crossed her legs and cooled herself with the church fan as she remembered the way Tyson sucked on ice cubes before he sucked her nipples and her ass and her clit. "Have mercy," she whispered. "Whooooo."

"Hi, Sister Bell. You okay?"

Her eyes popped open and she flushed in embarrassment to see church was over and people were filing out of the church. *Nothing but the devil.*

She rose to her feet and gave Henry Lyons a friendly smile. Every Sunday since he first introduced himself to her after church he made sure to speak to her and to ask about her well-being. "I just lost my train of thought," she said, falling in beside him as they walked out of church together.

"It happens," he said, forming his wide and friendly face into a smile.

"Yeah, lots of things . . . just happen."

"Well, I believe God already has each person's life laid out and pre-planned from birth to death, so things don't really just happen."

Jessa paused in her steps and looked up at him. "So even the missteps are a part of God's plans?" she asked, sounding doubtful.

Henry paused to look down at her with a nod. "I had to learn that everything in life happens for a reason. There's a lesson is everything: the good, the bad, and the ugly."

Jessa still looked doubtful.

"People give the devil way too much power."

"I cannot see God cosigning death, affairs, pain, and wars," Jessa insisted as they continued out the open double doors into the sunshine beaming outside.

"When I was fighting to get off drugs—"

Jessa side-eyed him with a slight frown.

Henry laughed. "Yes, I was strung out pretty bad about ten years ago. Thin. Damn near homeless. Stealing. Just wilding out and doing anything to get high."

Jessa remained silent and had to fight the urge to clutch her purse tighter. *Judge not, Jessa. Judge not.*

"But as I was saying, when I was getting high I thought the Lord turned his back on me, but it was because he never left me even through the darkness that I didn't die. I didn't completely lose my faith. I didn't go crazy or worse. I made it through it."

Jessa paused again at the sound of victory in his voice. He was giving testimony and honor to God. She knew he meant every word. That gave her chills.

"Sometimes I look at my life now and compare it to the man I was and it blows my mind like heroin never could."

They were standing on the steps of the church. As Jessa watched him and saw his conviction, she knew she had a long way to go. She read the Bible, said the prayers, went to Bible study, endlessly asked for forgiveness, but she didn't feel it as deeply as he did.

"There is nothing better than giving it to God and letting him guide your path," Henry told her. "He will move mountains when needed and He will place them in your path when needed to make sure you go in another direction. God is amazing."

She followed an impulse and reached out to squeeze his wrist. She honestly wanted to feel closer to him and what he was feeling. As if he understood her struggle, he placed one of his strong and warm hands over hers. Jessa had never felt so protected. So covered.

But even as she stood there absorbing his words and trying to understand the power of God and the way that He worked in someone's life, she felt more confused than ever.

Why does the Lord keep blessing me when I continue to trip on my path to him? The baby. The TV exposure. The speaking engagements. The magazine interviews. The book deal. All of it.

Was she supposed to make mistakes as a part of her learning? Was all the goodness making up for her almost dying? Or was he testing her? And if she failed, would he snatch it all away?

Jessa had come straight to church from New York, and she was glad to finally climb back in the SUV and tell the driver to take her home. She hadn't seen her house in a week, and although she loved the luxury of her hotel suite, there was nothing more comfortable to her than her own bed and thousand-count sheets lightly scented with lavender and vanilla.

She was playing on her iPad when the SUV stopped at the security booth for clearance before rolling through the gates of Richmond Hills. Jessa's stomach growled and she briefly thought about going to the Terrace Room but quickly squashed the idea. She wasn't one of the down-home, make you smack your mama kind of cooks, but she could handle baked tilapia and seasoned rice.

No, I'm going home. Bathe. Get in my most luxurious pajamas. Cook. And stay huddled in my beautiful home for the rest of the—

"Aaron! Be careful!"

The driver slammed on the brakes and the tires screeched as the SUV skidded to a stop, barely missing slamming into the driver's side of Renee's car. Jessa reached out to brace her hand against the rear of the driver's seat as she looked at Renee's son, Aaron, quickly maneuver the steering wheel of the car to turn it and speed off down the street.

"You okay back there?" her driver asked.

Jessa nodded and licked her lips as her heart continued

to pound hard. She looked through the rear passenger window as Renee's daughter, Kieran, went stomping into the house before slamming the front door as Renee argued with Jackson. Jessa leaned over and lowered the window enough just in time to hear.

"He's your son and it shouldn't matter to you that he's gay," Renee roared.

"Could you be any louder?" Jackson snapped.

Renee's eyes widened. "So you're ashamed of your son? The child should be ashamed of is that illegitimate bastard you made on me," she told him coldly as she pointed her finger at him accusingly.

Jackson reached for her arm and she snatched it away just as the driver rolled ahead.

"Get the fuck off of me and go home to sign the divorce papers. Your old family will make it just fine without you."

Jessa settled back against her seat as she raised the tinted window. *So Aaron is gay? Never saw that one coming.*

"Y'all have more drama going on than anything near what pops off in my hood," the driver said.

Jessa cut her eyes up to his reflection in the mirror and recognized him as the driver who walked her through the mob of wives who had been waiting at her front door. "You're right," was all that she said.

He pulled up to her home and Jessa spotted a black four-door Lexus sitting in her drive. She recognized the car. It was Eric's parents. Jaime had to have let them into the subdivision unless they still had Eric's security code. Either way, here they were waiting on her.

Without a doubt it was about the baby.

Jessa smoothed the edges of her skirt and arranged the layers of her jet-black hair behind her ears as the SUV slid to a stop. She placed her iPad back into her Louis Vuitton tote and gathered her pocketbook just as the passenger door opened and the driver extended his hand to help her out.

Determined to maintain her composure, Jessa smoothed her white linen dress over her curves and literally flexed her shoulders before making her way to her front door. She had barely passed the hood of the car when both front doors opened and the Halls climbed out. Jessa unlocked her door and pushed the door open wide just as the driver jogged up the steps with her luggage and set it in the foyer. She gave him a stiff smile and slid a fifty-dollar tip into his hand without a word of thanks.

"Jessa, I think it's time we all talked. Don't you?"

She turned on the doorstep to eye Eric's father. She hadn't seen him since the day of his son's funeral when he escorted her out the church and proceeded to make a slick pass at her. He was an older, slightly shorter version of Eric with square features and deep-set eyes.

"If you think so," Jessa said coolly as she shifted her eyes to Mrs. Hall, looking prim and proper in her peach coatdress, wide-brimmed church hat, and pearls.

She stepped back and allowed them to enter the house before her. She closed the front door and saw them headed into her living room. "No!" she shouted out in a knee-jerk reaction.

They both stopped and turned to eye her.

She couldn't let them sit in the room where their son had killed himself. She just couldn't.

"So is it okay if we talk in my den," Jessa said, already turning to head down the hall leading to the rear of her house. They followed behind her.

Sunlight beamed through the entire room from the wall of ceiling-to-floor windows that showcased her beautifully landscaped backyard. Jessa waved her hand at one of the large oversized suede sofas as she took a seat in one of the two club chairs facing them across the large leather ottoman.

"How can I help you?" she asked as soon as they took their seat. Jessa wanted to gain and maintain control of the conversation.

"It has come to our attention that you claim to be pregnant with our son's child," Eric Sr. began, crossing his ankle over the opposite knee.

"Make I ask your source?" Jessa asked as she crossed her leg and settled back against the comfort of the chair.

"Does it matter?" Mrs. Hall snapped.

Jessa curved the corner of her mouth into a smile. "I guess not, Mrs. Hall."

The woman set up on the edge of the sofa and pointed her finger at Jessa as she gave her an Aunt Ester one-eyed stare. "Your attitude really disturbs me. You seem too cocky and damn cool for a woman who didn't have the gall or the class to let us now that you *may be* pregnant with our dead son's child," she said coldly, even as her eyes filled with tears.

"If there are any doubts about the paternity, one or both of you can submit a DNA sample for a grandparentage test that would prove Eric is indeed the father," Jessa told them.

"And you are considering suing the estate on behalf of the child?" Eric Sr. asked.

"Yes, I'm considering it. I'm sure you both know your son would want his child taken care of. I'm sure you want the same."

"What I want is for my son to be alive and committed to his marriage," Mrs. Hall snapped as her husband pressed his handkerchief into her hand. "And it's your fault he is dead."

Jessa looked at the woman as if she was crazy. "Excuse me—and I mean no disrespect—but no one is to blame for

Eric's death but Eric," she stressed as she felt her entire body tense.

"We don't know what *really* happened that night?"

Jessa sat up in her chair. "Then I'll tell you since you obviously did not read the police report *or* the autopsy. Your son, after weeks of harassing and stalking me because I *ended* the affair, came to my home and attempted to kill me by strangulation, and when I passed out he shot himself," she told the woman with ferocity in her eyes and her voice.

"Liar!" Mrs. Hall roared, jumping to her foot. "You lying whore!"

"Kittie," Mr. Hall said in warning, rising to his feet as well.

Jessa remained in her seat and forced herself to relax her body as she settled back in her seat. "I will excuse your bad manners because I can understand the delusions of a parent not willing to accept that the son they spoon-fed and raised was crazy," she said calmly, her eyes locked with the stormy ones of his mother.

"If that is my son's child you are carrying, we will sue you for custody and we will use any means to win. Do you understand me?" Mrs. Hall said, standing over Jessa.

Jessa rose to her feet and looked down into the woman's face as they stood close enough to kiss or fight. "I see where Eric gets his crazy from, and if you think I am going to turn over my baby to you to be turned into a fruitcake like your son, then you are out of your motherfucking mind. Don't *fuck* with me about my baby. Now, do *you* understand *me?*" Jessa told her in a cold and hard voice that still held nothing on the chill in her eyes.

Mr. Hall pressed his body in between them. "Jessa, you'll be hearing from our attorneys," he said, before guiding his crying wife out of the house.

As soon as Jessa heard the front door close behind

them, she lost all of her strength. All of her fight. Her knees gave out beneath her and her body sank to the floor as she felt fear like nothing else she ever knew evoke wretched tears.

She couldn't let them take this baby. She couldn't.

But secrets long hidden shook Jessa's very foundation, and she knew if they were discovered that she may very well lose.

Chapter 12

Two months later

Jessa looked in the mirror at the changes to her face now that her pregnancy was fully blossoming on her body. Her natural hair was fuller and thicker. Her face was glowing—she hardly needed bronzer. Even though she thought she had the cheeks of a chipmunk, the nose of a bulldog, and her neck was slightly darker than the rest of her caramel complexion. Her belly was swollen with life, her titties felt as heavy as punching bags, and sometimes her feet were too pudgy for her fabulous collection of designer shoes.

Still, she was loving every minute of it. She was glad to be in the moment and old enough to realize the gift of motherhood.

And that's why she would move out of the country and stay on the run before she let ANYONE else raise this child.

She hadn't heard anything from the Halls, and her attorney, Lincoln, assured her they were probably waiting for the birth of the child to confirm paternity. And because she had denied risking her pregnancy for a prenatal paternity test, she had, in turn, put her lawsuit against Eric's estate on hold as well.

Everything was in limbo as they *all* waited for the birth of her baby.

"You ready?" Myra asked as she walked up to Jessa as she sat in the makeup chair.

"A little nervous about an inspirational talk show, but I think I'm ready," Jessa said, splaying her fingers on her belly.

"Don't be nervous. We talk all the time and you honestly have increased the presence of spirituality and religion in your life, and that's what you're here to speak about," Myra crossed her arms over her shoulder as she leaned her buttocks back against the Formica counter.

"A friend of mine from the church has been really helping me to focus and see things different, and it's been good. I feel more connected and aware of God's presence, you know?"

That day after the Halls left her home with their threats still resting heavily on her mind, she had made her way to the church and Henry was there volunteering to help clean the church as a part of his tithing.

She had surprised herself when she confided in him about the threats of a custody battle from the Halls. That man had immediately set aside his broom and gathered her hands in his to seriously pray for her and then taught her how to pray.

And in the weeks following, Jessa called on him. To pray. To talk. To be counseled. To help her do physical things around the house. To laugh.

Henry had truly become her friend and she was grateful for him. Although many of the church members speculated that there was more between them, Henry had never stepped to her that way. And she was grateful for that.

If only I hadn't crossed that line with Eric.

"They are ready for you on the set, Ms. Bell," a stagehand said.

Jessa rose to her feet in her heels (three inches instead of four) and smoothed the peach metallic maternity trench coat she wore over a silk ivory cap sleeve sweater and wide-leg wool pants of the same color.

Once Jessa was seated in the leather club chair on the stage, she was glad that there was no studio audience and just lots of brilliant lights to make her sweat. Franklin Cash stepped his tall and wiry frame onto the stage and extended one of his large hands to her.

"Nice to meet you," he said, his voice surprisingly deep for his thin frame.

"It's nice to meet you as well," she said politely, when in truth she had never heard of the man.

Myra assured her that he was the minister of a megachurch of more than ten thousand members in New York, and his talk show was one of the highest rated shows on The Christian Network.

According to Myra, this interview could possibly be just as major as the ones she did on *Kerry Kay* and other national talk shows.

Jessa let Myra adjust her hair as Reverend Cash was equipped with his mic pac. "Thanks," she told her, as she shifted her body to a comfortable position in the chair that was not as comfortable as it looked, especially for a six months' pregnant woman.

Suddenly everyone cleared the stage as the director counted them down.

"And welcome to back to *Total Insight,*" Reverend Cash said.

Jessa fixed her face into neutrality as she faced the camera and prepared herself to tell her story—and relive it—all over again.

Over the next twenty minutes Jessa felt herself relax as the minister not only interviewed her but delivered words of encouragement.

"I think it's a wonderful testimony of God's ever increasing presence in your life that you survived and used that terrible act to attend church and study the Bible," Reverend Cash said. "To me, I think God was in your life before then and you just didn't recognize it."

Jessa nodded in understanding even though she thought, *How much longer is this interview?* She was feeling tired and had woken early to get to the station for hair and makeup.

"Jessa, when I was thinking about your story and the path you traveled during your journey and in researching you a little bit . . ."

Jessa tensed and fought to keep her face neutral.

"We learned you were raised by your grandmother," he said.

Jessa felt her left eye twitch. "Yes, I was, and she made sure I was in church every Sunday, and I'm grateful for that foundation even though I strayed away from it once I was on my own and in college. It feels good to be back in touch with my spirituality," she said.

"And you were raised by your grandmother because . . ."

Jessa crossed her hands in her lap as she flipped her hair behind her shoulder. "No disrespect, but it's not relevant to my story. That's very personal and I prefer not to discuss my mother," she said with what she hoped was finality in her tone.

"I can understand that . . . and her absence may very well be a part of some of the decisions you have made, and so we thought the best way to strengthen your walk with God would be to correct the lack of a mother-daughter relationship." Reverend Cash rose to his feet.

Jessa hated everything about that moment. Everything. *I know they did not . . .*

Her heart was pounding as she leaned past the minister's frame to see an older and overweight version of herself walking out onstage. Jessa gasped as her façade broke. Her usual perfectly placed control was shot as she rose to her feet as her mother, Darla, pulled her into a tight embrace.

"My baby," she sighed with tears in her eyes.

For a moment, Jessa was transported back to a time when she was six and her mother was her world. She pressed her nose into her mother's now fleshy neck and inhaled. She was hoping that familiar scent of her flowery perfume was nestled there. But it wasn't.

Instead, she faintly smelled alcohol.

"I missed my little girl," Darla whispered.

The scent of alcohol doubled.

And that brought all the warm and yummy feelings crashing to an end.

Jessa leaned back to look into her mother's eyes, and she found them to be yellowed and aged and glassy. As a little girl she didn't know that the clear liquid that looked like water but burned her throat was alcohol. And she didn't know that the little pills her mother swallowed were drugs.

She was all grown now and Jessa knew that standing before her was an addict. And she wasn't having that fact exposed on television.

"Revered Cash, I thank you for this moment and this reconnection with my mother, but this is definitely a private moment that I do not want to happen on television," Jessa said as she removed both her and her mother's audio.

"What? Why?" Darla whined dramatically as Jessa guided her off the stage.

"Cut!" someone barked over the loud speaker.

"Ms. Bell, we still have one more segment to record," Reverend Cash called behind her. Myra scrambled to catch up with Jessa's long strides. Several producers followed them down the hall leading to her dressing room. Her mother jerked away from her in anger.

"You been all over television!" Darla screeched, her eyes wild and big as she pointed her finger in Jessa's face. "Why can't I be on TV just like you? Huh? Are you ashamed of me? Or . . . or . . . are you afraid that they'll like me more than you? Or is being some man's mistress a bigger deal than your mother?"

Jessa stiffened from the attack. "Mother?" she said snidely.

"Jessa, don't," Myra said in gentle warning.

"A mother doesn't leave their child behind for a life of men, liquor, and drugs," Jessa said coldly, all the years of pain, disappointment, and rejection surfacing in a rush that made her heart pound and her head spin. "How dare you question me when I haven't seen you in over twenty-five years?"

Darla pushed up off the wall of the hallway and swung, slapping Jessa harshly.

Everyone gathered in the hall gasped as Jessa's head swung to the left as she pressed her hand to her cheek where it stung.

"I am your mother and you will respect MEEEEEEEEEEEEEEEE!" Darla screamed at the top of her lungs, drawing the word out for what seemed all eternity, before she suddenly broke into a maniacal laughter that was eerie.

Jessa stepped back from the craziness she saw in her mother's eyes. She felt weak and confused and a little a dazed from the slap.

Everyone watched Darla with their mouths slightly ajar and the area around them was library quiet.

"I see now the best thing you did for me was stay the

hell away," Jessa said in a soft voice that was still loud with her pain.

With one last look, Jessa turned to walk away. Everyone pressed their bodies against the walls of the halls to let Jessa through the melee.

"No, Jessa. Please don't leave me. I'm sorry. I'm sorry."

Jessa paused at her mother sounding like a five-year-old child. She turned and her eyes widened as Darla's eyes flittered wildly from left to right as she dropped to her knees with tears already in her eyes and flowing down her cheeks.

"Jessa, please don't leave me," Darla begged, moving forward on her knees to pull at Jessa's legs.

What the hell?

Darla's sobs echoed in the hall.

Jessa reached for her mother's pudgy hands and motioned for her to rise to her feet. "Stop crying, Mama. I won't leave you. I won't," she said, the switch in her mother's affect and demeanor completely shaking her. This was more than the emotional swings of a drunk.

Darla continued to sob as she rose to her feet. Jessa wrapped her arm around her mother's broad shoulders and hugged her close. "Come on, Mama. Let's go home," she said softly, motioning for Myra to get her things from the dressing room.

"This, Jessa. My baby Jessa. See. I told you I had a daughter," Darla said, patting her daughter's hand. "Y'all thought I was lying about my Jessa."

Jessa led her mother out the studio, the bite of early winter nipping at them. *Who in the hell is she talking to?*

After motioning for her driver to pull up and help her mother into the rear of the SUV, Jessa turned to find Myra on her cell phone.

"If I see one word of this in print, your ass is mine, Myra," Jessa warned her.

Myra ended her call. "Jessa, please don't question my integrity. Your mother is obviously in need of care."

"Were you in on this?" Jessa asked, taking her tote and a rolling carry-on she assumed was her mother's from the publicist.

"No, definitely not. I would have prescreened everything before," Myra said. "I honestly think they were trying to do something nice for you."

Jessa arched a brow. "And no one saw she was drunk?"

"They claim she wasn't when they escorted her to the green room. They're thinking she must have brought it with her."

Jessa nodded in understanding.

"Well, I asked them to give you whatever info they found on her," Myra said, reaching in her briefcase for a thin green folder that she handed over to Jessa.

She pursed her lips and breathed deeply, pressing a hand to her lower back before she reached for the folder.

"Not the reunion you dreamed of, huh?" Myra asked gingerly.

Jessa opened the folder and looked down at its contents. "I can't say that because I never thought I would see my mother again," she admitted. "I better go."

Myra opened her mouth to say something and then seemed to change her mind. "I'll call you tomorrow."

Jessa closed the folder and tucked it under her arm before she turned and climbed into the back of the SUV before the driver even had a chance to leave the driver's seat to help her.

The heat was on and the interior was toasty. Jessa was glad for that. Her mother was slumped in the corner and her head was tilted back with her mouth ajar as she snored.

"You ready, Ms. Bell?" he asked.

"Yes, I already checked out of my hotel this morning. Thank you," Jessa said, reopening the folder. "Could you take me to One Hundred Tenth Street in Harlem, please?"

"Harlem?" the driver asked. "They have me routed to take you back to New Jersey."

Jessa flexed her shoulder a little bit as she felt her irritation spike. "Well, *they* aren't seeing that she gets home. *I* am. So *you* should let whoever "they" are know that *we* are most definitely headed to Harlem first and then Jersey on *their* dime. Clear?"

He said nothing, but he reached for his cell phone.

Jessa focused her attention back on her mother, eyeing her carefully as she mumbled in her sleep.

Gone was the stylish woman who was always impeccably dressed. Her bright red lipstick was smeared around her mouth, and her mascara ran in black tracks down her cheeks. She resembled a scary clown. Her fingernails were bitten down, and what little polish she wore was peeled and faded.

Jessa's eyes filled with tears. She was shell-shocked by all of it, and seeing her mother still under the effects of drugs and alcohol—and maybe much more—had her nerves shot to hell.

Had her mother been in Harlem all this time?

When Jessa was small enough to allow herself to care about her mother's whereabouts, she had imagined that the man in the red car carried Darla so far away that she *couldn't* get back to her. Harlem, New York, was barely an hour by car.

Feeling her anger rise again, Jessa looked back down at the folder, but there was no other info except her phone number and travel itinerary. Jessa slid the folder into her patent-leather tote.

In a perfect world, a perfect daughter would take her long-lost mother home, but Jessa was beyond hesitant to do that. She didn't know the scope of her mother's addiction and didn't know if she cared enough to help her fight any demons—and that's if Darla even wanted to.

No, I'll take her home where she's been hiding from being a mother any damn way and I'll call her later to make sure she's okay. Baby steps.

Jessa felt like she didn't really know this woman, and how could she after more than twenty-five years?

"Let me see my baby. Please just let me see her," Darla mumbled in her sleep.

That made Jessa suck air between her teeth. *Darla knew damn well where she left me and there I stayed until college. If she wanted to see me, all she had to do was come home.*

For the remainder of the ride Jessa sat quietly in the back lost in her thoughts of her past and future. *Just where does my mother fit into all of this now?*

"Stay away from me. Leave me alone," Darla mumbled.

Jessa started to call Henry and get his take on everything but decided against it. She was too busy trying to grapple with all of her emotions and getting a firm grasp on what she thought to take on someone else's advice yet.

The only thing she knew for sure was that she needed to get the hell away from everybody and everything and regroup. Period. Point blank.

They were in Harlem when Darla stirred awake, smacking her lips as if she couldn't stand the taste of her own mouth. She stretched and cleared her throat.

Jessa immediately put on her guard, not sure if Darla was about to show anger, paranoia, or histrionics.

"It's really good to see you, Jessa," Darla said, reaching over to pat her hand.

Jessa instinctively covered her belly.

Darla's eyes filled with anger. "You think I would hurt my grandbaby?"

Jessa stiffened her back. "I never thought you would leave me behind," she said, then regretted showing any sign that her mother had left her behind wounded.

The driver pulled the SUV into a parking spot in front of a brownstone.

Jessa sat up on the edge of the car seat and lowered the window as her mouth fell open. The entire tree-lined block was lined with renovated brownstones. It wasn't at all the ramshackle hood she was expecting.

"Home sweet fucking home," Darla said, picking up her purse. "You coming up or you have to get back to your fabulous fucking life?"

And the sarcasm was back. Jessa felt tired, but she allowed the driver to help her out of the SUV after he helped her mother.

Darla sniffed a dozen different times as she struggled to retrieve her keys from her purse as she climbed the stairs. Jessa motioned for the driver to help her mother, feeling like she couldn't risk her mother falling or stumbling and causing Jessa to fall backward down the brick stairs. She cupped her hand to her round belly in full protective mode.

As soon as Darla unlocked the door, their driver set her carry-on on the step and stepped back. But Jessa barely noticed because she was completely taken aback by the total disarray of her mother's home.

Dirty dishes. Piles of clothes everywhere. The smell of rotting garbage. Flies and gnats cruising through the air. A cat suddenly jumped from behind a couch and on top of a floor-model television.

Jessa screamed out and stumbled back.

Darla moved around like her life was not total chaos. She didn't even flinch at Jessa crying out.

This is madness.

Jessa covered her nose and mouth with her hand and swatted away gnats and flies with her other hand.

Darla swatted the cat away and then picked up a photo album. She whirled to hand it to Jessa and dust flew. "See all the pictures I have of my pretty baby," she said, opening the book.

Jessa spotted a photo of herself at age twelve. She reached out and took the album from her mother's hands. With her heart pounding wildly, she flipped through the pages. Nearly all of her school pictures were there.

"Where did you get these?" Jessa asked, her voice soft.

Darla pulled a flask from inside her brassiere as she slumped down on the couch, nearly flattening the cat, who flew from under her just in time. "My mama sent them to me," Darla said, looking down into the flask before raising it in mock toast.

That had to be true.

Where else would she get them?

Jessa slammed the album closed and let it drop to the floor with a *WHAM*. "So you wanted photos, but you couldn't be bothered with the real thing?" she snapped, reaching out to snatch the flask from her mother's hand.

Darla jumped to her feet and started to breathe in and out her nose like a bull.

Not exactly sure she wasn't about to be run over, Jessa tossed the flask back at her.

Darla caught it and took a healthy swig. "You don't know nothing about what went on. You don't know shit about what I been through," she said, her eyes filling with tears as she bent down and opened the album to the last page.

Jessa looked down as Darla rocked and fell on her ass, her legs splayed out in front of her as she pulled a thin bundle of letters out. "My own mama told me I wasn't good enough to raise my child," Darla said, stroking the cat, who moved up close to her side and purred.

Jessa squinted her eyes.

"She bought me this house and give me money every month to stay away from my baby," Darla whispered in a singsong voice that was eerie.

Jessa felt goose bumps race up her arms.

Let me see my baby. Please just let me see her.

Her mother's ramblings in her sleep.

"She said I would ruin my baby," Darla snapped in anger, her fingers balling up into a fist with some of the cat's skin in her grasp. It cried out and exposed its teeth and claws before angrily swiping at Darla's arm.

Jessa stood there in shock and horror as Darla cursed and flung the cat away from her. It flew in the air a little before landing on its feet and jetting off down a long hall.

Darla sat there among the chaos of her life crying like a child as she held on to the letters tightly. Jessa bent down as best she could and wrapped her hands around her mother's wrist. "Come on, Mama," she said gently. "Come on. I got you."

Darla struggled to her feet. "I'm so sorry, Jessa. She said I wasn't no good for you. And she wouldn't let me see you. I fucked up. I promised you I would come back. I promised you and I knew I wasn't. I'm sorry."

Jessa's heart ached to know that after all those years her mother remembered the promise she made. Even if she broke it. She couldn't leave her mother in this filth and to her own devices. She couldn't do it.

"Let's get out of here, Mama," Jessa said, easing the letters and photo album from her mother's hand as she walked her out the door.

Hours later, Jessa sat in the chair beside her mother's bed in the hospital's psychiatric ward. As soon as they left Harlem, she had the driver take them there and Darla was admitted for her addiction to alcohol and crack cocaine. But the psychiatrist also diagnosed her mother with bipolar disorder. They believe she used drugs and alcohol to defeat the symptoms of the mental disorder, not realizing it created a crazy and vicious cycle, with one further hindering the other.

Jessa had already contacted Keegan to get a cleaning and organizing expert and her team into the brownstone that Monday to get rid of the clutter and the cat. When Darla finished her treatment and got on her psych meds, Jessa wanted her to return to a home as clutter free as her life and her mind.

She felt no guilt about sticking to her decision not to move her mother into her home. Darla would have to prove herself for that, and that came in time. Jessa felt she had to be wary and cautious because more than just her feelings and her life were involved.

Rubbing her belly, she looked over at her mother as she slept peacefully. *Probably the best sleep she's had in years,* Jessa thought, looking down at an old photo of her mother in a form-fitting dress with curves that made Beyoncé look like a man.

Even then Darla struggled with her mental disease and didn't even know it.

Jessa swiped at the tears that filled her eyes as she lightly patted the letters. She felt betrayed and lost and confused as hell.

Every letter from her grandmother to her mother confirmed what Darla had said. She was literally paid to stay away. Warned not to call the house or be cut off. Threatened not to show up at Jessa's school to watch her from a distance. Who gives money and a free place to live to a junkie and not expect them to spiral out of control?

Someone who didn't know better would think her grandmother was just looking out for Jessa's best interests. Jessa wasn't buying it. She had felt the supposed wisdom of her grandmother's actions, and Frances Jordan looked out for herself first and foremost.

Jessa thought of her pain at her mother leaving—and Darla had some of the weight of that to carry for herself—but Jessa knew firsthand that Grandma Frances had a way of getting anyone to see, and do, things exactly how she wanted.

Aria

I woke up some time late during the night with Kingston cupping my nude body from behind with his hand warm and secure on my stomach. Before my body became swollen with the baby, he used to sleep cupping my breasts or with his hand snuggled down between my thighs.

Kingston claimed he loved me big and pregnant. God bless his lying heart—although the way he made love to me last night, gently but strong and passionate, made me feel damn sexy even though I was damn big. I smiled, remembering teasing him that we were putting sex on our baby's brain.

And because we were having a son, Kingston joked he was getting him ready early to please the ladies.

A son.

I smiled in the darkness, letting my hand stroke Kingston's at the memory of how happy he was to have a boy on the way.

His nursery was done and I knew the baby shower Renee and Jaime were throwing me next month would supply so much of the smaller things he would need like bottles, Pampers, and blankets. Still, I had his drawers stocked.

My mother was already packed to move in for a few weeks after his birth to guide me in the right direction, an-

swer all my silly questions, and keep me from overreacting to the small things most first-time mothers panicked about.

We were all set for his arrival.

The only thing left to do was give birth and then name him . . . once we laid eyes on him. Kingston was very adamant that he didn't want or need to make his son a junior. He wanted him to have his own identity. I agreed.

And even if he was our miracle child and we would never be blessed with another pregnancy, I was happy for him. Our son.

To think I almost threw this—my family—away because of my own fears and bullshit. I thank God every day for bringing Kingston back to me and blessing us with a family. We made it through some tough times, and I had faith nothing could defeat us. Nothing.

Feeling thirsty and needing to pee, I eased free of Kingston's body and sat up.

"Where you going, baby?" he asked, instantly waking up from his sleep.

"To the bathroom," I told him, rubbing his strong arms reassuringly before I padded barefoot and nude to the bathroom.

Soon his snores filled the air again and I just chuckled as I relieved myself and then pulled on a thin cotton robe that hung on a hook behind the door. Pausing by the bed long enough to put on my slippers, I made my way out the bedroom.

Sighing, I pressed to my lower back as I made my way to my office down the hall. Being eight months' pregnant and having gained nearly fifty pounds, I felt all of my pregnancy in my lower back. I was taking my baby weight in stride and found it funny when my mother teased I looked like I was ready to float up to the sky like a balloon in a holiday parade.

I grabbed my iPad and snuggled down in the oversized

chair in the corner. Not feeling too sleepy, I updated my Baby on Board blog site, read a few online magazine articles, and checked a few of my favorite daily blogs, like A Belle in Brooklyn.

Lastly, I checked some industry sites for writers and in a flash my night when straight to hell.

You have got to be kidding me with this bullshit?

Frowning in disgust, I read for a second and third time the announcement for the major book deal Jessa signed.

I have lost all faith in the publishing industry.

Renee

I couldn't sleep and I was standing at my bedroom window when a light January snow began to fall. It was a really beautiful winter scene of the snow sticking to the trees and bushes of my neighbor's front yards. Nothing in the neighborhood moved or stirred but the snow. If it continued, it meant digging out cars and shoveling walkways, but I loved the winter.

Jackson and I used to love the winter together. Playful snow fights. Making love in front of the fireplace. Drinking hot chocolate spiked with brandy. Decorating the house for Christmas.

Although I missed him, I knew I was on the road to recovery because I didn't cry not once this Christmas because he was not there at my side. I had no urge to lose myself in a drunken stupor so as not to face the dissolution of my marriage. Or the fact that my children had a sibling that wasn't borne by me. Or . . . or that my husband and son weren't speaking because of my son's sexuality.

Something about knowing that Jackson would lose his relationship with his son than accept that he's gay made me so hurt and disappointed by him.

The baby put the nail in the coffin holding our dead relationship, and his treatment of our son hammered the nail in all the way.

And so, yes, our divorce was almost finalized. We both were ready to move on.

Jackson had signed the papers. We worked out dividing our properties, alimony, and child support. We were just waiting for the final divorce decree.

And truly, I was okay with it.

"Renee, come back to bed."

I looked over my shoulder at the man waiting there for me.

I met Davin Thorne a few weeks ago at my Alcoholic Anonymous meeting, and tonight a long talk over coffee led to a flirtation that led to him following me home. And I hadn't been disappointed by my choice.

He flung back the cover, exposing his naked body to me.

Nice, I thought, dropping my robe and feeling damn good about his thick dick rising from lying across his thigh to stand erect.

"See something you want?" he asked.

I licked my lips as I climbed onto the bed and straddled his hips. "I see lots of good dick and someone who is good with it," I said softly, bending to circle one of his nipples with the tip of my tongue.

The kids were away and Mama was going to play.

I sighed as his hands massaged my lower back and then cupped my ass deeply as I moved my lips up to suckle his neck.

I leaned up and he lifted his head to take one of my nipples into his mouth as I heard the tear of the condom wrapper.

I pushed pillows behind his head to prop him up as he

lifted me up by my hips and slid me down onto his hard dick. I gasped and bit my lip from the feel of him pressing against my walls.

"Damn, it's hot," he gasped, looking up at me as I grabbed the headboard and took control.

I closed my eyes and let my head fall back as I circled my hips, bringing the base of his dick against my swollen clit. His hands teased both of my full, undulating breasts as he gently rolled my nipples between his fingers.

I locked my legs beneath his and popped my hips, riding just the tip of his thick dick. He freed my breasts and they hung above his open and panting mouth as his fingers dug into my ass and tried to control the movement of my hips.

I resisted him, loving the control. Loving that he felt he would cum if he didn't stop. Loving that I was so near my third nut on his dick that night.

I looked down at him intensely as he licked my nipples wildly. "Yes. Yesss," I moaned, adjusting my ride to take all of his dick into me as I continued to glide back and forth on him.

He slapped my ass as he fucked me back, sending his dick even deeper inside of me.

I sat up straight and then turned on his dick to ride him backward.

He sat up behind me and wrapped his arms around my body as I worked my hips until my heart pounded and my sweat soaked the sheets.

"I'm gonna come," I moaned, gasping hotly when his hands covered my breasts again as I glided back and forth on his dick like I rode a log.

I cried out as the first explosion burst inside me and made my clit extra sensitive. I didn't give a damn who heard as I flung my head back and released all of my pent-up sexual frustration in a shout that was primal.

He didn't feel like Jackson.
He didn't taste like Jackson.
He didn't smell like Jackson.
His touch didn't electrify me like Jackson.
But it was nice. It was satisfying.
In time, with him or someone else, the rest would follow.

Jaime

I woke up with a start and realized the house was cold. Icy cold. At first I tried to bury my entire head and body beneath the covers, but even that didn't keep enough of the chill from seeping into my bones.

Dammit, I swore, before I jumped from under the covers and raced on my tiptoes to the digital thermostat on the wall. I kicked the heat up another five degrees and raced back beneath the covers.

Everyone knew winter was the perfect season to have a man in one's big lonely bed to provide the heat. It had been six months since Eric's death, and I was ready to get out and date again. Something I truly had not done since before I married Eric.

My relationship with Pleasure had never involved anything outside the bed—or in whatever locale we chose to have sex.

And although it would be so easy to call Pleasure to bring that dick to me, I refused to budge. Pleasure turning me down to fuck another woman who had the money in her hand had hurt me. I could admit that. Yes, I knew he was a whore, but I really thought I was first on his list. That I was special. That my pussy was better. That he would never turn me down. That his dick was mine.

That reality check slapped me hard as hell in the face and I knew I had to wean myself off my drug. I had to. It was all well and good that he fucked other women for money as long as I never saw it. We never talked about it.

But I was looking for more than just dick in my life. I wanted a relationship. Not marriage. Not even something completely exclusive, but someone of similar style and class to escort me to social functions, hold an intelligent conversation—and still be able to bang my back out when I wanted.

The thought of that made me smile as I shifted my hands to the edge of my pajamas. I had just scooped my hands down to cup my pussy when my phone rang. Frowning, I sat up in bed and picked up my cordless. Aria? Aria!!

"Are you having the baby?" I asked, already throwing back the covers.

"No, I'm going to have a coronary over that crazy bitch!" Aria snapped.

Jessa. It was always Jessa. I was tired of talking about the bitch.

I dropped back down on the bed and ran my chilled fingers through my hair. "What is she up to now? I haven't really seen her the last month or so."

"Do you know that bitch is writing a goddamn book? On what?"

I opened my dresser drawer and took out a suede box. "Listen, after that bitch came at me about suing Eric's estate, I don't put anything past her ass," I said, shoving the phone between my ear and shoulder as I opened the box and took out my vibrator. I turned it on to test the batteries.

Bzzzzzzzz.

It jumped to life in my hands.

"What the hell is that? A chainsaw?" Aria asked.

I turned it off. "Nothing," I lied.

"Whatever happened with that lawsuit?"

"We're assuming she's waiting for the little bastard to drop, because we told her if she pursued it we would push to make her have a prenatal paternity test," I said, rising to walk into the bathroom to rinse it off. I smiled as I lathered it with soap and worked it like a real dick.

"Jaime, do you really have to call the baby a bastard all the time?" Aria asked.

I paused. "Oh, so now you're Jessa Bell's best friend again?" I asked coolly.

"No, but I'm mad at her, not the baby. The same should go for you."

"Well, Aria, that's fucking easy for you to say; she didn't fuck your husband and get pregnant. Did she?" I snapped.

"Bitch, you tripping. I'll call you in the morning when you get your head and your thoughts together."

Click.

I shrugged and tossed the phone on a chair before I climbed back under the covers with my little friend. Soon the vibrating motion of it against my clit made forget every damn thing.

Bzzzzzzzz.

Chapter 13

Two months later

Jessa couldn't lie and say she wasn't nervous about the Halls' threats of suing her for custody as the time neared for her to have her baby. She hadn't heard from them since the day they ambushed her at her home, but they were never far from her mind.

Even though Lincoln assured her that grandparents rarely ever won a custody battle against a fit mother. *But Lincoln doesn't know everything.*

Sighing, she picked up the remote and flipped through the channels before she gave up on that and picked up her laptop to try and finish the detailed outline for her book. *Boredom is a bitch.*

Myra had put any further interview requests on hold and advised her to focus on the outline for her still untitled book. Considering she had already signed the contract and deposited the check for half of her advance, she knew her publicist and literary agent were right when they pushed her to get it done.

Jessa looked down and read what she had so far, starting with a prelude detailing her original plan to steal Eric from Jaime:

* * *

"Where do I begin? How do I tell the story? Our story. His and mine. He was my lover and her husband. You would think that wasn't possible–like saying dry rain or cold heat–but it was true. She had the ring and the certificate . . . but I had him."

Those words came easily. She had thought them in the days when she felt like she couldn't live without Eric.

The difficult parts—her past, her relationship with her mother, her near death, her closer relationship to God—those words she struggled for. Those were things she felt were out of her control.

But when she was still deluded about her feelings and her power over Eric, she had thought it all out and felt everything was of her own design.

Setting the laptop aside and needing to feel more activity than shifting her wide ass on the bed, Jessa eased her cumbersome frame off the bed and walked out onto her balcony. It was hard to miss the colorful pastel balloons and streamers floating around Jaime's backyard.

Aria's baby shower.

Jessa knew she shouldn't dare let anyone see her taking a gander at their festivities for Aria's baby when she knew they all damned her baby to hell.

But she did allow herself a moment to take in the colorful rose topiary arrangements on each table. The bartender serving of fruity drinks. Four to five tables of food laid out buffet style. A huge, round table filled with brightly wrapped gifts that grew in size as more and more people strolled into the backyard.

Jessa felt a pang of sadness as she finally turned and moved back into her bedroom. She continued across the floor and out the door to the nursery directly across the hall.

Again, Keegan had worked wonders. The nursery was soft and warm and inviting with its creamy vanilla décor and furnishings with just a tiny hint of pale pink for the girl she was having.

No, there would be no baby shower celebrating the arrival of baby Delaney.

But there were people in Jessa's life who cared.

She lightly touched the creamy afghan folded over the rails of the crib. Her mother had knitted it for her grandbaby, and Jessa was surprised when she gifted it to her during her last visit to the long-term rehabilitation facility.

Keegan gifted the beautiful Italian recliner chair and waived her usual fees for the interior design.

Henry gifted the bassinet that was ready to be pushed into Jessa's room once the baby arrived.

Jessa laughed at the basketload of newborn clothing Myra dropped off. All designer, of course.

Still, that would have made one sorry shower. Four people and five gifts. Hell, she counted at least twenty gifts or better on Aria's table and the shower hadn't even started yet. *I oughta crash it*, Jessa thought spitefully even though she knew she never would.

She had outgrown that kind of childish drama. Plus, she honestly didn't think her ex-friends were worth the effort anymore. She was trying to stay right with God, and those heifers were not worth a trip to hell.

Giving the nursery one last look, Jessa made her way back to her bedroom. Jessa settled back against the many pillows on her bed just as a twinge radiated across her lower back. She whistled until it disappeared and closed her eyes, taking deep breaths. She wasn't due for another two weeks and figured they were just Braxton-Hicks contractions.

Ten minutes later, the twinge returned.

In another ten minutes, the twinge intensified in pain.

And every ten minutes after that.

Jessa frowned and popped her eyes open. Oh shit.

She picked up her phone and dialed Keegan's number.

"Hey, sugar," Keegan said in her usual big and bold voice.

"Lookey here, *sugar*," Jessa bit out, swinging her legs off the side of the bed to sit up on the side. "Remember the plan for you to stay here with me the last week before my due date?"

"Yes."

"Huge failure," Jessa drawled. "Where are you?"

"Oh Lord, I'm in upstate New York. It'll take an hour or better for me to get there, honey bell," Keegan said in obvious distress. "Are you sure it's time?"

Jessa felt a gush and she looked up to the ceiling. "My water just broke . . . on my custom duvet!!! Like really, God? Really?!"

"Oh Lord," Keegan drawled.

"Just call my doctor for me and come to the Overlook Hospital as soon as you can," Jessa said, hanging up on Keegan before another of her affectionate and sugary nicknames made her literally vomit.

As she rose and calmly peeled off her soaked satin nightgown and robe, she tried to call Henry. His phone went straight to voice mail. Reverend Dobbins. He was at a church revival in Philadelphia. Her attorney, Lincoln, was in court. Her mother was in rehab. Myra's phone just rang endlessly.

"WHAT THE FUCKKKKKKKKK!!!!" Jessa screamed at the top of her lungs, fighting the urge to throw her cell phone against a wall.

Standing there nude with her thighs still damp, Jessa gripped the edge of the dresser and forced herself to just breathe. "Calm down, Jessa. This is your baby and this is not the first time you've had to face things alone. You can do this. Don't lose it."

The phone rang in her hand, she answered. "Yes," she sighed, feeling another labor pain building.

"I called an ambulance and it's on the way, sugar,"

Keegan said. "I'm already in my car heading to Livingston. GET DOWNSTAIRS AND OPEN THE FRONT DOOR!"

Jessa made a face. "Keegan, I'm in labor. Not deaf."

"I'm sorry. I want to be excited for the baby coming, but right now I am as scared as a near-death hooker who ain't been read her last rites until you get some medical help."

Jessa paused in pulling on a strapless maternity maxi dress. She actually laughed. "Boy, a ho never gets a break," she joked.

"At least you're laughing."

"I was," she moaned, before another pain gripped her as she slid her purse over her shoulder and slid on a pair of flip-flops.

Jessa breathed through it.

"Don't worry about the bag you packed, I'll get it later—"

"Keegan, fuck that bag!" Jessa bit out just before the contraction subsided. She left her room and held up the hem of the dress as she made her way down the stairs slowly.

When she neared the bottom she heard the sirens of the ambulance, and it was in that moment that the reality of her life hit her. She was pregnant and in labor without a familiar face to support her. Jessa released a sharp breath as she lowered her chin to her chest and blinked her eyes to keep the tears from falling.

This shit is pitiful, Jessa thought, as she gingerly made her way to the front door and set her alarm to activate in ten minutes. *Just pitiful.*

But as the medics rolled the stretcher into the house and helped her on it, Jessa remembered something Henry always told her. "It is when you are at your lowest that God is truly with you, seeing you through to the other side. He never leaves you. Never."

She forced herself to relax as the mix of her impending labor and the sound of the sirens evoking memories of that night ate at her. Jessa closed her eyes and breathed, hating that the image of Eric—an image she hadn't been haunted by in months—suddenly appeared.

"It is when you are at your lowest that God is truly with you, seeing you through to the other side. He never leaves you. Never."

"Be with me God," she prayed, as the medics rolled her out the house and closed the door.

Jessa ignored her neighbors already gathering outside her door and around the ambulance, whose sirens still flashed red and echoed throughout the subdivision. She closed her eyes, not wanting to see anyone gloat or glare as the ambulance sped her away from her house.

"Hello, Delaney," Jessa cooed to the swaddled bundle the nurse placed in her arms. "We did it. You're here and healthy and all mine. Me and you are one helluva team."

Jessa lightly kissed her daughter's chubby cheeks and longed for her to open her eyes and look up at her. But she slept peacefully. "It's okay. It's been a long night," she whispered, opening the blanket a little to guide her finger into Delaney's tiny palm.

Her heart surged when tiny little fingers wrapped around hers. "Are you strong like your mama?" she asked into the quiet. "You look like me, so you better be strong like me. But don't make the mistakes I did. We're both lucky to be here."

Memories of the night Eric almost killed her caused her emotions to choke in her throat, and Jessa tilted her head back and closed her eyes tightly to try to free herself from the thoughts.

"I will fight for you. I will die for you. I will not let anyone take you from me. Or make me leave you. I promise.

I'm your mother. Nobody else. And I never knew I could love someone so much." One of Jessa's tears raced down her face and fell on Delaney's brown cheeks.

"I can't believe God has blessed me like this," Jessa admitted. "Thank you, God. Thank you, thank you, thank you."

The door to her private room opened. Jessa looked up as a nurse walked in with a smile carrying a pale pink chart. "How is Mama and baby?" she asked.

"You're not coming to take her, are you?" Jessa asked.

"No, not yet," the nurse said, coming to stand by the bed. "I just wanted to let you know that we have been bombarded with calls from the press about you all night."

Jessa figured as much. When Myra called to check on her, she alerted Jessa that the news had broke that she had the baby. Although Myra had released a statement asking for respect of Jessa's privacy at this time, the press had other plans.

"Also . . . we caught a photographer trying to sneak in to the unit to take a picture of the baby."

Jessa's heart damn near stopped as she sat up and clutched the baby closer.

The nurse held up her hands. "We have let everyone know they are to treat you as a high-profile client and we are being even more strict with everyone on the unit—even those people coming to see other patients."

Jessa forced herself to relax as Delaney stirred. She looked down and cooed to her.

The nurse set the chart down on Jessa's nightstand and moved around the bed to grab a bottle from the rolling crib. "She may be hungry."

Jessa nodded, forcing herself to calm down as she accepted the bottle. She didn't want her sudden fears and anxiety to upset the peace of the baby. She nuzzled the nipple of the bottle to the baby's lips and Delaney latched on.

Jessa's breath caught as Delaney's eyes opened. "I know she can't see me really, but just knowing her eyes are on me . . ."

The nurse smiled.

"If the press calls and they're harassing you guys, please refer them to my publicist and let the staff know I am so sorry about all the hassle," Jessa said, before the nurse could walk out the door.

"No problem."

Jessa finished feeding Delaney and changed her Pampers before she swaddled her back in her blanket and laid her down inside her crib. She darkened the lights of her room and moved to stand by the window. She felt a little lightheaded from suddenly being up on her feet, but she leaned against the wall as she looked out at the night.

The press releasing the news of the baby's delivery might have set the Halls on her ass just a little quicker. And that's all Jessa could think about. So much of her life and her sins had been exposed, but there was more to her story that she wanted to stay in the past. Even they could stumble on the truth, even after all the years that had passed . . .

What the fuck am I going to do?

And that wasn't the only decision she had to make.

Jessa turned and walked over to the small clear crib to look down at her sleeping daughter. She wasn't giving Delaney Eric's last name, and giving her Marc's last name wasn't right either. "Delaney Logan," Jessa said.

She loved Marc, but she had made the choice to go back to using her own maiden name as well. She wanted her and her daughter to have the same last name . . . and it would kill the whole Jessa Bell/Jezebel reference.

But what about the lawsuit? Jessa thought. *Do I have the time or energy to fight Jaime when the Halls are gunning for me?*

The door opened and another nurse came in. "We need to do an assessment of the baby."

Jessa moved to stand in front of the crib. "Can I see your badge please?" she asked.

The nurse handed it over. "I understand completely and don't worry, we'll take good care of her until we bring her back."

Jessa turned over the badge. "Could you also let everyone know that I need to give approval for anyone before they're allowed on the unit to see me?" she asked, moving to climb back into the hospital bed.

"Of course."

Jessa pulled the cover up to her chest and closed her eyes. The Halls were Delaney's grandparents, but they started the war and now Jessa was playing her hand. They would not lay eyes on her daughter until she said so, and Jessa doubted she would ever feel comfortable enough for that. Ever. *Fuck them.*

Her job was to protect her child and the more she thought about, she didn't know if she trusted her neighbors of Richmond Hills enough to send her daughter out among them once she was older. As she had many times over the last few months, Jessa wondered if perhaps it was time to say good-bye to the subdivision. Maybe even the state.

Yes, there were a lot of decisions Jessa had to make and she prayed to God that she would make all the right choices.

The next day, Jessa was bombarded by guests and she enjoyed every chance to show off her beautiful daughter. First Myra—before she jetted off to work. And then Lincoln—before he rushed off to court. Keegan sat with her and the baby nearly all morning before she too had a meeting that called her away.

By the early afternoon, Jessa was yawning and ready for a light nap as Delaney slept peacefully on her own.

She was just closing her eyes when her room phone rang. She rushed to grab it before it awoke the baby. "Yes?"

"Ms. Logan, there's Eric Hall Sr. and his wife requesting to see the baby."

Being addressed by her maiden name sounded weird to her. She'd made the change weeks ago in preparation for the baby's birth and she was still getting used to it again. "No, absolutely not," Jessa said finally, sitting up in bed as her heart pounded.

The line went quiet.

"They are insisting, Ms. Logan."

"Can I speak to Mr. Hall?" she said, her hand gripping the phone so tightly that her palm hurt.

"Yes, Jessa, you cannot be serious keeping us away from the child you claim belongs to our son."

"And you can't be serious coming here to swoop down on my baby like a couple of vultures after the way you insulted me in my home," she told him coldly, reaching over to stroke Delaney's back.

"This isn't going to make things any better, Jessa," he said.

"Are you still planning to go forward with fighting me for custody of my baby?" she asked, as she held out hope that they would just fall back and let her be.

"Listen, we just wanted to see the baby," he answered, dodging the question.

Jessa was many things, but dumb was not one of them.

"No, you want to play I Spy and see if she resembles Eric. So the answer, without any doubt, coming straight from my mouth to your ears is for you and your wife to get the fuck away from me and my baby."

"Jessa, you're far too beautiful a woman to use such language."

His voice was warm. Too warm. Too inviting.

Again, Jessa wasn't dumb. She knew men all too well.

She flashed back to his obvious interest the day of Eric's funeral. "Listen, you sick son of a bitch. Grab your troll of a wife and get out of here before I have security drag your asses out of here."

Jessa hung up the phone and massaged the bridge of her nose with her free hand.

Two seconds later, the phone rang again. "What?" Jessa snapped, still upset.

"We're sorry to bother you, Ms. Logan, but you *did* request we call the room for approval for all visitors."

"Yes, I did. Are the Halls gone?" she asked, forcing a calmness to her voice.

"Yes, they are. This is a Mr. Tyson—"

"Tyson?" Jessa gasped, her mouth falling open as she pictured the sexy captain she hadn't seen since their one-night stand in New York. *What the hell is he doing here?*

"Yes," the nurse said with a hint of impatience.

Jessa couldn't blame her.

"Okay. Let him back. Thank you."

Jessa climbed from the bed as her heart raced in anticipation. She went into the bathroom and made sure her long uncurled hair didn't look too crazy before she dug in her purse and put on a light amount of clear lip gloss; then she pinched her cheeks for a little color to her caramel complexion.

She was freshly showered but wished she was in one of her sensuous nightgowns and not the hospital generic, bulky and unflattering gowns. *Then again,* she thought, turning her mirror to see her stomach still as round and full as if she was six or seven months' pregnant. Her uterus hadn't shrunk down yet.

Jessa quickly checked on Delaney before climbing back in bed and arranging the covers neatly around her body.

"Well, hello stranger," Tyson said as he strolled in the

door carrying what had to be two or even three dozen long-stemmed pink roses.

He completely changed the energy in the room and Jessa felt breathless from seeing him again. Maybe it was the surprise of his appearance or just simply how sexy he looked in his navy blazer, white shirt, and jeans.

"Hi, Tyson," she said. Her heart pounded as she smoothed her hair behind her ear.

He set the floral arrangement in the windowsill next to the ones she received from the church, Henry, Lincoln, and Myra. He towered over them like trees over bushes.

Jessa watched his every movement and remembered every technique he used on her that night. Then, like now, everything about him spoke of power and strength.

Big dick self, she thought, letting her eyes drop down briefly to take in his imprint against his jeans.

"You're a hard lady to find," Tyson said, coming over to stand by her bedside.

Jessa briefly noted that he hadn't even looked down at her baby in the crib. "Um, yeah . . . well, I can be reached when I want to, and obviously you can find me when you want to."

He reached down and stroked the back of her hand.

Jessa got chills as she forced herself not to free her hand from his touch.

"You been on my mind since that night in New York," Tyson said, looking down at her. "I thought I left enough of an *impression* for you to call me."

Jessa leaned back against the pillows and slyly cut her eyes up at him. "So what are you doing now, putting in your bid for the first one to get the post-pregnancy pussy?" she asked.

Tyson shook his head and laughed, his white teeth flashing against his bronzed skin. "Still sassy as hell I see."

Lord, this man is fine.

Jessa said nothing as she continued to look up at him

even as her heart beat so loud that she wondered if she would be able to hear Delaney if she cried.

"I heard on the news you had the baby and I figured this was my chance to reconnect with you and let you know I'm still interested."

"Right now?" she joked, with a horrified expression.

Tyson held up both of his massive hands with his eyes wide. "Nooooo. No. No. No."

Jessa laughed huskily.

He joined her in her laughter. "That's what I like about you. You're fun and sexy and you know how to make a man feel good. You know?"

In truth, Jessa had thought a lot about Tyson and the night they shared over the months that passed, but she knew being around him was a threat to her promise to stay celibate—and her even bigger promise not to have sex while pregnant with another man's child.

Jessa wasn't looking for strictly a lover, and with all the chemistry they shared—and now that she was no longer pregnant—maybe they could see if more could develop. Maybe God was sending her the man to fulfill all her wishes.

"You look beautiful," he told her, his voice deep and low.

"Listen, once I get settled down with motherhood and get my body back together in bikini shape, maybe we can go on a couple of dates and see what happens," she told him.

Being alone when she went into labor and all through the birth made her realize just how much she hated being alone.

"Does that mean I can have your number now?" Tyson asked teasingly.

Jessa shrugged. "We'll see," she said, flirting.

Delaney began to stir in her crib and Jessa climbed out of bed to check to make sure she didn't need a diaper change. She found her daughter's eyes open wide. They were big and bright. Jessa bent down close to her and nuzzled her cheek. "Who loves the baby? Hmm? Mama loves the baby?" she cooed softly. "Mama loves Delaney?"

She leaned up just in time to see a soft smile spread on her daughter's face. Jessa giggled, feeling the innocent joy like that of a child again. Something she hadn't even felt as a child after her mother left.

"Look, she's smil—"

Jessa words faded as she looked up and saw Tyson in the opposite corner quietly talking on his cell phone. She looked back down at Delaney, who was lying quietly and sucking the side of her hand.

"Oh my God, I love you so much, Delaney," Jessa sighed, feeling her love for her child burst in her chest. It was better than the other love she even thought she had for her own mother, Eric, or even Marc.

Deciding to fight the urge to hold Delaney and spoil her, Jessa climbed back in bed and pulled the crib close to its side.

"Okay, reschedule the meeting for the morning and make my apologies," Tyson said in a no-nonsense business tone, before ending his call and sliding his iPhone into the inside pocket of his blazer.

Jessa let her eyes take in his swagger as he came back up to the bed on the side opposite from where she had the crib. He had just reached down to stroke soft circles onto the back of her hand when the door opened and Henry strolled in.

Jessa's face lit into a big smile. "Hi, Henry," she said, genuinely pleased to see her friend. He was on her list of approved guests and so no call ahead was necessary. She looked down at Delaney. "Look, it's Uncle Henry."

Henry eyed Tyson for a few seconds before he nodded in greeting and made his way straight to the crib. "Mornin', morning', Delaney," he said in his big booming voice.

The baby smiled again.

Jessa looked on as he went to the bathroom to wash his hand and then rubbed them to warm them before he scooped her right up into his arms with ease. "I guess having all those brothers and sisters paid off," Jessa teased, enjoying the way Henry walked back and forth around the room holding the baby.

"Jessa."

She tore her eyes away from them to look at Tyson. "Yes?"

"Maybe I should come back," he said.

Jessa shook her head. "No, Henry is like family. You're fine."

Henry looked over at Tyson. "That's me. Henry the family friend," he said, his voice slightly odd.

Jessa eyed him, but he was busy eyeing Tyson.

Then she turned her head to eye Tyson, but he was just as busy eyeing Henry back.

She eyed Henry. Then Tyson. Then Henry again.

Jessa bit her bottom lip.

Jessa knew men. Well. And standing before her were two men eyeing and shaping each other up like primal animals who sniffed out their first piece of tail and was ready to spar for it.

She eyed Henry again. But he had finally turned away to talk in quiet tones to the baby.

Henry isn't interested in me. My radar is off. Maybe he's just being overprotective like a big brother or uncle. Not every man wants me. Well . . . most, but not all.

Right?

Tyson smiled as he handed her a piece of paper and a pen.

Jessa hesitated briefly as she looked up at him with soft eyes and an even softer smile before she finally took it and scribbled her cell phone and landline numbers on it.

Tyson smiled broadly like a wolf about to jump on its prey. He bent down and pressed his lips to her cheeks and then again on the corner of her mouth. "You'll be hearing from me soon," he whispered against her lips.

Jessa gasped a little and nodded, stepping back to watch him turn and walk out the room without even acknowledging Henry. She smiled and lightly pressed her fingers to her lips.

Chapter 14

Six weeks later

Jessa parked her new cherry red Land Rover in the parking lot of her mother's long-term residential care facility. Darla had finished her inpatient drug and alcohol rehab a month ago and chose to move directly into a sober living environment. The halfway house of sorts served as a bridge between rehab and returning back to her normal life. It was meant to strengthen her resolve, not to relapse.

The high-end facility was costing Jessa a pretty penny, but it was worth it to her.

She climbed from the SUV and opened the rear door. "Hey, Delaney," Jessa said, as she removed her carrier/car seat from the strapped down base. Flinging her Burberry baby bag over her shoulder, Jessa used her hip to bump the vehicle's door closed.

Covering the carrier lightly with a blanket to shield the April winds, Jessa made her way into the renovated mansion that housed ten currently sober-living clients.

Jessa frowned at the empty check-in desk. She waited for a solid two to three minutes before simply turning and heading up the stairs to her mother's room at the end of the hall. She knocked and opened the door.

Jessa gasped in shock as a man pulled his dick out of

her mother from behind. Darla's skirt was up around her waist and her lace panties on the floor around her feet.

"Sorry. Excuse me. Sorry," he apologized profusely as he tried his best to shove his erection inside his jeans. Tried and failed.

Jessa grabbed the short man by the back of his balding head and guided him out the bedroom to securely close the door behind him while he still apologized profusely. "I hope by the time I turn, your ass is still not tooted in the air, Mama," Jessa snapped, bending down to remove the blanket from the carrier.

Delaney was fast asleep.

"I have *needs* like any other woman, Jessa," Darla cooed.

Jessa sniffed. The smell of their sex hung in the air. *Oh. Hell. No.* She looked over her shoulder. Her mother was in her adjoining bathroom with the water running. Jessa opened the bedroom door and the window. Wide.

"He was actually about to get me all finished before you interrupted," Darla called from the bathroom.

"I came to see my mother, but that was *way* too much for my eyes," Jessa drawled, grabbing one of her mother's perfume bottles to lightly spritz the air.

She paused and pressed the bottle to her nose. The scent made her feel nostalgic. This was the perfume her mother wore when she was child. She looked at the bottle: Chanel No. 5. Of course.

She allowed herself one last long sniff before setting it back on her dresser where everything was neatly arranged. The room was neat and orderly, just like her mother had always kept their homes when she lived with her.

Stopping herself from sitting on the bed, and picking up any "drippings," Jessa set Delaney's carrier on the small sofa in the corner as she watched her mother stroll out of the bathroom. She smiled.

Darla had lost nearly twenty pounds, and the casual but stylish clothes Jessa brought for her fit her newly svelte frame. Gone was the craziness she saw in the early days of her recovery; she fought the addiction, and the psych medicines were able to work.

In that moment, as it did now and in the weeks since Delaney's birth, Jessa thought about the fact that her child had crazy running in the family on both sides. She could only pray God watched over her daughter and did not let her be afflicted by mental disease.

"Oooh, let me see my grandbaby," Darla said as soon as she sat down on the sofa. "I can't believe you finally brought her here for me to see."

Jessa swallowed down her fears as she removed the baby from the carrier and handed her over to her mother.

Darla looked surprised. "You're actually letting me hold her? Wow, I was just testing you," she said slyly.

Jessa said nothing as she handed her mother a thin baby blanket from her Burberry baby bag.

Sober and mentally clear, Darla was smart, quick-witted, flirtatious, and funny. Jessa genuinely liked her, and it felt good to have family.

"Oooh, she looks just like us," Darla said, removing Delaney's shoes to kiss the bottom of her feet.

Delaney smiled.

"And you're doing so good with her." Darla looked up at Jessa. "I'm proud of you."

Jessa turned to keep her mother from seeing how much her praise pleased her. She was nervous about going all in with loving her mother. Her fear of love and being hurt remained.

Her cell phone rang from the side pocket of the baby bag. Jessa kept her eyes on her mother and her daughter as she moved across the room to retrieve it. "Hello."

"Hey. You busy?"

Jessa immediately felt her insides warm at the sound of Tyson's deep voice. "No, not really," she said, her eyes widening as her mother held the baby precariously.

She moved back over to sit next to her mother, taking Delaney and pretending to check her diaper. "Are we still on for dinner tonight?" she asked.

"I can change her diaper. You not fooling anyone. I invented slick, baby girl," Darla said dryly, moving across the room to light a cigarette.

"Who's that?" Tyson asked.

"No one," Jessa said, as Delaney belched and threw up a bit onto Jessa's lightweight linen jacket.

Darla snorted in derision.

"You sound busy. I'll pick you up around seven," he said.

Jessa ended the call. "Mama, hand me a bib please," she requested, holding her hand out.

She looked up when after a few moments her hand remained empty. Darla was sitting on the bed swinging her crossed leg and smoking her cigarette. "You sure I have sense enough to hand you a bib?" she snapped.

Jessa placed Delaney on her shoulder and walked across the room to grab the cigarette from her mother's hand. "You have sense enough than to smoke around a baby."

Jessa tossed it out the window before she grabbed the bib herself. "What's wrong with you?" she snapped as she cleaned the baby's chin.

"How long you think you gone keep me hidden here?" Darla snapped back.

Jessa looked down at her mother. "This isn't prison, Mama. You can leave when you want."

Darla nodded. "And go where. Back to hiding in Harlem?"

Jessa walked back across the room and put Delaney in

her carrier. "Um, I didn't know a damn thing about you being in Harlem all these years and you know that."

Darla moved to sit on the window bench and open the window higher before she lit another cigarette, exhaling the fumes outside. "What I do know is my daughter is ashamed of me. Won't answer questions from the press about just where I am and how I'm doing after our big re-union. Rather hire a live-in nanny than ask me to help her. You're scared to have the baby around me, like I'm gonna literally eat her for lunch or throw her out the window."

Jessa shifted her eyes from her mother, afraid she would see just how true her words were.

Darla laughed huskily and low in her throat. "Remember, daughter, sometimes what is not said is more telling than what is," she advised her before turning her head to exhale a long and full-bodied stream of silver smoke out the window.

Jessa waved her hand dismissively. "I just don't want to argue with you, so I'm not saying anything."

"I don't want to lose another twenty-five years with you and so I pretended not to notice," Darla countered.

Jessa looked up and hated the tears in her mother's beautiful eyes. "I'm sorry if I made you feel some kind of way. I am doing the best I know how to deal with all these changes in my life," she admitted.

Darla wiped her eyes with the sides of her hands.

"You have to understand that you leaving really fucked me up, Mama," Jessa admitted for the first time out loud. "I didn't know then what I know now. About the bipolar disorder and Grandma keeping us apart. So I was a kid who grew up thinking her Mama didn't love her. Because of that I don't give out my trust to anybody that easily . . . and it's going to take time for me to get over my natural instinct to protect myself from getting hurt."

Darla looked out the window for a long time before she

looked back at Jessa. "I just don't want you to feel about me the way I feel about my mother. She was wrong for what she did and I hate her for it. You were all I had Jessa and she took that from me."

But you could have turned down the money and kept me.

Darla shook her head. "You don't know my mother. She would have done anything to keep me from you. She wouldn't stop there," she said, as if she had read Jessa's mind.

Jessa felt her past trying to come forward and be acknowledged, but she pushed it back down. *Trust me, Mama. I know all too well.*

"Next Saturday, I'm gone pick you up and you're gonna spend the day me and Delaney and, Mama, just wait until you see my house."

Darla cried even harder as she put out her cigarette and held her hands out for the baby with a plea in her eyes.

Jessa lifted Delaney from the carrier and placed her in her mother's arms.

Jessa glanced at her diamond watch before she turned this way and that in the full-length mirror of her dressing room. 6:45 P.M.

Tyson was always punctual and she knew she had exactly fifteen minutes or less to finish getting ready for that date. *He might be early but never late.*

She checked herself one last time. She had lost the majority of her baby weight, but another ten pounds would get her back to a slimmer version of her hourglass shape. Thankfully, her Spanx snatched it all together and the silk wrap dress was pressed against her curves like an artist had poured the dress on her body like paint.

"Pow!" Jessa teased her reflection, finger-combing the deep waves of her jet-black hair and reapplying another layer of peach-colored lip gloss that made her lips completely suckable.

About two weeks after she left the hospital, Tyson had become a regular fixture in her life. Phone calls. Surprise visits. Gifts. Flowers. Intimate and romantic dinners. The works. The brother was coming on strong, a full-court press, and Jessa was enjoying every minute of his attention and their chemistry.

She even explained her presence in the church and her desire to remain celibate until she got married. He respected that—but let it be known that he was the man made for a sexy backslide on a promise to the Lord.

Jessa was remembering a heated kiss they shared against the fridge when the ringing of her cell phone interrupted the sexy memory. Grabbing it from the console, she answered the call, "Hello?"

"The doctor gave you the okay, so let that man slide that big ole dick on home, sugar," Keegan teased.

"No, thank you, Keegan. We're good." Jessa slid her feet into stilettos.

"How long you think that big sexy man is going to walk around with the dry dick syndrome?" she balked. "At least suck it."

Jessa frowned. "No, *the hell* I will not."

"I'd suck it . . . and swallow it."

"I bet you would," Jessa drawled.

"Trust me, darling, that ex-husband of mine was out in the streets because he just ain't no damn good. It wasn't for lack of good pussy."

"The more we're friends, the worse your mouth gets," Jessa complained.

"Had to make sure you could take the real me before I turned her loose."

Ding-dong.

"That's Tyson. I wanna kiss Delaney before I have a mommy date night."

"Humph. Kiss him below the belt to top off your mommy date night. Now that sounds like a fucking helluva plan, honey bee."

Jessa hung up on her and rushed into the nursery. Delaney was sleeping, and her nanny was quietly folding her laundry and putting it up in the dressers. "I'm leaving now, Yari. I won't be too late," she said softly before walking over to the crib to blow a kiss at her baby.

"Yes, ma'am."

Jessa left the nursery and made her way down the stairs on her five-inch platform heels. As soon as she opened the door, the warm scent of Tyson's cologne nudged at her. She smiled up at him, instantly feeling that chemistry that seemed to brew between them all the time.

"Damn, that dress is a killer, Jessa," he said, raising her arm to spin her slowly.

"Yes, isn't it?" she flirted, spotting his black Rolls in the drive. *Let the nosey neighbors marinate on that.*

"Where are we going for dinner?" Jessa asked.

"Your kitchen," Tyson said, reaching down to pick up two grocery bags.

He chuckled as he breezed past her with his bags and indeed headed for her kitchen.

Jessa frowned a bit. She wanted four-star or better cuisine, not some homemade bull—

"You coming?" he called from the kitchen.

Jessa arched a brow in annoyance. "Let me tell the nanny we're staying in instead," she called back before she kicked off her lovely Louboutins and jogged upstairs.

She stopped at the door of the nursery. "Yari, we're dining in tonight," she said, her face showing her displeasure.

"I'll steer clear of the first floor then."

Jessa shrugged. She *hated* a change of plans.

Deciding her dress was far too over the top for dinner

at home, she changed into a silk maxi dress and peeled off her Spanx and ditched the bra. She refused to sit at home all night and be uncomfortable.

His choice. Not mine.

By the time she checked on Delaney again and made her way down the stairs, Tyson had her kitchen smelling of garlic and herbs. Jessa's stomach grumbled loudly and she could only pray he didn't hear it.

Tyson handed her a glass of white wine. "Sit. Sip. See a master at work."

Jessa moved over to stand close to him by the sink where he was rinsing thick fillets of salmon. "So your dickplay isn't your own handiwork?" she asked in her huskiest tone as she looked up at him and sipped her wine.

Tyson looked down at her. "Don't start something you *won't* finish, Ms. Celibate," he warned, his eyes dipping to take in her hard nipples pressing against the thin silk.

"The devil made me do that," Jessa said, playfully apologetic before she turned to look out her window.

She frowned a bit and opened the thick slats of the wooden blinds. What she saw caused her mouth to open a bit in surprise. "I'll be right back," she told him before walking to her front door to open it wide.

Jessa shook her head and sipped her wine as she watched Kingston trying his hardest to keep Jackson from completely whooping the ass of some man she didn't know who was in his bikini briefs on Renee's lawn. "Well, I'll be damned."

Jessa chuckled as Jackson literally flexed his arms and sent poor Kingston flying through the air like a fly before he used his strong hands to pick up the bikini-clad man by the throat.

"Jackson. Stop it before you hurt him," Renee cried from the porch in nothing but a short robe.

"Kingston, stay out of it," Aria snapped, standing on her porch holding her baby in her arms. "Get your men,

Renee, before I jump in that shit and somebody get fucked up. For real."

Jessa thought about it for a second and realized their shenanigans bored her. She couldn't even muster enough energy to take pleasure in the fools they made of themselves as their Richmond Hills neighbors looked on.

She had more interesting things to occupy her time.

Jessa sipped her wine as she made her way back into her spacious kitchen. "You finding everything you need?" she asked softly before she leaned back against the island and watched him stir a pot of seasoned rice before he began to pan sear the salmon.

Tyson glanced at her over his broad shoulder. "Not everything."

Jessa arched a brow. "Really?" she asked.

Tyson slid the metal pan with the fish into the oven and turned the rice down on low before he put the lid on. Just as quickly, he took two big steps and gathered her into his arms.

Jessa hissed at the feel of his hard dick pressing against her belly. "Wow, hello, down there," she teased softly, as she tilted her head back to look up at him.

"So you just want to strut around with no panties on and your nipples swinging and think *this* wasn't going to happen?" he asked, gripping her ass to pull her body even closer to his.

Jessa's eyes searched his as he lowered his head to taste her lips. She set her wineglass on the island and brought her hands up to hold the sides of his face just as he deepened the kiss. She shivered at the feel of his tongue slowly dragging against hers before he captured it and then suckled it into his fresh-tasting mouth.

Everything with a pulse on her body pounded as Jessa felt herself lost in the heat. Not even the sound of glass shattering outside broke the mood for her.

It had been so long since she gave in to the sensuality of being a woman aroused by a man.

He lowered his head to kiss from the corner of her mouth to the base of her neck. “Let me make love to you again, Jessa,” he moaned near her ear before he kissed behind her earlobe.

She shook her head even as she slid her hands down his body to grip his hard buttocks.

He wrapped one arm around her waist and lifted her up to sit on the island. Inching her dress up around the top of her thighs, he stood between her legs and brought his hands up to twist in her hair before he kissed her again. And again. And again.

Jessa eagerly released the hem of his shirt from his pants and went underneath the cool cotton to enjoy the warm strength of his back.

“Your doctor give you the okay?” he asked, tugging the top of her strapless top down to free her breasts before his gentle hands guided her upper body down to the island.

Jessa arched her back from the chill of the granite.

Tyson bent down to suck one of her brown nipples that were hardened and pointed up to the ceiling.

He moaned in pleasure.

Jessa gasped hotly.

He licked a trail to her other taut nipple.

Jessa’s entire body shivered in anticipation.

“Man, Jessa, let me just put the tip in,” he asked, lifting his head to look down at her.

She smiled as she shook her head. “I haven’t heard that since high school,” she teased.

He laughed and lowered his head to her chest. “Oh man, my dick is so hard.”

“Aw, poor baby,” she said huskily.

Tyson looked up at her as he eased his hands down to stroke her pussy. “Aw, poor baby,” he copied her. “Your pussy is so wet.”

Jessa lowered her eyelids halfway as he played in the moist folds before he used his thumb to press deeply against her throbbing wet clit. "Oooh," she moaned low in her throat.

Tyson's dark eyes intensified as he slid one finger deep inside her tight core and put his thumb back to work massaging her sensitive clit.

Jessa worked her hips in a tight circular motion as she licked her lips.

"Sexy ass," he told her, his eyes locked on the varying expressions of pleasure and passion that she made as he finger-fucked her slow and easy and deeply.

"Damn you," she cursed him as she worked her hips against the thrust of his fingers buried deep inside her.

"Man, let me have some of this good pussy," he demanded throatily before he slipped his fingers out of her and quickly turned his head to suck them clean of her pussy juices.

Jessa cried out at the move.

"I need to taste this motherfucker," he said, inching down her body to spread her legs wide before he licked her from her ass to clit before he suckled it between pursed lips.

Jessa's hips seem to lift of their own accord.

Tyson bit each of her ass cheeks before he wet her thoroughly and then eased his thumb into her ass as he licked her clit crazily.

Jessa's arm reached out frantically for anything to clutch as she bit her bottom lip to keep from crying out too loudly. "Fuck me," she begged. "Give me that dick."

Tyson picked her up from the island and set her on her feet in front of the sink. He bent her over it with his arms as he quickly covered his dick with a condom.

Jessa raised up on the tip of her toes as Tyson spread her ass cheeks with his hands and guided his dick inside her pussy slowly. She dropped her head to the sink and bit her bottom lip with a grunt of pleasure. "Oh, that feels good," she moaned, working her hips to circle his dick and then pull downward on it.

Tyson reached for the pullout kitchen faucet as he lightly sprayed Jessa's ass as she worked his dick.

The cool feel of the water shocked her, but Jessa kept going.

He dropped the faucet. "Nah, let me do this before you make this dick cum."

Grabbing her waist, he worked his hips back and forth, gliding his dick in and out of her. As her walls tightened and released his dick, he picked up the pace until the sweat from his stomach dripped down onto her ass.

The juicy sounds of their bodies smacking against each other echoed into the air.

Jessa looked back over her shoulder as she panted. "I'm coming," she told him.

Tyson brought his hands around her to lightly tease her nipples as he fucked her harder and deeper. "Me too," he roared, flinging his head back as he shot off round after round of cum.

Jessa used her hips to back him up until his ass pressed against the island before she worked her hips and her pussy walls to drain his dick.

Ding-dong.

Jessa heard the bell. She didn't stop.

Tyson took back the lead and thrust the last of his hardness into her, watching her fleshy ass vibrate with each hard thrust.

Ding-dong.

Tyson eased his dick from her and Jessa felt like he suctioned her pussy. Stumbling on shaky legs, she let her dress drop back down around her body and jerked her top up over her sweaty breasts. She looked over at Tyson as his chest expanded with each deep breath he took as he panted.

Ding-dong. Ding-dong. Ding-dong.

"You can clean up in the bathroom back there," she told him, pointing to the half bath next to the pantry before she hurried to the front door.

"Yes," Jessa snapped as she snatched the front door open.

Henry stood there and everything about his stance let her know he was angry. "I hate to interrupt the little freak show, but I thought you should know that anybody walking by can see that chump sexing you through your open blinds."

Jessa's eyes widened and she looked down the hall at the kitchen . . . and the blinds she cracked open to watch Renee's drama. Jessa closed her eyes in shame unable to even look at her friend. "Henry—"

Something slammed and she opened her eyes to see two oversized boxes of Pampers. She looked up at him. Again, she saw his anger and this time the hurt in his eyes.

"See, I'm the kind of man who respects you and cares about your daughter, so I brought these while Costco had them on sale. But I see you're not into looking for that. You want somebody to help you break your promise to God to stay celibate and could care less if he ever lays eyes on your baby," he said coldly. "Has he once picked her up? Changed her diapers? Asked how she's doing?"

Jessa was confused by Henry's reaction. This was more than just the embarrassment of a friend catching another friend in sticky situation.

"Henry—"

He waved his hand and turned to walk away. "I'm the fool sitting back being a gentleman while the scoundrel wins the prize he shouldn't have gotten unless he wanted to marry you . . . like I did."

Moments later, he was reversing his pickup truck down her driveway and peeling away.

Henry wanted to marry her? What the hell?

Jessa thought about that day at the hospital when she thought she saw him and Tyson sizing each up other.

Brrrrnnnggg . . .

Literally scratching her head, Jessa swung the door closed and raced down the hall to snatch up her cordless phone just as Tyson walked out the bathroom.

"Hello." Jessa's heart was already pounding from Tyson's sex and Henry's revelation.

"Jessa. Hey, this is Lincoln. How are you doing?"

She felt her entire body tense. She hadn't really heard from him the last month, since she told him she wanted more time to decide whether to pursue the lawsuit. "Hey, Lincoln. What's up?" she asked.

"Interesting news. You ready?"

"Go," she demanded, watching Tyson pull the salmon from the oven before he stirred the rice.

"Both Jaime's attorney and the Halls' attorney have contacted me requesting that a grandparentage paternity test be done."

Jessa's mind felt like it was ready to explode as she smoothed her red-tipped fingers across her chin nervously. "So these motherfuck—"

She stopped herself and licked her lips. "So they are tag-teaming me?" she corrected herself, vaguely realizing premarital sex with Tyson AGAIN was a much greater sin than profanity.

"To be honest, I'm not really sure when this connection of the attorneys came about and why," Lincoln admitted. "But I do know that there's a court order for the paternity of the baby that has to go in before the week is up."

Shit.

Jessa could care less about Jaime. It was the Halls that worried her—or the thought of the two of them now working together against her.

Shit.

Jessa left the kitchen and rushed up the stairs to the nursery. The nanny was napping in a chair by the crib.

"This doesn't necessarily mean they are still going to pursue custody of the baby—"

"Delaney," Jessa said, almost absentmindedly.

"Huh?"

Jessa stepped close to the crib to look down at her baby. "Her name is Delaney Jordan," Jessa said, tightly clutching the phone as fear consumed her. "And she is *my* baby and I will do *anything*—including destroy them—to make sure they understand that I am not going to lose *this* baby," she swore with a hardened heart.

Chapter 15

One week later

Jessa was focused. She was in full war mode. Her life had never been so swamped with problems to be fixed and decisions to be made. She loved Delaney, her life, her stronger ties to God, and even her new relationship with her mother, but she knew she had to get back a little of the old Jessa to fight off the demons coming at her.

True, Reverend Dobbins said the Bible said to put your total faith in God, but Jessa had never been one to not control what happened. She just couldn't take the chance.

"You really have a good life here, Jessa."

She side-eyed her mother as they sat on a bench by the lake enjoying the early May weather; her mother sat beside her, rocking Delaney, who was deep into her favorite pastime of gnawing on the side of her hand. "I used to before all the drama," she said, hating the raw burning feeling of her stomach, like an ulcer was developing. "I used to be the queen of the ball and everyone would be happy to see me coming."

"Do you miss all that?" Darla asked.

"I used to."

"And now?"

"Fuck 'em."

"That's *my* daughter," Darla said in approval.

Jessa crossed her legs and looked down at the patent-leather square-toe flats she wore with linen pants. "Would you ever move?"

"Give up my house in Harlem?" Darla asked. "Shit no. I lost way too much to have that house. Nooo, I wouldn't sell it."

Jessa nodded. "It's just I have to figure out a lot of things and one of them is trying to raise your grandchild here. I don't trust all of these people to be nice to her when she gets older."

"So why be here?"

"To prove they couldn't *make* me run," Jessa said with a streak of vengeance in her voice.

"Humph. Don't cut your nose off to spite your face."

Jessa fell silent. She was stressed beyond belief. The results of the paternity test come back today, and although she was one hundred percent sure of the results, she still had no clue what the Halls would do once they knew without a doubt that Delaney was indeed their grandchild.

Bzzzzzzzzz . . . Bzzzzzzzzz . . . Bzzzzzzzzz.

Jessa looked down at her cell phone sitting beside her on the bench. She scooped it up. "What you got for me," she asked. "Give me something good, Salvatore."

"I got nothing on them, Jessa. Not even anything that I can make look like something. They're clean," he said in his heavy Italian accent.

Jessa let her head fall back as she closed her eyes and released a heavy breath as the private investigator just crushed what little hope she had of gaining some leverage to use against the Halls. Just in case.

"And you are absolutely telling me the truth that you aren't working for them or Jaime?" Jessa asked, fixing her eyes on the sun in the distance.

"Nah, not me."

"Not even if I tell you I will triple whatever rate they

are paying you to feed me a false story?" she asked, her eyes squinting as she pressed the phone closer to her ear.

"I don't work like that and you know it."

The baby cried and Jessa looked on as her mother held her securely on her arm as she reached in the diaper bag for a bottle. Soon Delaney was suckling away and Darla was singing to her softly. "Sal, if I find out you did me dirty with those motherfuckers, I will stop at nothing to make sure you never forget who the fuck I am. I love you, but this is business," she told him coldly. "You got me."

"I got you, beautiful. Trust me, we're good."

"I hope so because I am thinking of starting a new business and I could really throw some major work your way once it gets rolling," she told him.

"What kinda business?"

Jessa shook her head. "That's for me to know and you to find out later . . . *if* you don't fuck me over."

She ended the call on that note.

Darla cut her eyes over at her daughter. "Wanna tell me about it?" she asked, taking the bottle out just long enough to belch the baby before letting her finish the rest of the small bottle.

"Not yet, but I will."

Her phone vibrated again, but it was Tyson and so she let it go to voice mail. She was avoiding him and Henry was avoiding her. With a possible custody battle looming, the last thing she needed was man drama to preoccupy her time and her thoughts. There was truth in Henry's observation that Tyson wasn't particularly demonstrative toward Delaney, but their chemistry had been undeniable. Henry was completely in love with her baby, but Jessa never thought of him as anything but a friend. The battle of a good fuck versus a good stepfather for Delaney would have to be fought another time.

She dug a folded lightweight blanket out of the bag and put it over Delaney's pudgy little legs as she felt it become more breezy. She was pressing a kiss to her cheek when she spotted Renee, Aria, and Jaime coming up the walk with Aria pushing a stroller.

Jessa ignored them. The days of trying to be a factor of any kind in their lives had passed. The friendship was over. She was making no more apologies. She honestly could care less if she ever saw them again. Seriously. *It is what the fuck it is,* she thought, using her thumb to wipe her lip gloss from Delaney's fat cheek.

As they neared, Jessa opened the blanket and covered her mother's shoulders and arm to shield Delaney from their curious eyes.

Darla frowned. "Jessa, why you covering her up like that?" she asked.

"I don't need them bitches to see my baby," she muttered.

"Who?" Darla asked, looking around.

"Don't worry about it, Mama," she said, taking the empty bottle and putting the cap back on it before she pushed it into the diaper bag.

The ladies walked by on the paved path behind the benches. Their voices carried.

"I bet she's beautiful," Renee said in a low voice.

"Ms. Kingsley said she is," Aria said.

Jessa rolled her eyes.

"Well, we'll find out today if she's Eric's bastard or not," Jaime added.

"Jaime!" Aria and Renee snapped in reprimand.

Stupid bitch, Jessa thought.

"Jessa, take Delaney," Darla said. "My arm is killing me and I think she needs her diaper changed."

Jessa forced the anger caused by Jaime's words from her body as she took her daughter. She buried her face in her neck and inhaled deeply of the scent of innocence and love.

"I *dare* you to call my grandbaby a bastard again,"

Darla said coldly. "I triple double dare you, bitch, for you to do it again."

Jessa's eyes popped and she whirled around surprised to see her mother had made her way over to get straight up in Jaime's face.

"Matter of fact, you don't have to say it again," Darla said, then swung.

WHAP!

Jessa's mouth fell open as the slap sent Jaime's entire body to roll down the slight incline and into the lake with a splash.

"Oh shit!" Aria cussed.

"Who is that?" Renee asked.

They both rushed forward to help Jaime, who stood up waist deep in the water with green algae covering her hair and face. "Are you crazy?" she roared at Darla across the distance.

Darla calmly slid the baby bag on her shoulder. "Some things are just fighting words, Jessa. You hear me? You don't let nobody call your child a bastard and get away with it. And I mean it. You hear me?" she asked again, still fired up, as they walked away from the scene.

Jessa nodded and pressed her face into Delaney's neck as she smiled. Her cell phone rang and she reached in her pocket for it. "Yes."

"Jessa, this is Lincoln. We got the paternity results and Eric Hall is indisputably the father of baby Delaney Logan."

Jessa arched a brow. "Of course."

"Of course," he conceded. "As you know, the Halls also have received notification of the results. The ball is in their court. Now for you and the case against Eric's estate, how do you want to proceed?"

"Drop it," Jessa said without any doubt.

"You sure?" he asked.

"Yes, I have to focus all of my time and resources on the Halls. My gut tells me they are going forward with it and I don't have time to play with Jaime anymore. Keeping my child is more important to me than winning money."

"I agree and don't forget you're eligible for social security benefits on behalf of the child. This paternity proves the eligibility and I would go forward with that and leave the rest alone."

"Okay, I'll look into it," she admitted.

"Not that you need it, but it is hers and there's no reason you shouldn't get it."

Jessa ended the call. All of her stressors were kicked up a notch. Were the mistakes of her past going to completely shatter her future?

Later that evening, after Jessa dropped her mother back at the sober house to make her curfew, she made her way home. She had just turned into her driveway behind her Jag when she spotted Dina. *What did this bitch want?*

"I need your help," she said as soon as Jessa got out her vehicle.

"Dina, I got problems of my own, and right now I am going inside to kiss my baby and enjoy a glass of wine while I figure out how to help my damn self," Jessa told her coolly before breezing past her to climb her steps.

"I think my husband is cheating again."

Jessa turned with an incredulous expression. "Duh, I'm not surprised. Are you?" she snapped. "I showed you proof he was begging me for pussy and you stayed with him. What the hell do you want from me now?"

Dina came close to the base of the steps. "But I am done and I want to catch him and use it to make sure I get all the alimony I can."

Jessa sighed. "I don't have the video anymore," she said, finding patience for the woman. "I deleted it."

Dina looked nervous as she wrung her hands. "I talked

to my attorney and he said we could call you as a witness—"

"What!" Jessa exclaimed.

Dina jumped back. "I'm sorry—"

"No, you're not sorry, but you're going to be if you pull me into you and your perverted husband's bullshit," Jessa told her in no uncertain terms as she came down the stairs to stalk toward the petite woman, who looked ready to shit her pants.

Dina started to cry hysterically.

Jessa flung her hands up in the air. "Seriously, are you twelve?" she asked in exasperation, reaching in her tote for napkins to push into the woman's hand.

"I thought you were going to hit me," Dina said, wiping her eyes.

"I'm too pretty to fight," Jessa said truthfully.

Dina smiled through her tears.

"Look, if I help you catch him, will you keep me out of court?" Jessa asked.

Dina held up her right hand to God. "Yes, I swear."

Jessa reached out and pulled her hand down. "This is not godly, let's not involve him," she said dryly.

Dina nodded.

"Give me about a week to get some things set up," Jessa said. "Do not tell anyone, especially your husband, and we'll catch him. Can you deal for another week?"

"I been dealing with him since we were twelve."

Jessa frowned. "That is way too long with the same dick. You raised it like a child."

Dina smiled. "Yeah, and it's not even full *grown,*" she snapped with a little spice.

Jessa held up her hands. "Terrible damn situation!"

"O-kay."

Jessa took out her cell phone. "What's your cell phone number?" she asked.

Dina recited it and Jessa saved it in her contacts. "Go home, keep up the front, and I'll call you in a week or so. Good?"

"Great!" Dina reached out and hugged her.

Jessa's body remained stiff and she gave the woman a forced smile as she finally walked away and carried herself home. *Where she belongs instead of on my damn porch.*

She finally entered her house, then locked the door securely behind her. She kicked off her shoes and massaged her own neck. "Yari, I'm home. I'll be up in a minute," she called up the stairs before she padded barefoot into her living room.

At the fully stocked bar she poured herself a full glass of white wine before she settled in one of the club chairs situated by the windows. She sipped and looked out at Richmond Hills. Her thoughts were full and heavy and varied.

Her fears of her secret being exposed remained in the forefront. *Maybe God will be on my side. He knows the whole truth. He has to understand.*

She missed calling Henry and hearing his guidance, receiving his comfort and security. His presence always calmed her. Reassured her. Made everything seem better. But she didn't love him and didn't want to marry him. *Did I lead him on?* she wondered, as she had many times in the last week.

Jessa forced herself to push those thoughts aside as she filled her mouth with wine and savored the flavor and aroma before swallowing it gently.

Her publicity events were becoming few and far between. Her book was almost done, but there was no guarantee anyone would want to read her story when it dropped later in the year. The modeling agency was still interested, but Jessa was still on the fence about it. She hadn't heard from Myra in over two weeks—a first since they first started working together. And in truth, it didn't bother her. Delaney made her yearn for her privacy again.

The idea she had for a new business was CRAZY and she knew that, but she saw firsthand that there was a need for such a thing. *Business was all about supply and motherfucking demand.*

Jessa took another sip just as her phone rang. She reached for the cordless. Someone from the security gate. "Yes?"

"Keegan Connor is at the gate."

"Let her in. Thank you." Jessa dropped the phone in the chair and rose to pour another glass of wine, which she carried to the front door. She sat one of the glasses on the floor to unlock the door and then picked it up again just as Keegan walked through the door.

Jessa handed her the glass.

"Good," Keegan said, immediately taking a sip. "Chardonnay?"

"Of course," Jessa assured her as she led her back to the living room.

"Great."

"I want to run something by you," Jessa said, reclaiming her seat as Keegan took the one directly across from her.

"I want to run a business with hired mistresses who help wives catch their husbands cheating." Jessa stood up to retrieve the entire bottle of wine to replenish their goblets.

Keegan frowned. "Like prostitutes, sugar?"

"*Hell* no," Jessa balked. "I'm not a pimp selling ass. No sex involved. Just pretty women—*or men*—to reel him in just enough to show his hand or that he's willing or that his ass is not to be trusted."

"Side note: You're cursing again?" Keegan asked.

Jessa waved her hand dismissively. "I'm stressed the fuck out and sometimes it takes a well-placed "fuck you" to get your point across. God understands."

"Ha!"

"Hell, I was thinking it, so I might as well say it. You can't fake it with God."

Keegan just smiled into her goblet as she took another sip.

"*An-y-way* . . . what do you think?"

"To be honest, when I wanted to catch the wandering dick ex-husband of mine, something like this would have been right up my alley, darling," Keegan admitted.

Jessa gazed out the window at the lit homes of Richmond Hills. She thought of all the wives who clamored around her door the day after she announced that one of her neighbor's husbands was actively pursuing her.

"There are so many women with doubts about their husbands who just want to know if the man they love is to be trusted."

Keegan looked thoughtful.

"And who better than a former mistress to help them offer their husband Eve's apple?" Jessa asked, her voice soft but still filled with excitement.

"You're serious about this?" Keegan asked, moving to sit up on the edge of her seat as if she was being pulled into Jessa's words.

Jessa settled back in her chair and crossed her legs. "I think so. And what better way to fix the negative karma of being a mistress than to help wives catch their own cheating husbands."

Keegan settled back in her chair and flipped her red hair behind her shoulder as she eyed her friend. "I want in, sugar," she said.

Jessa arched a brow. "What? Why? You have a business."

Keegan arched a dyed red brow. "I need some of that good karma too, and maybe the next man I marry won't live life like he ain't used to pussy."

Jessa felt all of her red trust flags waving around her. She dampened the appearance of her excitement. She was regretting telling Keegan about it. Big time. "First, I have to see what's going on with Eric's parents. Today they received their confirmation that their son is indeed the daddy like I said," Jessa said, picking up the remote to swivel and turn on the flat-screen television over the fireplace.

An image of the nursery filled the screen. Delaney was sleeping peacefully.

"Nanny cam?" Keegan asked.

"Of course." Jessa switched to another view and found Yari in her own room reading a book as she sat in the windowsill with the baby monitor beside her.

"I hate that she's sleeping because I'm sure going to wake her for some kisses before I leave here tonight," Keegan said.

"Oh no. Night duty is all mine, you kooky redheaded bitch. Don't you do it," Jessa warned her playfully.

Keegan laughed as she refilled her glass.

"If you keep drinking, your ass is not going anywhere."

Keegan shrugged. "We can put on our jammies and talk about Henry all night."

"Henry?" Jessa balked. "You're confused. It's Tyson the captain that was . . . *blessed*."

"I'm know exactly whom I'm talking about. Henry is the one I heard about all this week. Henry is mad. I didn't know Henry wanted to marry me. You really think Henry loves me? I wonder what Henry would say about that?" Keegan mimicked her. "Henry, Henry. Henry. Not Tyson. Not once. Haven't heard a peep out of you about Tyson or his good dick."

True. Very true.

"Well, I don't have time for either one. So fuck them both right about now."

Keegan rolled her eyes. "Whatever, you delusional weave-wearing bitch."

Jessa ran her fingers through her hair. "This is *not* a weave."

"Yeah, okay, honey bunch, and my pussy hairs ain't blond either."

Jessa and Keegan laughed at that.

"I did not need the visual!"

"Oh, right now it's as bald as your baby's," Keegan drawled. "I swear."

Jessa laughed until tears filled her eyes. "Oh, Keegan, thank you for coming over. I needed a good laugh," Jessa admitted.

Keegan shook her head. "What you need is a good business partner," she said, her eyes serious. "Come on, darling, two brains and pussies are better than one."

Jessa eyed her as Keegan extended her goblet into the air between them. *Maybe I should keep her close since I opened my big mouth about the idea.* "Okay, *if* I decide to go forward and *if* the Halls do not sue me for custody, then I will *think* about starting this business with you as an *investor,*" Jessa said.

"Sounds like a plan, sugar," Keegan said. "And your ex-friend across the way gave you the perfect name."

Jessa knew exactly what Keegan was referring to. "Isn't that tacky, though?"

"No, it fits perfectly."

Jessa finally raised her glass in toast as well. "Okay, then here's to Mistress, Inc.," she said before they touched glasses.

Ding.

The next morning, Jessa skipped church; she was not ready to face Henry. Although he never made his feelings clear, she knew him seeing her getting sexed—and well—by Tyson had to have hurt him. Yari had the day off, Keegan had already headed home, and Jessa was lounging in bed rereading the last couple of chapters of her book to reclaim the rhythm and flow to finish. Delaney slept on the bed beside her and the house was quiet as she read.

Hindsight is 20/20.

I know now more than ever how true that is. But it is too late for regrets and what-ifs. The time to make different—better—decisions has passed.

It's ironic how the thought of stepping forward into my future without my man, my lover, my everything had been hurtful. Scary. Disappointing.

I cannot help but recognize that I drove the car that led my life down this road. I was the maker of my own destiny. The ruler of the domain of my life. Keeper of my pussy.

Now?

Now I know that welcoming him into my life and my bed was the biggest mistake . . .

A cold shiver passed over Jessa's body as she looked away from the page. She had written her actual thoughts up until the moment Eric tried to choke her to death. She remembered the night with vivid clarity.

Setting the manuscript aside, Jessa lay on the bed on her side and lightly rubbed Delaney's back. As she had many times since she discovered she was pregnant, she wondered what the future held for a child born to a mother who was almost killed by her father.

"I will do right by you. I swear. I will make *everything* right," Jessa promised in a whisper.

Brrrrnnnggg . . .

Jessa picked up her cordless phone. "Yes?"

"Mr. and Mrs. Hall at the security gate for you."

Jessa sat up straight in bed. "No. Hell no," she said.

Click.

Jessa dialed her attorney Lincoln's cell phone number. It went straight to voice mail. "Shit," she swore.

Do they have a court order or something? What the fuck do they want?

Jessa tried Lincoln's number again. And again. And

again. "Okay, this motherfucker is so fired," she snapped, pacing as her heart pounded. *I hate this shit. I hate it.*

Ding-dong. Ding-dong. Ding-dong.

Jessa called the security gate.

"Yes, Ms. Bell?"

"Logan. My last name is Logan," Jessa snapped. "Did you just let the Halls in?"

"No, Ms. Bell—uh, Logan. They called Ms. Hall and she told me to let them in."

"Were they alone? No police?"

"No, just them."

Click.

Jessa eased Delaney up and hurried her into her crib in the nursery. She turned on the baby monitor before she headed down the stairs. She looked out the peephole of the front door and there they stood. Eric Hall and his wife. She looked around them.

She just knew Jaime was somewhere smiling, thinking she was clever.

Ding-dong. Ding-dong. Ding-dong.

Jessa grabbed her keys and slid them in her pocket before she opened the door and stepped out, closing the door behind her and forcing them to step back.

"Is this type of behavior really necessary, Jessa?" Mr. Hall asked, the lines in his face even more pronounced as he frowned down at her.

"What do you want? To insult me again? To blame me for Eric's death again? To disrespect my home again?" Jessa asked them, glaring at Mrs. Hall standing there with her mouth pressed into a flat line.

"No, we would like to see our grandchild," he said, before giving his wife a stern eye.

Mrs. Hall's hands gripped the handle of her straw bag as she looked in Jessa's direction without really focusing her eyes on her. "Our son is dead and we will never see him again. He was our only child. And now God has blessed us with a grandchild by him, and I am asking you to please let me just hold my grandbaby one time," she said, finally looking at Jessa. *"Please."*

Jessa shook her head as she crossed her arms over her chest. "Are you going to pursue a custody battle for her? Are you still planning to try and take *my* baby from me?" she asked.

Mrs. Hall opened her mouth.

"No," Mr. Hall said smoothly. "We have discovered that our rights are very limited and it's of our best interest to call a truce so that you allow us some involvement in her life."

Jessa still shook her head. "And how do I know that is true?"

Mr. Hall slid his hands into the pockets of his black slacks as he eyed her. "Jessa, our son is dead; you have his daughter. Do you have any empathy for how we feel?"

No. Fuck y'all.

But Jessa turned and unlocked the front door, allowing them to enter. Everything in her screamed not to do it. "Stay here . . . please," she said, before she jogged up the stairs to the nursery.

"I don't want you around these people, Delaney," Jessa said when she found her quietly lying in her crib watching the mobile with tiny stuffed animals turn above her. "But maybe if I let them come and see you, they won't go digging around in my past. I know you don't understand, but there are things I am ashamed of. Things I don't want you or anyone else to know."

Delaney cooed as Jessa picked her up in her arms. She pressed her face to her daughter's as she carried her down the stairs.

"Oh my goodness, Eric, she's beautiful," Mrs. Hall sighed, coming forward to stand at the base of the stairs with her hands already open and ready to take her.

Jessa paused and pressed kisses to her daughter's cheek

before she forced herself to continue down the stairs. The toughest thing she ever did was place her daughter in the other woman's arms and lead them into the living room for a chance to visit with their granddaughter.

For the next hour, Jessa patiently sat across the living room and watched the Halls enjoy holding, kissing, and cooing over the baby. When Delaney cried she had to force herself not to run across the room and snatch her baby from them.

Ding-dong.

The doorbell surprised her.

"Excuse me," she told them, rushing to the door to shoo away whoever it was so that she could get back to watching them with her baby.

Jessa opened the door and was surprised to see a thin white man standing on the step. "Jessa Logan?" he asked.

"Yes?"

He handed her a folded stack of papers before he turned and walked back to the small pickup truck she now saw parked in front of her house.

She looked down the street at Jaime standing in the street waving at the process server as he drove by. She obviously let the process server in just like she did the Halls.

Jessa ignored her as she looked down at the court papers. She felt like she was just gut punched as she read them. The Halls *were* suing for custody of Delaney. She slammed the front door and stormed back into the living room. "You lying mother—"

She bit back her words, not wanting to give them any further ammunition against her. They tricked her to see the baby knowing she wouldn't dare allow it once they served her with the papers.

Tossing the papers onto the floor, she reached for her daughter.

"Not so fast," Mrs. Hall said calmly.

Too calmly.

She handed her tote to her husband and he pulled out a black folder, which he sat on the middle of the coffee table.

"Have a seat," he offered with a smug expression. "Let's discuss your past and how that affects little Delaney here . . . or should I say little Georgia?"

Jessa felt like the room was spinning as she eyed the folder. Her knees nearly gave out beneath her and she felt completely nauseous as her past came hurtling at her like she was trapped in the path of a massive truck.

She shifted her eyes and the joy on their faces at her expense filled her heart with pure hatred.

Chapter 16

Jessa was afraid at the sharp, burning feel of her first labor pain. She pressed her hands to her swollen baby, and sweat covered her naked body on the thin bed. "It hurts, Nana," she cried out, her tears flowing freely.

"You're having a baby. What did you think it was going to feel like?" Nana asked as she mopped the brow of her thin face with a cool cloth. "The midwife will be here soon."

Jessa licked her lips, struggling for courage. "Can I please keep the baby, Nana? Please."

"Don't be silly, child, you're thirteen years old. I'm struggling enough to take care of you after your mama ran off. What are you going to do with a baby?" Nana snapped, her eyes flashing.

Jessa closed her eyes as she cried even harder.

"Don't you want to go back to school and have fun with your friends and enjoy your life. Huh? Don't you want to forget what happened?" Nana wiped her brow again.

Knock-knock.

"That's the midwife." Nana dropped the rag in the bowl of ice water by the bed before she lifted her tall frame and walked out of Jessa's bedroom to the front door.

Jessa cried in silence, not even letting herself cry out when another labor pain hit her. Even at such a young age, she was steeling herself to be able to take her child being born from body and then taken away from her. Forever.

A thirteen-year-old body wasn't meant to carry or bear a child. Nothing about their minds or their bodies was ready for it. Everyone knew that. But how was she suddenly supposed to mature enough to understand never raising her child. That made no sense to her.

Biting her bottom lip, she turned and looked out through the thin lace of her window. She could hear the sounds of children outside playing. She hadn't been to school or even outdoors since she started showing.

No one knew her secret.

No one but her grandmother, the doctor she went to in another state, the midwife, and whoever was scheduled to come and take her baby away from her.

They act like I'm just supposed to forget, *she thought, biting her bottom lip and turning her head again to face the wall as her bedroom door opened.*

Many hours later, too many to count, her Nana held her slender legs as she gave one last strong push to free her baby from her body and into the world.

Even in her fatigue, she raised her head from the sweaty pillow to look up at and glance at her crying baby. But the bodies of her grandmother and the midwife shielded it from her.

"Is the baby okay?" Jessa asked, fear instead causing her heart to pound behind her small breasts. "Is she normal?"

Nothing. They said nothing.

"Please let me see the baby," Jessa cried out.

The midwife turned back to tend to between her thighs as her grandmother carried the baby out the door.

"Where she taking the baby?"

The midwife pulled a long thread as she stitched Jessa.

She stopped for a second to look at the young girl who had seen and been through too much. "It's for the best. She will be adopted and some couple will love her real good for you."

Jessa's head fell back on the pillow. They weren't even going to let her see her baby. Not once. Ever. "Is she normal?" Jessa asked.

But she never got an answer.

In time, Jessa had trained herself to never think about that baby. Her Nana kept saying it was for the best. Eventually, she was back at school and caught up in schoolwork and being a teen.

She had to force herself not to think about it because whenever she did, the pain was too much to bear.

Just like now.

Jessa took her baby from Mrs. Hall's arms, hating the tears that filled her eyes. "Get out of my house. Now!" she roared, wanting them gone.

Mr. Hall pushed the folder toward her. "But we're not done and you know it, Jessa. See, we know the whole story. All of it, and you wouldn't want us to contact Georgia and tell her all about her history. Would you?"

Jessa locked eyes with him and she knew in that moment that if she owned a gun she would have easily put a round dead between his eyes and saved one to pierce his wife's heart.

Cold-hearted evil motherfuckers like these deserved to die.

"That would be a hard pill for any twenty-year-old girl to swallow."

Yes, she would be going on twenty now. Her birthday was in June. June 17th.

Jessa stepped back from feeling like their evil would rub off. And what she hated the most was that she knew he was right. What person could stand the truth. *That* truth.

No one.

Jessa felt nauseous from the memory of it herself. . . .

Jessa bopped her head and shoulders to the music playing in her earphones as she sat on the couch in her nightgown. She looked up when the front door opened and he walked in carrying a bag of McDonald's.

"I'm not really hungry yet," she said, taking her earphones off to use the remote to flip through the channels.

"I'll leave it on the stove and you can eat when you're ready," he said.

"Okay."

He came to sit on the sofa beside her.

Jessa frowned at the smell of alcohol. He left an hour ago to get food. She looked over at him and his eyes were slightly glassy. She smiled when he turned his head to look at her.

"You enjoyed the weekend?" he asked.

Jessa nodded.

"Yeah, me too," he said, licking his already wet lips. "I should have searched for you sooner, baby girl."

Jessa smiled again and turned to watch the television.

"You're such a pretty girl," he said.

She visibly jumped when he reached out to stroke the back of her head.

"Don't be scared," he said in a low voice, his eyes dipping down to her small breasts.

Jessa tried to move away from him, but his grip on her head tightened as he jerked her head forward and came up to touch her thigh.

"Such a pretty girl.

Jessa's eyes filled with alarm as she pushed his hand away. "No. Please stop!"

He pressed his hand between her thighs.

Tears fell from Jessa's eyes as she started to fight his hands off her. "Please, no, Daddy. NO!"

* * *

Jessa shook her head to free herself of the memory, the images, the nightmare of her own father raping her. She covered her hand with her mouth to keep her nausea from quickly turning into a vomiting spell.

Please, no, Daddy. No!

Her father had reappeared in her life when she was twelve. He began to visit once a week, and then one day he asked her if she wanted to spend the weekend with him. Her Nana had gladly sent her on her way with an overnight bag, but who would have ever suspected . . .

Please, no, Daddy. No!

"Having a baby by your own father," Mrs. Hall said in disgust. "That poor girl is probably severely retarded."

Jessa's eyes locked on them even as she grappled with the memories. "Get the hell out now!" she screamed, pointing toward her front door. "Get out!"

Delaney started to cry.

Mrs. Hall jumped to her feet and rushed toward Jessa. "You're upsetting the baby."

Jessa sidestepped her and picked up her cordless phone with her free hand. "I'm calling the police," she said coldly. "Get out of my house."

Mr. Hall rose to his feet. "Inside the folder are also legal forms giving us custody of the baby. You have twenty-four hours to sign them or we will reveal your dirty little secret and contact your daughter/sister to tell her the truth of her parentage."

Jessa shook her head in disbelief at their cruelty.

"Let's go, Kittie," he said.

They left the room and Jessa moved to stand in the doorway of the living room and pierce them with hate-filled eyes until her front door closed behind them. Holding a still-crying Delaney tightly, she ran to the door and locked it securely before she turned, pressing her back to the wood before her body gave out and she slid to the floor on her ass.

Her world felt so unsure. All of her chickens were home to roost. All of her sins were being thrown back at her. Karma was winning.

"Ssshhh, Delaney. It's okay," she said softly, pressing kisses salty from her tears to Delaney's cheeks. "I swear Mama will fix this. I swear."

Darkness had set and Jessa was a woman with a plan. A desperate plan that was the only solution she could think of. What other choice did she have? The Halls had pushed her to the ledge and left her there to decide just how to save herself.

With a calm that was unnerving even to herself, she walked down the block to Renee's house dressed in all black and slipped into the backyard where she slowly took the steps and tried the lock on the patio doors.

Richmond Hills was safe. The first show of major violence was Eric's attempt on her life. Just as she thought as she sat and plotted, the door was unlocked. Renee had no alarm. Never did.

The house was dark and quiet. There was nothing but the odds creaks of a house settling as she made her way to the office. It took her just a few seconds to find the drawer where the gun sat and she took it, holding it up to the stream of moonlight coming through the window to see the metal gleam in her hand.

Holding the gun at her side, she boldly and uncaringly left the office and walked out the front door with the gun at her side, making her way back to her home.

Cloaked by darkness, she climbed the stairs back to her bedroom and slid the gun under her pillow before making her way out to the balcony. She sat there with her knees pulled to her chest. Waiting.

They have given me no choice.

She had nothing but murder on her mind.

These people wanted to destroy her by attacking the most vital things to any mother. Her children. They wanted to snatch the baby from her and then ruin the life of her eldest daughter with a past that was far too disturbing. Her children were victims in all of this.

Just as she was a victim of her own father.

Even he knew what he did was vile and despicable. Once he awakened from his drunken stupor and found his daughter bloody and crying in a corner because of his incestuous actions, he cut his own throat.

Jessa flinched.

She had almost forgotten it all. Pushed it away. The Halls brought it all rushing back. All of it.

People like that deserve to die.

Sighing, she thought of the daughter she never laid eyes on. She hadn't even known her name until today. Georgia. The folder the Halls left for her still sat in the same spot. She couldn't bring herself to open it. To know more. To face her guilt and her shame.

Who knew her affair with Eric would lead her right down the road to a past she fought so hard to forget?

Jessa sat there on the balcony, knowing the nanny was taking care of Delaney, as she struggled with every possible emotion she felt. She was so lost in her thoughts and her memories and her regrets that she didn't even realize how many hours had slipped by until the sun broke in the sky.

Nothing in her life would ever be the same again.

Wiping away fresh tears, she made her way to the nursery. She picked up Delaney and held her close as she eased down into the chair by the crib. She was still sitting there humming softly to her baby when Yari walked in. The woman stopped in surprise to see Jessa sitting there.

"Yari, would you dress Delaney and take her to the mall for me. She needs . . . um . . . clothes. She needs clothes," Jessa said softly, rising to her feet.

"Yes, ma'am," Yari said, taking the baby from her. "Are you okay, Ms. Logan?"

Jessa nodded, even though she knew her face had to look a sight from a night of tears and fears. Her eyes ached and they felt swollen and puffy. "I will be. Thank you," she said, pressing one last kiss to Delaney's soft mat of shiny black curls before she left the room.

She took a long, steaming hot shower and dressed in a tank and a white linen skirt before she took the gun from beneath her pillows and made her way downstairs barefoot. She unlocked the front door before walking into the living room. Jessa slid the gun behind the pillows of the sofa.

Brrrrnnnggg . . .

She moved to answer the cordless phone on the base sitting on the bar. It was the security guard at the gate. Jessa glanced at the clock. 9:00 A.M. *Right on time.* "Let the Halls in. Thank you."

Click.

Jessa didn't move from her spot on the couch. She was trying to decide if she should shoot them on sight or hold the gun on them until they shit themselves begging for their lives.

Ding-dong.

"Come in," she called out, shifting her eyes to her view of the front door.

Her face momentarily filled with surprise and then disappointment when only Eric Hall Sr. walked through the door and closed it behind himself. He looked around before he took a few steps forward that echoed in the large foyer.

"In here, Mr. Hall," Jessa said calmly.

She watched as his eyes squinted a bit as he swung his head in the direction of her voice. Before yesterday, Jessa had always been careful not to invite the couple into the room where their son had taken his own life.

And now?

Jessa thought it was a fitting, ironic end to kill them both in this room.

Mr. Hall stepped into the room looking distinguished in his charcoal single-breasted suit. Jessa felt a chill at just how much his son resembled him as he glanced down at his watch. "I wasn't looking to hear from you for a few more hours," he said.

"And your wife? Where is she this morning?" Jessa asked, crossing her legs.

His eyes dipped down to take in the move. "She's getting Delaney's nursery ready for her at home," he said smugly, walking into the room to pick up the same black folder.

Jessa watched him aloofly.

He frowned and looked taken aback as he viewed the contents of the folder. "These aren't signed," he said, looking down at Jessa.

"Have a seat, Mr. Hall," Jessa offered with more politeness than she felt.

"I don't have time for this—"

Jessa reached behind the pillow for the gun and pointed it at him. She arched a brow coldly. "I would love nothing more than to kill you in the same room where your son killed himself. Have a *fucking* seat."

His eyes went from her face to the gun and back up to her face before he finally folded his tall frame into the chair directly across from her.

"Do you know that I held my baby in my arms preparing myself to say good-bye to her forever," Jessa began, rising to her feet to walk over to the bar and pour a glass of wine. She took a deep sip and looked at him over her shoulder.

His eyes slowly rose from her ass and up to her face.

Jessa looked at him in loathing over the rim of the glass. "I had decided that I would kill you two evil motherfuckers and rot in jail before I let you raise my baby or hurt my eldest daughter, who has absolutely *nothing* to do with this," Jessa told him with emotion, her eyes brilliant with anger and hate.

"I had every intention of killing you," she admitted with a bitter laugh as she fought tears.

"Do you think I would sit back and let people willing to use the fact that *my own father* raped me raise my child?" Jessa asked, her voice rising with each second until she roared and her eyes bulged with emotions as she stalked over to him with the gun raised in her hand. She sniffed and wiped her nose with the back of her free hand. "Do you understand that I would rather see you dead than have you raise MY CHILD?"

Jessa nearly choked on her emotions as she pressed the barrel of the gun to his head. She lowered her head in her hand as she gasped for breath.

"Don't do this," Mr. Hall said in a low voice, as if trying to calm her.

Jessa backed away from him, shaking her head. "I can't kill you now because your wife isn't here. I kill you. I go to jail. And there is no one else to raise Delaney but that bitch."

"Especially with your mentally ill, drug-addicted mother," he said.

"You were really thorough in your research," she said snidely. "At least my mother has a chemical imbalance for the illness. What's your excuse for being a sadistic asshole?"

He settled into his chair like he was getting comfortable. As if he had no fear for the gun she pointed at him. "I'll tell what you what. Sign the papers, put down the gun, and I'll forget you pulled this little stunt."

Jessa fought for control as she moved back to the bar for another sip of her drink.

"Or you sign these papers, put down that gun, give me some of the good pussy I know you got, and I'll let you visit your daugh—"

Jessa tossed the drink into his face and threw the glass at him. He ducked and it crashed against the floor.

"You will not force my hand. You will not raise my baby. You will not hurt my daughter. You will NOT FUCK ME!" Jessa told him coldly. "What is wrong with you? You think I would trick myself—"

He held his large hands up. "Once a trick always a trick," he told her.

Jessa stalked back over to him and slapped him hard before she pressed the barrel against his dick. "You talk a lot of shit when I'm the one with the motherfucking gun."

Eric opened his legs wider and thrust his hips up once, causing the gun to stroke his nuts, as he continued to boldly meet her hateful stare. "You are in between a rock and a hard place, Jessa. You don't want to go to jail and have those big dykes in there fucking you with broom handles and making you eat their pussy."

Jessa hated that her plan had unraveled right in front of her. Without Mrs. Hall there to take a well-placed bullet between her eyes, shit was not working out as she planned. She had been willing to kill to save her daughter, and not even that had worked. Not when her time was almost up.

What the fuck am I going to do?

"Maybe there is another deal you and I can make," Mr. Hall said.

Jessa saw the intent in his eyes as they moved over her entire body. Disgust for him filled her and she visualized her pussy juices drying up.

"Give me a month—no, two months—of pussy on call and allow us to keep the baby once a month and I'll convince Kittie to drop the lawsuit," he said.

Jessa stepped back from him with the gun at her side. "You're actually sitting here negotiating for custody of your grandchild over some pussy," Jessa asked, her tone disparaging.

"I know what I want. That's why I'm successful, and right now I want you, Jessa."

"Your son's ex-mistress?" she asked in disbelief.

"Who will now be my mistress," he countered, adjusting his tall frame in the seat as he continued to watch her.

Jessa shook her head at the shame of it.

"Besides, my wife and I are too old to raise a newborn," he said. "I'm about to retire and we're going to see the world. A baby would tie us up."

I can't do this. I will not do this. "And you'll never contact the daughter I gave up for adoption?" Jessa asked.

Mr. Hall rose from his seat and walked over to stand in front of her. He placed his hand on the small of her back and pulled her body forward as he pressed his lips to her temple.

Jessa shivered in revulsion as she tightened her grip on the gun and brought it up to press to his side as his hand dipped down to grip her ass tightly. She closed her eyes as one lone tear raced down her cheek.

"Do we have a deal?" he asked, pressing his hard dick against her belly.

Jessa's hand shook as she held the gun and fought for the courage to pull the trigger.

But his death won't change shit.

Jessa wanted her daughter. She wanted to see her grow. To see every milestone. To teach her the bullshit games men played. To help make her a better woman than she could ever be.

"Do we have a deal, Jessa?" he asked again, shifting his lips down to press against the corner of her mouth.

She fought not to hurl as she dug the gun in deeper to his side. *It would be so easy to pull this trigger.*

But she didn't want her secret exposed. Selfishly, to keep her shame hidden, but also because she didn't want the life of the daughter she gave up for adoption to be destroyed. Who wanted to have a mother and father who were a daughter and father?

I have to do what I have to do.

Jessa dropped the gun to the floor and Mr. Hall brought his hands up to the back of her head to guide his mouth down on hers.

Jessa was stiff in his embrace as her tears blended in their kiss. She forced herself not to cry as she allowed him to hitch her skirt up to her hips and play in the folds of her pussy as he pressed her body down onto the sofa. As she blocked out his actions between her thighs, Jessa looked over his shoulder and locked her eyes on the recording nanny cam disguised as the innocent teddy bear sitting harmlessly in a chair.

Her eyes glinted with victory.

Never underestimate me.

Epilogue

One year later

Life goes on.

When I said I was done being a mistress, I meant it. I am by no means perfect, but that is one line I will not cross again.

To do this day I hated that Eric Hall Sr. took me to that place. Hated it. But I will never forget the joy I felt when I showed that creepy a-hole the video taken by the nanny cam. A wealthy married man without a prenup didn't need that kind of pressure being exposed . . . not even for his grandchild.

Having the last laugh felt damn good, even if I had to compromise myself to get it.

Did I plan to fuck him that day? No, definitely not.

Did I end up fucking him. Yes, most definitely.

I truly planned to let my rage and shame fuel me into pulling the trigger and sending Eric's parents straight to hell, where he surely waited for their arrival. It was just a coincidence that the bear was even in that room, but once I spotted it, I turned it on when I went by the bar. The rest of the show he supplied . . . along with the deal to drop the custody case.

I didn't know what lie or tale Eric Sr. came up with to tell his wife, and I truly didn't give a fuck. I had to garner my daughters' safety on my back, but they were safe and that's all that mattered to me.

And that's why I decided it was best to let my eldest daughter, Georgia, be. I couldn't face her or the truth of my past and was just happy to know she was alive and well living in Connecticut. I had her contact info, but I had no plans to use it. I rather her be happy and blissfully lost to her parentage than be able to hold her in my arms. Our lives had continued on two different paths for this long. No need for them to collide now.

It was just too big of a risk.

I asked for God's forgiveness for the thousandth time, and all I can do is begin my walk again.

Sighing, I slid my hands into the pockets of the strapless polka dot dress I wore with bright red heels. I smiled a bit at the memory of Tyson and making love by the sink as he sprayed our union with water. It was a fitting final memory.

I never saw him again. Truthfully, Henry was right; Tyson was all about my pussy and nothing else—including my daughter Delaney. That was unforgivable.

Just as Henry was never able to forgive me for not recognizing or reciprocating his love. I never spoke to him again either. I missed his presence in my life but . . . C'est la vie.

"There you are."

I looked over my shoulder at my mother breezing into the kitchen with Delaney on her hip. She looked amazing in a pale pink wrap dress and neutral heels. Sober, mentally fit, another twenty pounds lighter, and absolutely beautiful. We looked more like sisters than mother and daughter.

She was well. We were well. I thank God for that.

"Ma-ma," Delaney said, reaching out for me with her chubby little hands.

My mother stooped down to let Delaney stand on her own two feet and take a few tenuous steps toward me. Love for her nearly knocked me over as I clapped and hugged her body close.

"You ready to go?" Darla asked.

I nodded as I picked Delaney up onto my hip and used my free hand to pick up my oversized red crocodile tote and slide on my shades.

Our heels echoed against the floors as we made our way out the house. It sounded like a death march.

"Looks like somebody's getting married?" Darla said as we stepped out onto the porch.

We both looked up the street as Jaime and Aria helped Renee into the back of a limousine, looking beautiful in her wedding gown. There was a time I would have been in her bridesmaid's dress helping her as well as she took a second chance on love.

Humph, Jackson won the fight in the front yard, but Renee's new lover won her in the end.

To be honest, when I allowed myself to give a fuck for a few seconds, I actually thought Renee and Jackson would reunite. After over twenty years of marriage and two kids, I knew even my shenanigans wasn't enough to tear them apart.

I guess an affair and an outside baby is too much to swallow, *I thought as I watched the limo pull off with a shrug.*

Again, c'est la vie.

"Did it feel good to come back and have a last walk-through?"

My real-estate agent looked up from sliding the SOLD banner on top of the realtor's FOR SALE sign.

"Yes, it was time to say good-bye," I said, handing the woman the keys to what was once my beloved home in Richmond Hills. "And this time for good."

I had moved out Richmond Hills just weeks after my

tryst with Eric's father. I relocated to a small town in upstate New York, and I was enjoying my new home and my new life. My mother even agreed to put her renovated brownstone up for rent and move with me. I finally knew what it felt like to have a family again.

I was truly starting over and I swore the next thirty years of my life were going to be damn better than the first. My book, The Mistress Memoirs, *had just hit* The New York Times Bestseller List, *and my agent and editor were both trying to talk me into trying my hand at fiction. Something about having a great voice. I was considering it. I was open to whatever life had in store for me because I felt blessed to be alive.*

My mother took Delaney and strapped her into the car seat in the backseat of the Land Rover as I allowed myself one last glance at the house and then the surrounding neighbors. It was time to say good-bye to Richmond Hills for good.

I waved good-bye to the realtor as I slowly walked down the stairs. I was just about to climb behind the wheel when a small lime-green Beetle came screeching to a halt at the end of the driveway.

What bullshit is this now? *I wondered, looking over my shoulder.*

Dina climbed from the car and came rushing up the drive to grab me into a hug I couldn't avoid. "I heard you were at the house and I just wanted to thank you in person for that help you gave me last year," she said.

I smiled. "A deal is a deal, right?"

Dina nodded. "And he is long gone."

"I hear that," I said in congratulations.

Dina stepped back. "I don't want to hold you up, I just wanted to thank you again in person."

I watched her as she rushed back to her car and reversed in the cul-de-sac before she pulled off with a brief honk of her horn.

Bzzzzzzzzz . . .

I reached in my bright red bag for my business cell phone as I eased behind the wheel and reversed down the drive. I didn't recognize the number and if the call was coming directly to me, then it was a heavy hitter. Business was booming. Sad for the wives and the current state of marriage, but damn good for Keegan and I.

"Hello, Mistress, Inc.," I said in my husky voice as I sped out of Richmond Hills without even looking back.

Discussion Questions

1) For the readers who have already enjoyed—or been frustrated by—*Message from a Mistress* and *Mistress No More*, how did you feel about Jessa Bell surviving Eric's attempt to kill her? Do you feel she deserved to die? If so, why?
2) Jessa's decision to attend the funeral of Eric was "questionable" to say the least, but Jessa felt that Eric's death had put the entire weight of their affair completely on her shoulders. Does she deserve any absolution since she ended the affair with Eric?
3) Do you feel "the other woman/the other man" gets more blame for an affair than the married person? Should they?
4) Do you believe Jessa was genuine in her attempt to apologize to Renee, Aria, and Jaime? Also, Kingston, Aria's husband, demanded an apology from Jessa for himself? Did you agree with his reasoning?
5) Jessa said she was truly trying to "live right" with God but constantly found herself asking for His forgiveness for her actions when she messed up. Do you think a person who "gets saved" never makes mistakes—or never should make mistakes?
6) Did learning more about Jessa's past help you to understand some of the decisions she made in the past or was it a cop-out for her behaving badly?
7) Once Jessa discovered she was pregnant, she made the decision to sue Eric's estate on behalf on her child? Bold and brash, or responsible and right? If you were in her shoes, would you even consider such a lawsuit?
8) Jessa did make her former position as a mistress into a profitable hustle where she spoke out on her decision to enter an affair and made quite a profit. Aria sarcastically called it "Mistress, Incorpor-

ated." What are your thoughts on Jessa's new business venture, and what do you believe her true motivations were?

9) Jessa saw that there were plenty of wives curious about the fidelity of their husbands. If you were a wife suspicious of your husband, would you ever use the services Jessa planned to offer via her business Mistress, Inc.?
10) Were Eric's parents wrong to want to fight Jessa for custody? Were their blackmail actions wrong, or do you feel Jessa was getting the payback she deserved? Would you ever be able to trust your child with them if you were Jessa?

About the Author

Niobia Bryant is the acclaimed and best-selling author of more than twenty works of fiction in multiple genres. She writes both romance fiction and commercial mainstream fiction as Niobia Bryant. As Meesha Mink, she's the co-author of the popular and best-selling Hoodwives/Bentley Manor series (*Desperate Hoodwives, Shameless Hoodwives,* and *The Hood Life*) and the solo author of the best-selling *Real Wifeys* trilogy (*Real Wifeys: On the Grind, Real Wifeys: Get Money, and the untitled third Real Wifeys book*). The proud Newark, New Jersey, native writes full-time and lives in South Carolina. She is busy at work on her next piece of fiction.

Connect With Niobia:

Web site:	www.NIOBIABRYANT.com
E-mail:	niobia_bryant@yahoo.com
Twitter:	/InfiniteInk
Facebook (Fan Page):	Niobia Bryant/Meesha Mink
Shelfari:	/Unlimited_Ink
Yahoo Group:	/Niobia_Bryant_News

If you enjoyed *Mistress, Inc.*, don't miss Naomi Chase's

Deception

On sale now from Dafina Books

Chapter 1
Tamia

Houston, Texas
November 4, 2011

Tamia Luke's heart pounded violently as she watched the twelve jurors file into the jury box and reclaim their seats. She was so nervous, she wanted to throw up. These men and women held her fate in their hands. Their verdict would determine whether she spent the rest of her life in prison or walked out of this courtroom a free woman.

She searched their faces, hoping for something—*anything*—that would give her insight into the decision they had reached. But their expressions were unreadable, and none of them would make eye contact with her. Not even Juror Number Eight, an attractive, middle-aged black man who'd hardly been able to keep his eyes off her throughout the trial.

But today he seemed to go out of his way not to look at her.

Like the other jurors.

With mounting anxiety, Tamia leaned over and whispered to her attorney, "They won't look at me. Why won't they look at me?"

"Relax," Brandon murmured soothingly. "It doesn't mean anything."

Tamia hoped to God he was right. She'd spent the past five months behind bars, serving time for a crime she hadn't committed. She didn't know *what* she would do if the jury found her guilty of Isabel Archer's murder. It was unthinkable.

When the judge emerged from his chambers, Tamia and Brandon rose from the defense table. Her insides were shivering, and her legs were so wobbly, she thought she'd collapse to the floor. Without thinking she grabbed Brandon's hand and held tight, comforted when he squeezed her back.

"Ladies and gentlemen of the jury," said the judge, "have you reached a verdict?"

The jury forewoman stood. "We have, Your Honor."

As the judge read the folded note that contained the jury's verdict, the silence that had permeated the packed courtroom was now deafening. You could literally hear a pin drop.

The judge looked at the forewoman. "What is your verdict?"

Tamia closed her eyes, her heart slamming against her rib cage as she braced herself for the woman's next words.

"We, the jury, find the defendant—"

Tamia held her breath.

"—not guilty."

Pandemonium erupted in the courtroom, loud cheers from Tamia's supporters dueling with shouts of protest from Isabel Archer's outraged relatives. The judge banged his gavel, calling for order. But it was the sight of Brandon's beaming face that gave Tamia permission to believe the verdict she'd just heard.

"WE WON!" she screamed, throwing her arms around Brandon's neck as he laughingly lifted her off the floor. As he spun her around, she caught a glimpse of Dominic Archer, seated behind the plaintiff's table across the aisle.

He looked so stunned that Tamia might have felt sorry for him—if she didn't despise his motherfucking ass.

"Thank you, Brandon," she said earnestly as he set her back down on her feet. "Thank you for believing in me. Thank you for saving my life!"

"You're welcome," he told her. "I never doubted your innocence."

"I know. And that meant *everything* to me."

His expression softened. "You know I—"

"Congratulations," a new voice interrupted.

Tamia and Brandon turned to encounter a pretty, brown-skinned woman dressed in a navy Dolce & Gabbana skirt suit that hugged her slender figure. Her dark, lustrous hair flowed past her shoulders in a way that made Tamia more desperate than ever to get into her stylist's chair. Sporting months of nappy new growth and wearing a pantsuit that did nothing for her shape, she felt raggedy next to Cynthia Yarbrough—the scheming hussy who'd stolen Brandon from her.

She forced a smile. "Hey, Cynthia. You're looking well."

"Thank you, Tamia." Cynthia didn't insult her intelligence by returning the compliment. "Congratulations on your acquittal."

"Thanks." Tamia smiled gratefully at Brandon. "I couldn't have done it without this man's amazing legal prowess. I don't know if I can ever repay him, but I'm determined to try."

Brandon chuckled. "You might feel differently after you receive my final bill."

Tamia laughed, then leaned up and kissed his smooth, clean-shaven cheek. She didn't miss the way Cynthia's eyes narrowed with displeasure.

Don't get it twisted, heffa, Tamia mused. *He was my man first!*

Soon she was surrounded by a group of supporters who'd been there for her throughout the trial. Lou Saldaña scooped her up and swung her around, while her best friend, Shanell Jasper, took one look at her attire and promised to take her shopping ASAP. Distant cousins Tamia hadn't seen in ages had shown up, along with a few of her neighbors.

Everyone who mattered was there.

Except Fiona.

And she *doesn't matter anymore*, Tamia thought darkly.

"YOU BITCH!"

The enraged outburst came from the other side of the courtroom, where a sobbing woman was being restrained by several members of Isabel Archer's family. As Tamia watched, the woman pointed at her and screamed, "You're gonna burn in hell for what you did to Isabel!"

Before Tamia could open her mouth to defend herself, Brandon silenced her with a warning look. "Don't say anything. The jury has spoken for you, and that's all that matters."

Nodding grimly, she watched as the hysterical woman was led out of the courtroom. Although Tamia knew she was innocent, it bothered her that there were people who would always believe the worst of her, that she'd killed her lover's wife in a jealous rage. The worst part was that she *knew* who the real killer was—and there wasn't a damn thing she could do about it. She'd sworn not to tell anyone, and no matter how horribly she'd been used and betrayed, a promise was a promise.

After accepting more congratulatory hugs and kisses, Tamia followed her small entourage out of the courthouse and into the bright November afternoon. She and Brandon were met by a buzzing swarm of reporters who shouted questions at them.

"Miss Luke, do you feel vindicated by today's verdict?"

"Mr. Chambers, do you stand by your strategy to portray Dominic Archer as the real killer?"

"Do either of you believe he really murdered his wife?"

"Miss Luke, do you regret having an affair with a married man?"

Taken aback by the barrage of questions, Tamia looked askance at Brandon. He gave her a reassuring smile, then stepped to the cluster of microphones. Calmly he surveyed the crowd, waiting for the noise to die down before he spoke.

"Miss Luke and I are pleased that justice was served today. I commend the men and women of the jury for weighing all the evidence and coming back with the only verdict they could have: not guilty."

The reporters fired more questions at him.

"With all due respect, Brandon," one voice rang out above the rest, "how difficult was it for you to defend the woman who cheated on you? Throughout the trial, you were forced to hear the lurid details of Miss Luke's affair with Dominic Archer. How in the world did you remain objective?"

Tamia's face heated with shame, while Brandon didn't so much as flinch. "My prior relationship with Miss Luke wasn't on trial," he answered evenly. "If I didn't think I could handle hearing the 'lurid details' of her affair, as you put it, I wouldn't have taken her case. But I did, because I believed in her innocence. Clearly the jury did, too."

Tamia beamed at him.

"Is there any chance that you and Miss Luke might reconcile?"

Brandon paused, giving Tamia a sidelong glance.

She met his gaze, holding her breath as she waited for his response.

After several moments he turned back to the reporters, chuckling and shaking his head. "You guys are always looking for a romantic Hollywood ending. All I want to do is celebrate this victory, which reaffirms my belief that the justice system can and *does* work."

"Given your winning track record," someone retorted, "I'd say the system works just fine for you."

Brandon grinned as laughter swept over the crowd.

Tamia was also grinning, but not for the same reason as everyone else. For the first time in several months, she had reason to hope that all was not lost between her and Brandon. Because whether he realized it or not, by dodging the reporter's question, he'd left the door open for the possibility of him and Tamia getting back together.

Today's verdict had given her back her life. Now that she was a free woman again, nothing would stop her from trying to reclaim the only man she'd ever loved.

Nothing.

And no one.

Turning her head, she saw Cynthia standing off to the side by herself.

Their gazes met.

Tamia smiled.

Cynthia's eyes narrowed with suspicion.

That's right, bitch, Tamia thought. *I'm taking back what you stole from me. And this time, I'm never letting him go!*